CAPTURING CATE

A NOVEL BY

ANNABELLE WINTERS

Copyright Notice

Copyright © 2022 by Annabelle Winters
All Rights Reserved by Author
www.annabellewinters.com
ab@annabellewinters.com

If you'd like to copy, reproduce, sell, or distribute any part of this text, please obtain the explicit, written permission of the author first. Note that you should feel free to tell your spouse, lovers, friends, and co-workers how happy this book made you. Have a wonderful evening!

Cover Design by S. Lee

ISBN: 9798409299484

0 1 2 3 4 5 6 7 8 9

Books by Annabelle Winters

The CURVES FOR SHEIKHS Series
Curves for the Sheikh
Flames for the Sheikh
Hostage for the Sheikh
Single for the Sheikh
Stockings for the Sheikh
Untouched for the Sheikh
Surrogate for the Sheikh
Stars for the Sheikh
Shelter for the Sheikh
Shared for the Sheikh
Assassin for the Sheikh
Privilege for the Sheikh
Ransomed for the Sheikh
Uncorked for the Sheikh
Haunted for the Sheikh
Grateful for the Sheikh
Mistletoe for the Sheikh
Fake for the Sheikh

The CURVES FOR SHIFTERS Series
Curves for the Dragon
Born for the Bear
Witch for the Wolf
Tamed for the Lion
Taken for the Tiger

The CURVY FOR HIM Series
The Teacher and the Trainer
The Librarian and the Cop
The Lawyer and the Cowboy
The Princess and the Pirate

The CEO and the Soldier
The Astronaut and the Alien
The Botanist and the Biker
The Psychic and the Senator

THE CURVY FOR THE HOLIDAYS SERIES
Taken on Thanksgiving
Captive for Christmas
Night Before New Year's
Vampire's Curvy Valentine
Flagged on the Fourth
Home for Halloween

THE CURVY FOR KEEPS SERIES
Summoned by the CEO
Given to the Groom
Traded to the Trucker
Punished by the Principal
Wifed by the Warlord

THE DRAGON'S CURVY MATE SERIES
Dragon's Curvy Assistant
Dragon's Curvy Banker
Dragon's Curvy Counselor
Dragon's Curvy Doctor
Dragon's Curvy Engineer
Dragon's Curvy Firefighter
Dragon's Curvy Gambler

THE CURVY IN COLLEGE SERIES
The Jock and the Genius
The Rockstar and the Recluse
The Dropout and the Debutante
The Player and the Princess
The Fratboy and the Feminist

ANNABELLEWINTERS.COM

CAPTURING CATE

A NOVEL BY

ANNABELLE WINTERS

1

"What else you selling, Senorita?"

Cate Bonasera looked up into the man's eyes. She couldn't tell what color they were in the blue light of the men's room at the back of the Angel City Club. She could, however, tell that they were wild and wide, hopped up and bugged out.

Cate followed his gaze. It led down to her own chest. She was in her white V-neck cashmere sweater that was light and thin and hugged her breasts and showed a slash of cleavage. She'd packed for summer in Los Angeles, and this was her most conservative top. She'd paired it with black jeans that had a lot of stretch to them, New Balance sneakers that were whiter than Kim Kardashian's teeth. No wedding ring on her finger.

She'd pawned it and pocketed the cash.

She needed cash.

As much as she could get.

As fast as she could get it.

"The only other thing I'm selling is your own life," Cate said softly, blinking coolly and moving her gaze back up to the man's face, dragging the asshole's wild eyeballs along with it. "You wanna buy it back?"

"Huh?" grunted the guy, clutching the bag of cocaine she'd just sold him for eight hundred dollars in a greasy wad of bills that Cate desperately wanted to spray with Lysol—preferably the lavender scent, though lemon would do.

She kinda wanted to spray his eyeballs too, but she settled for sticking the snub-nosed .38 Special handgun against his purple silk shirt, right above his belt buckle.

"Your life," she explained. "I'll sell it back to you for . . . oh . . . let's see . . . three hundred?"

The man swallowed so hard his Adam's apple almost popped out of his strained neck. He glanced down at the gun, gulped again, didn't look up. He was staring at the silver metal barrel pressed against his purple shirt.

Cate relaxed a little. America was the land of guns and cowboys, but this guy wasn't that kind of American.

And that was a good thing.

Because Cate didn't particularly want to kill another man today.

"Thank you, Senor," she said sweetly as he dug into his trouser pocket and pulled out a Gucci wallet.

Cate hadn't seen the wallet before. The eight hundred had come from his other pocket. The wallet was dark green patent leather. It had a neat little zipper holding it together.

Purple-shirt fumbled with the wallet, still staring at the gun. Cate waited for him to get the zip undone, then she helped him out with the rest.

Took all the paper money and quickly stuck it into her back pocket with the rest of the day's haul. It was a tight squeeze. Her large round butt used up most of the stretch in these jeans.

"Get in there," she said, gesturing to one of the four stalls set against the dark red walls.

The entire restroom was empty. Four in the afternoon wasn't peak partying hours in Los Angeles. It was, however, peak market hours at the Angel City Club.

Cate waited until Purple-shirt closed the stall door. She hadn't asked him to lock it, but he did it anyway. She heard the rustle of plastic. He was dipping into his baggie.

She'd considered taking the cocaine back to sell to someone else, but that wouldn't have been right. He paid fair-and-square for the blow. But then he'd been rude, and so it cost him the rest of his cash. Fair and square.

Cate glanced at the square face of her gold Cartier watch. The man at the pawn store had eyed it greedily, but she'd only sold the wedding ring. The diamond was big but reasonably anonymous. It would take a long time to trace. The watch, however, had an inscription on the back.

To Catherine:
My time is more valuable than your life.
Never be late again.
- Boro.

Cate's fingers tightened into a fist, thickening her wrist to the point where she could feel the inscription against her smooth olive-brown skin. She wanted to fling the watch into the Pacific Ocean, except it was worth too much. She'd file off the inscription when she had the time. Maybe melt down the gold and mold it into a coin. A pirate's doubloon. That would be fitting, wouldn't it?

"Boro is descended from pirates, they say," Cate's mother Renata Bonasera had fumed when she'd been informed by her husband that a match had been arranged for their eighteen year old daughter. "And Boro is still a pirate. His business is smuggling that filthy white powder into the United States, is it not, Romero? Why do you do this? How can you agree to such a thing, with such people, without seeking my agreement? Boro has no bloodline that can be traced. He does not even use a last name. He could be descended from goats or aliens or sea dragons, for all we know. He is a thug. A monster with the thick neck of a toad."

Romero Bonasera had rubbed his own thick neck and sighed. He took his seat at the head of the dinner table stiffly that evening. It was ten years ago now, but Cate remembered it like it was playing out before her eyes. She'd considered commenting that nobody was asking *her* permission, but she held her tongue. There was something in her father's posture that made her hold back. Something in his voice. Something in his eyes.

Romero settled into his high-backed wooden chair and waited for the white-aproned server to pour the claret. "Red as blood and sweeter than Satan," he declared after swishing and sampling and sending away the server. He drained the glass in uncharacteristic fashion, poured himself more from the heavy cut-glass decanter. Only after another long sip did he dare look at his daughter.

His gaze lingered on her, but he said nothing. Cate stayed silent. She was often silent at the dinner table, content to watch the Italian house staff expertly serve piping hot pastas and cream-topped marinaras, always accompanied by enormous platters of monkfish fillets from the Amalfi coast or succulent lamb chops from their own stock. Romero was often on the phone during dinner, speaking loud and fast in Italian, Spanish, English, French, even Russian sometimes.

When Cate was younger she believed it was because her impressive white-haired father was head of an Italian mafia empire that stretched across Europe, from London and Paris through Milan and Rome, reaching the frozen cobblestones of Kiev and the colorful spiral domes of Moscow. It was only as she grew up and learned some of those languages herself did she realize that Romero's conversations were involving fewer crooked union bosses and more European bankers.

Less about protection payments and more about overdue debts.

Less about issuing deadlines and more about asking for time.

Begging for more time.

Always more time.

"No time for a drink?" the Angel City barman called as Cate hurried out of the restroom area and past the black-glass bar.

She smiled tightly. She wasn't sure what he knew. Best guess was he figured she'd given the guy a blowjob in the men's room. Cate didn't give a damn what he thought. Better he remembered her as a street hooker than a cocaine dealer.

Though of course she wasn't a dealer. Not really. Besides, she was out of product. The three bags she'd taken off the pony-tailed thug were long gone. Within a few hours she'd sold them for pennies on the dollar so she could move them quick and then move her ass before Boro discovered that his wife wasn't going to be late coming home.

She was never coming home.

Never going back.

Not back to that life.

Not back to him.

Cate stepped into the street and stumbled when the sunlight hit her face like a fist. She'd been in the dark club for over an hour, waiting for a prospect with expensive clothes and a nosebleed. According to what she'd hastily read online that morning, the Angel City Club was known as a place to score blow in the afternoon, before it got crowded, before the undercover LA cops recovered from their own drug fueled benders and dragged themselves to work.

Cate wondered why Ponytail had so much coke on him when he was supposed to be her local bodyguard. He'd met her outside LAX Airport, hanging back behind the limo drivers with placards. She didn't know anyone did the placard thing anymore.

Ponytail didn't have a placard. He had a teardrop tattoo under his left eye, though. Cate knew what that meant, but she also knew that so many people knew about it that it meant nothing these days. A suburban pre-teen with a few dollars and a fake ID could get one of those anywhere from Bogota to Boston, no questions asked.

"I am told you are here for a shopping trip?" Ponytail had asked in Spanish as they crept along in heavy traffic to the Beverly Hills Hotel, where Nico, Boro's right hand man, had booked her a suite.

"Yes, I am very excited to be shopping in Beverly Hills," Cate had answered from the backseat of the silver Range Rover Discovery that she noticed had bulletproof glass and no interior handles on the back doors.

She glanced at Ponytail's dark round eyes in the rearview mirror. He was looking directly at her without blinking. She held the gaze until he flicked his eyes towards the front again.

But Cate noticed that Ponytail took his time averting his gaze. In Colombia no man of Boro's would have dared hold eye contact with her for that long. Also, Ponytail did not address her as Senora. It told her something.

It told her that Boro's name did not carry much power in Los Angeles these days.

That made sense, of course. Ten years ago the American Drug Enforcement Agency had joined forces with the CIA to take the War on Drugs overseas, beyond America's own borders. There had been massive raids on Boro's Colombian operations. They had bombed his warehouses, burned his fields, frozen his bank accounts, destroyed his haciendas.

But apparently none of it had been a surprise to Boro.

He'd told her that proudly on their wedding night, as

he sprawled naked on the red-stained sheets, smoking a Cohiba cigar that made Cate want to vomit. She'd been turned on her side, facing away from him, staring at the cream-colored walls of the mansion nestled deep in the jungles outside Medellin, Colombia.

She'd never even been kissed before that night, and it occurred to her that she still hadn't been kissed. Boro had taken her with clinical efficiency, instructing her to strip like it was a routine doctor's visit.

Boro was not a tall man, but was very thick. His neck was thick. His head was thick. His chest was thick. His arms were thick. Even his eyebrows were thick, as were the black curls on his belly and back.

The first time she'd seen Boro was when she arrived at the Medellin mansion. Boro's man Nico had picked her up at Bogota International Airport and driven her six hours to the hidden mansion without speaking a single word. Nico had been so silent that Cate had assumed he was Boro, and she'd spent the entire car ride petrified at what would happen on their wedding night.

Indeed, Nico was pockmarked, grizzled, and looked much older than she'd been told Boro was. He was balding on the front and top, but kept his hair long and drew it back into a ponytail. The hair was streaked with gray, dry like straw. The portion of scalp she could see from behind was horribly sunburned, like it was permanent. He wore four rings on each hand, all of them platinum bands, each of them studded with a large diamond.

It was only later, when Cate's personal maid Marya, a round faced Italian nineteen-year-old who'd accompanied Cate from Italy as was tradition, had picked up the lay of the land from the house help, that Cate learned the story behind Nico's eight diamonds.

Each had come from a wedding ring.

From women whose husbands had been punished.

Punished by being forced to give up their wives to Nico.

"They say it inspires loyalty in Boro's men," Marya had explained wide-eyed with horror one evening when Cate was just nineteen and Marya only twenty. "The rings belonged to the wives of men who betrayed Boro."

Cate had stared at Marya, looking for a sign in her sweet maid's dancing blue eyes that this was a joke.

It was not a joke.

"If a man betrays Boro, his wife is given to Nico," Marya had explained, almost sick with disbelief. "Nico finishes them and wears their diamonds as a reminder to the troops."

Cate was young, but she wasn't an idiot. She knew what kind of family she'd come from, and she knew what kind of man she'd been given to.

Still, seeing her sweet, gentle Marya's lips tremble with fury as she explained that Nico "finished" the wives of traitors and wore their rings as spoils of war made Cate lightheaded when she thought of all the times she'd been close enough to Nico to smell his armpits.

And, oh yes, she was married to the man who'd issued those orders.

"What . . . what happens to the men who betray Boro?" she'd whispered to Marya.

Marya had shrugged, her eyes shining with hatred for Boro. "Nothing. They get another chance. Boro says those men become his most loyal soldiers."

Cate had felt the blood rush to her cheeks until her face burned with anger. "So the women pay the price for the sins of their men?"

Marya had laughed, shrill like a blackbird. "Is that a surprise to you? That is how it is in Italy too, is it not?"

Cate had been silent. She'd felt her anger spread like a cloud of locusts. It moved from Nico to Boro, then cast its shadow over her own mother and father. She'd had a sheltered life, been fed and clothed and protected from wind and rain, sex and violence. She'd never been struck by her father, been slapped just twice by her mother.

But then she'd been given away like she was theirs to give away.

A piece of property to be traded.

An asset to be bartered, sold, used as collateral, valued in dollars and cents, grams and kilos, like she was a thing and not a person.

"I suppose it is like that everywhere, maybe," she'd said after waiting for the anger to subside. "But that does not make it right." She'd looked down at her left hand, touched the large diamond protruding like a headstone on a grave. "What happens if Boro decides to give *me* to Nico?"

Marya had laughed like that blackbird in the spring. She seemed thrilled that Cate had dared to pass judgment on what was right and wrong.

"So long as you control your tongue and hide your true self, I think you will be all right," Marya had said in that sweet way that had a hidden edge. She'd turned her attention back to laying out the day's clothes for Cate.

And Cate had turned her attention back to the rest of her life.

She controlled her tongue.

Hid her true self, whatever that was.

Went about her life like a silent bird in a golden cage.

But she never needed to control her dreams.

And those dreams were always of escape.

Dreams that slowly coalesced into a plan.

A plan for freedom.

Except this wasn't the plan, Cate thought now as she put her Carolina Herrera shades on and patted the wad of cash near her left buttcheek, felt the weight of the handgun in her Prada mini-pack, smelled the anxious odor of her underarms from beneath the white cashmere.

"No, this was not the damn plan," she muttered in a mixture of Italian and English.

The Italian words sounded strange to her, she'd been speaking Spanish so long. It was even stranger to speak English, but thankfully the words came easy if heavily accented. English was the world's language, and she'd been tutored since she was five. Netflix and Social Media did the rest from how it exported America's euphemisms, slang, and pop culture to every isolated village, every distant city, every lonely girl's bedroom.

The plan had been to take this shopping trip to Los Angeles and then return home to Colombia like a good wife, a well-behaved woman, a docile creature who did what was expected, did what she was told. As Boro's trust in her grew, she could slowly take longer trips, go farther away, perhaps one day on her own without a chaperone, a bodyguard, a watchdog.

It had taken almost a year just to get Boro's permission for a solo trip to the United States. Granted, Boro himself barely left the walls of their hidden compound outside Medellin, so he was a prisoner as much as she was—perhaps even more so, given that he was exiled from the richest country in the world, sworn to never show his face at the designer stores of Rodeo Drive.

"The attacks were mostly for show," Boro had explained proudly that first night as he smoked his Cohiba and she bled on the white sheets. "They did not burn my best fields, did not destroy my underground warehouses, took just the paltry two million dollars I left in the official banking system. The whole thing was a ruse, the DEA shaking the tree to see if I will fall out and land at their negotiating table. They play these games with all the big Cartels. I was expecting them to get to me someday. And I knew I would have to accept their terms if I wanted to stay in business."

Cate had listened, wondering why Boro was telling her anything. She kept her back to him, the covers high on her bare shoulders, her body shivering in dreadful anticipation that he would be angry that she wasn't facing him. The blood was pounding in her ears, and his words barely registered. She was thinking only of what had happened.

It had been very fast, she thought. It had hurt, but only a little. He had seemed pleased that she bled. She knew of course that a virgin bleeds on her wedding night. This wasn't the dark ages where a woman wonders which hole does what.

She knew enough to make sure she was always careful with herself when she touched herself in her white-linen bedroom. She never used more than one finger, never pushed too deep. She'd enjoyed her time alone as a teenager.

She'd never been ashamed of it. After all, there were lots of lonely girls alone in their bedrooms with nobody but the entire anonymous Internet. She'd seen stuff online. She'd seen a lot. She'd imagined a lot. She'd anticipated a lot.

Which was why that first time had been disappointing.

She'd felt nothing except that sharp pain as he pushed himself into her. Then he'd propped himself up on his thick hairy arms, pumped in and out many times. His cigar-smoky breath came out in short bursts as he did it. He looked blankly at her face as he drove his thick hips back and forth.

He did not kiss her lips, and she was glad of it. She'd stared up at him, wincing a couple of times but staying silent. She counted how many times he pumped into her. She counted till twenty-six, then stopped counting when Boro's breath caught.

His bug-eyes bulged. His frog-neck thickened. A vein the size of a python throbbed along the left side of his throat.

She felt him spurt twice inside her. She wondered if she'd get pregnant immediately. She prayed that she wouldn't.

She prayed like she'd never prayed before.

She prayed because even that first night she knew that if she got pregnant, she'd never leave.

Never escape.

Never be free.

Of course, she knew that prayers would not be enough. She needed more than a prayer, and she found it on an anonymous Spanish-language chat forum where South American prostitutes discussed things such as this.

She ordered the seeds online, then grew the potent herb on the East-facing verandah of her private quarters. She followed the instructions to the letter, grinding the bitter leaves and stems until they oozed their milky-white elixir. One teaspoonful on the first day of her period was supposed to be enough to prevent pregnancy.

A whore's birth control.

A wife's secret.

Except now that secret had twisted around on her like a viper catching its victim unawares. For ten years nobody but Cate and Marya knew. But what was the old Spanish proverb?

The best way to break someone's spirit is to give them ten years of good fortune and then, just when they start to believe in fate, in destiny, in magic, you take it all away.

"He knows," Marya had texted in Italian just fourteen hours earlier. "You cannot come back. He will give you to Nico if you return. Nico will wear your ring for everyone to see. Do not worry about me. They are not concerned about me. I will work in the infirmary with the nurses like I do sometimes in my free time. I am safe here. But you must run. It has to happen now. Go, Cate. *Amore sempre.*"

The message came at two in the morning California time. Cate was in a new black silk negligee that no man would ever see. She'd dimmed the lights of her glamorous suite to a shady golden glow. She was propped up against the silver satin pillows, her manicured hand snaking up along the smooth skin of her thick thighs. She almost didn't reach for the phone.

When she did, the moment was lost.

And everything after that was one long moment.

A single unbroken stream of time.

Events and actions that flowed like a river.

Decisions made as if in a trance.

The first decision was what to do about Ponytail. She knew it before she even thought it. She'd never killed a man, but she'd seen some die. Not many, but enough to know she could stand it.

She'd grown up in the shadow of violence. She knew her sheltered childhood had been paid for with the blood of others. She knew her own soul was tainted with that same blood, regardless of who pulled the trigger or swung the sword.

The knowledge put a sadness in Cate, like there was no salvation for her, like she was destined to pay for the sins of her father and her husband, that they were her sins because she'd benefited from them.

Still, it didn't stop her from hating Boro.

Didn't stop her from imagining his death.

Didn't stop her from running for her life.

Running to a new life.

Without Boro.

Just like her dreams.

Her fantasies.

Fantasies that had started when she was a young newlywed. Ah, how she imagined Boro being gone, being dead.

An accident would be lovely.

An assassination would be perfect.

An act of God or the Devil, either would suffice.

The fantasies progressed as Cate grew older and more jaded. Her hatred for Boro turned inwards, turned to herself. She asked herself what sort of woman spends ten years married to a murderer and a thug. She told herself a strong, honorable woman would have slit his throat while he slept. Pressed a pillow to his face after a long night of tequila and sangria.

She thought of all the ways she'd kill Boro. Sometimes she touched herself as she imagined it. She fantasized that it was him bleeding on the bed and her smoking the cigar.

The thoughts made her tremble. She knew she was sick, twisted, damaged beyond repair. The hatred for Boro and her parents and herself all merged together as it grew inside her, thickening and hardening, twisting itself around her core like a creeper tightening around a tree, slowly strangling anything good and pure, destroying what was natural and free, dragging down what yearned to rise up.

Sometimes there were days she could barely rise up at all, days when all she wanted was to lean over her balcony and fall. Perhaps she would float away like a feather on the breeze.

But that was not in her, and she went on day after day, letting the darkness have its way with her. She was no better than Boro, she decided. Perhaps she even loved him, she thought in her sadder moments. Perhaps this was all that love really was.

Sadness.

Resignation.

Desolation.

It was only when she realized she'd been taking the herbal contraceptive for ten years without missing a cycle that she considered the significance of that monthly act.

It meant that there was still some part of her that hoped to escape.

Still a part of her that yearned to be free.

The day the thought came to her mind was the day she began to dream not of Boro's death but of her own life. It was like a switch had gotten flipped, negativity turned to positivity, darkness chased away by light, dreams of the future dragging her from the nightmares of the past.

But right now, surrounded by gilded luxury in the Beverly Hills Hotel, Cate knew the past was not going to let her go that easy.

Cate felt the weight of her inherited sins in that urgent message from Marya in the middle of the night. She'd sat stunned and silent, alone in the golden light of her lonely suite, surrounded by silk and shadows.

For a moment she'd almost given up, surrendered to her fate, submitted to the ever-present fear that she was no better than Boro, that she deserved no better than what she was getting, that her destiny was to end up as a diamond stud on Nico's thumb-ring.

But she didn't give up.

She didn't surrender.

Instead Cate decided that if she was going to die, then it would be in the Land of the Free, as a free woman, if only for a week, a day, a minute, even just one second.

The decision was like another switch getting flipped, sending a spark of excitement through her, the kind of excitement that bordered on manic, verged on suicidal, edged on homicidal.

Perhaps it was the intoxicating rush of danger, the anticipation of escape, an irrational certainty that this was fate helping her out. Perhaps it was her future self saying that the time had come, she had to decide now, she had to fight for her freedom if she wanted it.

Fight for it.

Kill for it.

Maybe die for it.

And then she flung the covers off her bare legs, leapt off the bed in her black silk negligee, ran barefoot from the bedroom like fate had given her wings. Her thoughts raced with furious clarity, the adrenaline making her breathe hard and heavy with excitement that made her head buzz.

She saw the room-service cart in the dining area of the suite. She hadn't called down to have it taken away. She'd ordered swordfish steak, eaten the entire thing to the backbone.

Her gaze fell on the serrated steak-knife that had cut

through the meaty fish like a hot razor through butter. She snatched up the knife, gripped the wooden handle tight, blinked and stared as the thoughts thundered through her mind.

Ponytail wasn't Boro's man. He was a local thug, probably a gun-for-hire from one of Boro's old contacts in the LA gangs. Ponytail wouldn't be given any details about Cate's betrayal. He would just get a simple order, probably from Nico:

Escort Senora Bonasera back to the airport. Make sure she gets on a direct flight to Bogota.

Perhaps Nico would explain that there was a family matter that required her presence back in Colombia. But nothing more. Boro would not show weakness to an outsider.

So Ponytail would expect a routine pickup.

He would knock on the door and wait.

He would not be expecting an attack.

She glanced at the knife and tried to reason with herself. Ponytail wasn't here yet. She might still have time. Should she run before Ponytail arrived?

Just then Cate heard the elevator ding down the hallway like it was destiny at the door.

Decision made, she raced to the bathroom, turned on the shower. She flung the bathroom door open wide so the sound carried through the suite.

She scampered back out to the main area of the suite. Snapped off the lights, stayed still like a statue, silent like death. Waited for the knock.

The knock came a second later.

"There was a message that you are needed home urgently," came Ponytail's voice. It was thick with drink, hoarse with smoke. She could smell the heavy mixture of marijuana and tobacco from under the door. "I am here to take you to the airport."

Cate held the knife and waited.

Ponytail knocked again.

Cate didn't move.

The shower was loud.

Was it loud enough?

Yes.

Just like Cate hoped, Ponytail muttered a curse in Spanish and walked away. She heard the elevator ding again. The metal elevator doors swished open and slid shut.

Cate walked to the suite's main door and leaned against it. She was sweating beads on her forehead. The perspiration evaporated in the dry air-conditioning, leaving her cold.

She took a breath and considered her actions again. If she did this, there would be no turning back.

Cate didn't want to turn back.

She turned her mind back to the task at hand.

The knife in hand.

She'd seen Ponytail talking in Spanish to one of the bellhops while she was checking in at the front desk the previous morning. It meant he had contacts in the hotel.

He would arrange for a keycard. He would let himself in and wait in the main area of the suite. Boro's man would not dare do that, but Ponytail would. She could tell from the way he'd held eye contact in the car. From the way he didn't call her Senora.

Cate waited for what felt like forever. Perhaps she was wrong. Perhaps Ponytail had gone to the hotel bar and would simply come up in an hour and knock again. She looked at her white-knuckled grip on the long, pointed steak knife which still smelled like the ocean.

Now she had second thoughts. This was stupid, she told herself. She should just run.

She had a thousand dollars in cash. She could pawn her jewelry for more cash. Perhaps her cards hadn't been cancelled yet. Perhaps they wouldn't be cancelled at all. Maybe she was overreacting. Maybe she could talk her way out of it. Lie her way out of it. Cry her way out of it.

She glanced at her silver phone blinking silently on the side-table. There was a new message. Cate listened for the elevator. No ding. She hurried to the phone.

It was Boro.

Come home on the five a.m. flight. Do not make me wait. I do not like to wait.

Cate blinked, stared, then blinked again. She looked at the message once more. Blinked twice more.

Then she turned off the phone. Snapped out the battery. Tossed the pieces onto the white leather couch.

Ten years of dark, dreamy fantasies to escape came together in a swirl of resolve. Cate suddenly knew what was happening to her, what was happening inside her.

Fate was forcing her to choose, and she knew it had to happen now or it would never happen.

She had to commit.

Cross the point of no return.

Make it so there was no turning back.

Like Cortez or Columbus burning their ships so there was no going home, Cate suddenly understood why she was standing here in a negligee holding a steak-knife.

Of the three possible paths she could take—surrender, run, or stand here and fight—this was the most final.

If she went home to Boro she would either be given to Nico like a discarded scrap of meat or she'd be back in her lonely bedroom with futile fantasies that she'd never follow through on.

If she ran out into the LA night, Ponytail would track her down soon enough. He knew the city, she didn't. He had contacts, she didn't. He'd also call Boro, who'd cut off her credit cards immediately if he hadn't already. Perhaps Boro would even let Ponytail use her while Nico flew out to escort her back for her final punishment.

No, she had to commit.

Burn her bridges.

Set fire to the sails.

Dive into the unknown.

And so she stabbed Ponytail in the eye when he walked through the front door.

She had thought it through and decided she couldn't push the knife through his breastbone. She didn't know which artery in the neck to cut or exactly where it ran. All she knew was that she'd have one shot, one chance, one moment where surprise gave her the advantage.

She remembered the teardrop tattoo above his left eye.

She practiced the move in her mind.

She took her shot and made it count.

Ponytail went down on the carpet with a thud. He convulsed like an electrocuted fish, clawed at the air like a mime artist, kicked out wildly like a dancer moved by the spirit.

Then he suddenly went still. The knife thrummed gently like a tuning fork before going silent. Its wooden handle stood like Excalibur in the stone.

Cate frowned at the scene, not sure if it was real or imagined. She waited for the sickness to rise in her, but to her surprise she was calm. Perhaps she *was* no better than Boro, she thought as her mind moved back into that cold state of focus.

She dragged Ponytail across the carpet. It wasn't easy, but she managed it. Cate had strong thighs and hamstrings, and she got him all the way to the bathroom.

The farther from the front door, the longer it would take for the smell to invade the hallways.

Cate searched Ponytail's jeans and denim jacket. She found one hundred and eighty three dollars in cash, a Range Rover key fob, and a sleek black Samsung phone that was locked with a passcode. There was also a very heavy black handgun in a shoulder holster beneath the denim jacket.

She took the cash and the keys but the gun was too large. Then she noticed a bulge near his ankle and found a snub-nosed .38 strapped above his boot.

She took it from the holster and placed it on the bathroom tiles beside the key fob and the cash. The phone was useless to her without the passcode, so she just removed the battery so it couldn't be traced by the signal. She wiped her fingerprints off the phone and battery with a wash cloth and left the parts on the floor. She lined them up neatly.

Cate thought of the police now. She imagined LA's finest homicide detectives searching for clues like in some TV show. She hadn't thought about the police before stabbing Ponytail in the eye. She didn't think much about them now either.

The hotel room was registered in her real name. Her passport was in her real name. They'd fingerprinted her at the airport, like they did with all foreigners entering the United States. It wouldn't be a huge mystery. An amateur sleuth with a cat sidekick could solve the crime in about three seconds.

But it was one thing to know who did it, another thing to catch who did it.

And perhaps catching Cate wouldn't be a huge priority for the police.

Would the LAPD put their best detectives on the hunt for Ponytail's murderess?

Would they spend thousands of taxpayer dollars pursuing justice for a gangbanger with a teardrop tattoo?

Cate decided they wouldn't.

So long as she didn't make it too easy to get caught, she'd probably be OK for a while. The more time that passed, the colder the trail would get. Soon it would become a cold case. One for the archives. Forgotten in the white mists of time.

She changed into her white cashmere sweater and black stretch jeans, took her .38 Special and stolen cash, stuck a wet towel under the closed bathroom door, and stepped out into the hallway. She closed the room door tight and hung a sleek black DO NOT DISTURB sign on the brass door handle.

Cate made her way down to the garage and found the silver Range Rover. She wasn't going to drive around in a murdered man's car, but she thought maybe there'd be something useful or expensive in there.

She found three bags of cocaine.

She'd seen bags of cocaine before. Many more than three. She stuffed them into her petite patent leather Prada mini backpack, left the keys in the car, and walked out into the night.

It was three in the morning.

The witching hour.

And she was free.

Her heart felt so full she wondered if it would burst.

And now at three in the afternoon Cate felt that burst of freedom again.

She'd sold the last bag of cocaine. She was walking down the sunbaked sidewalk in her shiny white New Balance sneakers. It was like walking on air.

She had four thousand dollars in her back pocket, a loaded gun in her purse, and a strange excitement in her breast. She felt giddy and lightheaded, like she was still in that continuous dream.

But somewhere in the back of her mind she knew she was a train that was heading downhill without brakes, nothing but disaster in her future. Common sense told her she was done for, finished, that this was her *Thelma and Louise* moment but alone instead of with a friend.

But somehow she still felt like a bird on the fly, free for once in her life. Perhaps it was the madness of the morning, but she almost skipped along the sunny sidewalk like a little girl playing hopscotch with an imaginary friend, a kid playing peek-a-boo with the shadows.

Then a shadow fell across her from behind.

It darkened the sunlit path ahead of her like a premonition.

She stopped with a jerk and turned around, her heart pounding so hard her boobs bounced.

The sidewalk behind her was empty.

There was a woman pushing a baby carriage filled with canned tuna across the street.

There was a rat sniffing the grease on a newspaper near the blue metal trash can.

Cate frowned and watched the woman bump her tuna-carriage over the curb and onto the sidewalk across the street. Then Cate glanced suspiciously at the rat. It had thick fur and appeared well nourished. It was investigating the personal ads, perhaps looking for the women-seeking-rodents section.

Cate exhaled and looked down to the end of the block. There was a small grocery store at the corner. Probably just someone dashing in there for some eggs or milk.

And so Cate turned back to her imaginary game of hopscotch, to those stolen moments of fake freedom before everything came crashing down around her, brought her face to face with the fate she feared, the destiny she dreaded.

2

"If this is some more bullshit about fate and destiny then I'm aborting the mission, Benson. Ax and Bruiser already warned me about your nonsense. Clearly they didn't warn you that I'm not as patient and tolerant as they are with this hokey crap."

Cody Cartright touched his clear-plastic earpiece and tried to blend in with the other grocery shoppers. Unfortunately for him there were only three other shoppers in the four-aisle corner grocery store that he'd ducked into when Benson called him just as he was about to make his move on the target.

Cody was about twice as tall and three times as broad as the largest of the other shoppers. He stood out like Gulliver in Lilliput.

He nodded at the young Hispanic woman who was running the cash counter. She glanced at his thick arms bulging out of his short-sleeved black tee shirt, then blinked and looked at her phone.

"I wouldn't call Ax and Bruiser patient or tolerant," came Benson's voice in Cody's earpiece. "Besides, you weren't carefully selected for this mission like Bruiser was for the last one. I picked you because you were already in California, and this thing came up quick, out of the blue. Besides, you're also the only Darkwater SEAL who hasn't shaved in a week. I needed a guy who looks a little rough. Down on his luck. Lost at sea kinda thing. One level above a street thug." He chuckled. "Or maybe a level below."

"Careful," Cody growled, dragging his knuckles along the cold glass of the dairy cooler. "You might hurt my feelings." He frowned at the strawberry milk that looked way too red to be natural. "Why'd you pull me back, Benson? I was within six feet of her. This mission would be over by now."

Benson chuckled again. He took a breath. "There's been a development."

Cody sighed, nodded at his scruffy reflection in the dairy-glass. Benson hadn't given him much to go on—just a description and a location. Cody's job was to grab the woman and wait for instructions. Clearly this was a mission in process—which meant Benson was making it up as he went along.

Cody was cool with that. A SEAL is trained to operate on incomplete information, to roll with the punches, go with the flow, float with the current until it became necessary to swim for his damn life, fight for the future of America and perhaps the world.

Dramatic?

Hell, yeah.

A soldier needs to see himself as a mythical god of war, fighting on behalf of all those who can't fight for themselves. Yeah, technically Cody and the rest of SEAL Team Thirteen were no longer part of the Navy or even the government, but old habits didn't die easy.

Cody waited for Benson to continue, but the wire was silent.

John Benson had his own habits, his own methods, his own way of seeing the world. Three decades as a double-dealing, triple-crossing CIA dog and now the head of Team Darkwater had given Benson his own set of twisted rules. Cody was just learning about them, but he'd been briefed by Ax and Bruiser.

Benson's voice came back on the line, but he was talking to someone else. Cody heard a woman's voice in the background. It was Nancy Sullivan, Brenna's mother. Nancy was a former Treasury Agent who was now handling Darkwater's finances.

Finances which had swelled beyond belief after Bruiser's mission with Brenna Yankova. There'd been a massive stash of cryptocurrency that was part of Bruiser and Brenna's story, and since it was secret money that had technically belonged to Brenna's late father Alexei, it was now the slush fund for Team Darkwater.

Cody rubbed his stubble and tried not to think about what he couldn't stop thinking about. Benson had paid out some of that money to the four SEALs as their first Darkwater salaries.

After all, they were no longer military men. There would be no more taxpayer-funded paychecks coming in. There was no free health insurance. Their retirement benefits wouldn't start for another twenty years. Yeah,

Cody had squirreled away pretty much all his money from ten years in the Navy. But still, Cody wasn't ready for *this* kind of money.

He'd grown up hard in rural Texas. His toys were made of wood whittled down by his dad. Could hammer in a horseshoe just as well as he could fix up a 1980s Camaro for drag night down past the dry oil pumps. He learned to shoot, track, and hunt before he was a teenager.

And back where he was from, if you didn't hunt, you didn't eat. So yeah, having this kind of money scared him. Scared him like no enemy fighter ever could.

"You're just gonna have to learn to handle it," Benson had said to the four former SEALs a few months earlier at a briefing on Ax's ranch in Marietta, Georgia. "You all need money to live, and I can't have my team worried about paying the bills when they're out risking their lives in the shadows. You're all providing a service to America and the world, and there's no shame in being paid for it. I realize it's a lot of money, but at least this way I know none of you guys will ever be tempted to take a bribe from some thug and double-cross my ass. Remember, I've got thirty years of experience with bribery and blackmail. So do it for me, OK, guys? Take the damn money, all right? Help an old man sleep easy at night."

The guys had all grinned and chuckled. John Benson's silver-gray eyes matched his hair, but there was a timeless quality about the man. Cody thought the guy could be sixty or six hundred and he'd look the same.

There'd been some protests, a little more discussion, but in the end all the guys understood. Learning how to handle big money without being twisted by it would be just one more challenge the former SEALs would have to face.

And it wouldn't be the hardest challenge for at least a couple of the SEALs.

Ax was a new dad, and Bruiser was hot on his heels. Amy had just given birth to healthy twin boys, and Bruiser's wife Brenna was seven months pregnant. It was crazy to see Ax and Bruiser turn that military-precise focus towards preparing to be the best damn fathers in America, perhaps the world.

Obviously Cody and Dogg relentlessly busted their balls, gave them shit about how they'd have to defuse diapers instead of bombs now. Of course, Cody and Dogg were still single and very much *not* looking—despite Amy and Brenna's constant offers to match them with girlfriends.

Cody strolled towards the grocery store window as Benson finished up with Nancy. He glanced out through painted lettering advertising tomatoes as big as your head.

His gaze swept across the sidewalk and street, taking in every detail in a single pass. Ax had been Team Leader and Bruiser was the sniper. Cody's specialty was reconnaissance. He was a top-class recon man. All those years learning how to track game and get close without spooking his target gave Cody an edge that none of the other SEALs could match. He could sneak up on a deer and pluck a tick off its nose without the critter noticing. Shave a terrorist's mustache before slitting his throat--all without waking the guy up.

Capturing Cate

Of course, Cody hadn't seen a need for that kind of stealth on the streets of LA in the middle of the afternoon. The mission seemed easy as pie. There wasn't even any tracking to be done, no real recon at all.

Benson had said the target was in the Angel City Club and Cody just needed to get in position and wait for her to come out. Follow her and wait for instructions.

And so he'd followed her.

But it turned out harder than he thought.

Not because she was elusive.

Because she was so damn distracting.

Cody's gaze had zeroed in on her as she walked along the sunny sidewalk. Her butt was beautifully big, with wide hips that swung effortlessly with each step. She seemed very happy, he thought. She almost skipped down the sidewalk, and he couldn't help but feel a spring in his own heavy steps as he followed that gorgeous ass.

She wore tight stretch jeans that were deep black and looked expensive. A white sweater that looked equally expensive. The sweater was fitted, and Cody had seen her from the front when she'd walked out of the Angel City Club.

The sight made him gulp and quickly glance away.

Not because he was too much of a gentleman to stare at a woman's boobs.

It was because he knew that he'd been distracted by how attractive she was, had been shaken out of the cool mental state that he called stealth-mode.

It was the frame of mind that lets you follow someone without them even knowing you exist. Every animal—even the human animal—has an instinct that warns them if they're being watched. An expert recon-man knows how to trick that instinct. The secret is to clear your mind, slow your breathing, don't even think about your target.

Except that was damn hard to do after Cody saw his target.

He'd been slammed by the sight of her long black hair framing a pretty round face with lips red like a Panama sunset. Her curves formed the deadliest hourglass he'd ever seen, and he'd felt his eyes widen like a teenager who'd never glimpsed a fully developed woman before.

It had taken willpower, but Cody had forced himself to let her walk by so he could reset, recalibrate, regain that dispassionate focus where he was a machine and not a man.

But as Cody followed her from behind, his gaze kept drifting down. So finally he just went with the flow, forced himself to take in the details of this woman. Might as well start putting the pieces together as he waited for Benson to fill him in.

Her jeans were filled out perfectly, and he could clearly make out the wad of money stuffed in the left rear pocket. The other pocket was empty.

No phone sticking out of her jeans. Interesting. Most women in designer jeans were also the type to keep their phones handy for a quick selfie with a filter that made their skin look flawless.

Not that this woman would need a filter. She was probably around thirty, but her light brown skin was smooth like the beach after the tide went out. Cody couldn't figure out if she was South American or Italian. Maybe she was both. Or neither. Benson hadn't told him. Benson hadn't even told Cody her name.

"Catherine Bonasera," came Benson's voice through Cody's earpiece. "Wife of a man named Boro. Daughter of Romero and Renata Bonasera. She kept her maiden name because I guess this guy Boro doesn't use a last name. Anyway, the Bonasera Family are an offshoot of the Sicilian Mafia family tree. Powerful back in the Nineties, but they weakened over the years. Old man Romero still has deep connections at the seaports along the western coast of Italy, though. The Bonasera name can still get anything through customs at the smaller Italian docks. That seems to be the point of the marriage. An old-world style business arrangement. Marrying Cate gave Boro access to the Italian docks, which meant he could get his Colombian product into Europe without having to hire mules to swallow condoms of cocaine on commercial flights. Good deal for him. Good deal for the Bonaseras too, considering Cate's father was deep in debt to some very powerful European banks. Boro paid it all off as part of the deal. Boro appears to have done very well even though he isn't affiliated with the big Colombian Cartels. Runs a tight operation out of a huge compound surrounded by the Colombian jungle outside Medellin."

Cody tried to digest the mass of information hurled at him. It was like swallowing an entire turkey at once. Italian and Sicilian mafia. An arranged marriage with a Colombian drug kingpin. Cocaine in condoms. European bankers. Jungles. The usual.

He filed away the information, knowing it would sit

there in his subconscious. Eventually his brain would make connections, see patterns, draw conclusions. It would form the scaffolding as Cody put the puzzle pieces together.

He already knew this was how John Benson worked. Ax and Bruiser had told him how the crafty old wolf never told you everything up front.

Sometimes it was because Benson himself didn't know everything up front.

Other times it was because Benson didn't want *you* to know everything up front.

"Got it," Cody murmured, his gaze resting on Cate Bonasera as she looked at a rat that appeared to be sniffing a newspaper near a blue trashcan. "So she's married to a wealthy drug kingpin who lives in a fortress. Why is she alone? No bodyguards. No protection." He took a breath as his stealthy gaze caught something. "And no wedding ring."

Benson was silent. Cody could hear him breathe.

"Good," Benson said quietly. "Ax was right about you. You pay attention to details. Read between the lines. Think two steps ahead."

Cody frowned. "You testing me, Benson?" he growled, not sure if he was pissed at being tested or pleased at passing the test.

Maybe pleased about that missing wedding ring.

"Always," said Benson casually. "Now listen up. I thought this was going to be a straightforward thing, but it turns out Cate Bonasera might not be exactly what I expected."

Cody moved towards the glass-and-metal door. He

slowly pushed it open, remembering that there was a bell above the door. It tinkled gently as he let himself out of the store.

Cate Bonasera had resumed her half-skipping walk. She was at the end of the block now, and Cody picked up the pace when she took a left and disappeared around the corner of a yellow stucco building that housed a bail bonds place next to a flower shop.

"What did you expect her to be?" Cody asked as he approached the yellow building.

He slowed down as he got to the corner, then stopped dead when he saw that she was inspecting the fresh-cut roses stuck in water-filled plastic buckets outside the flower store.

Cody leaned against the wall outside the bail bond store. He pulled out his black unmarked phone and held it to his ear so he wouldn't look like he was talking to himself.

He stole a glance at Cate. She was smelling the roses. She was smiling. It was an odd smile, genuine but somehow strained, perhaps even a little sad.

Cody glanced at her eyes. They were dark brown like the burnt Sierra hills. There was a wildness in those eyes, the kind Cody had seen in unbroken mustangs when they realized they were trapped in the round, that they'd have to surrender eventually, bow their proud heads and accept their fate.

Except they didn't want to accept their fate. They wanted to steal another moment of freedom, even if they knew they were close to the end.

Cody watched as Cate reached for a black rose the color of midnight. She pulled it out of the bucket, shaking diamond-like droplets of water off the bright green stem.

The florist looked up from where he'd been shaving the thorns off a batch of pink roses. She asked him how much in Spanish. He grinned wide and shook his head. Winked and waved her away with the single black rose.

"*Grazie*," she said in Italian. Those sunset-red lips parted in a brilliant smile that almost destroyed both the florist and Cody.

"Mamma mia," Cody muttered in Texan.

"Your record doesn't say you speak Italian, Soldier," crackled Benson's voice in his left ear.

Cody ignored the jab. "She's on the move again," he whispered. "You better start talking, Benson. In plain English, preferably. I assume the mission is more than just following a rich drug dealer's wife on an LA shopping spree."

"It appears she might not want to be his wife anymore," said Benson. "She's on the run, Cody. That's how we got wind of it. Early this morning Boro put out an alert through the underworld network in California. He's offered a bounty for the safe return of Cate Bonasera. Ten million dollars to the man who brings her back to Colombia alive."

Cody frowned as he passed the flower shop and turned the corner.

He stopped dead in his tracks.

The sidewalk was empty.

A ripple of embarrassment raced up Cody's spine. He

scanned the street, then groaned when he saw a blue-and-white taxi turning the far corner. License plate ending in 734. She must have hailed a cruising cab. Shit.

Cody's rental Jeep Liberty was still outside the Angel City Club, and so he turned and ran back the way he'd come. His well-worn military boots hammered the sidewalk as he tore down the street. It was hot outside, and he was breathing hard after sprinting full tilt.

He revved the engine and squealed the tires as he barreled the Jeep back towards where he'd last seen the blue-and-white cab.

"Panting. Car engine. Burning rubber," said Benson slowly in Cody's ear. "You didn't lose your target, did you, Soldier?"

Cody preferred not to lie, so he stayed silent. His eyes narrowed as he turned left, then right, then sped up, then slammed on the brakes.

Red light.

Traffic cameras pointing at him.

He scanned the streams of cars going left and right at the intersection. Locked in on a blue-and-white cab. Wrong cab.

Light flipped to green. It was a four-way intersection. Cody was coming from one way. That left three options. Odds were against him. He decided to go left.

"She went straight," said Benson. "She's six cars ahead, taking the ramp to 101."

Cody glanced at the traffic cameras. After the Patriot Act, those were all upgraded to live video feeds that could be tapped into by any government agency with authority and access. Benson was no longer a government agent, but he clearly still had authority and access.

Cody shook off the embarrassment and focused back on the mission. He saw the cab rumble up the ramp to the expressway. He threaded the black Jeep between Maseratis and Mazdas, merged into traffic at seventy miles an hour, locked into position three cars behind Cate Bonasera.

And then slammed on the brakes again.

Los Angeles traffic.

Cody sighed. A sea of brake lights going off and on. A caterpillar of cars inching along.

"Well, no way to lose her now," Cody said. "Gonna lose the earpiece, though. Switch to the phone, Benson."

Cody pulled out his earpiece and tossed it onto the seat. Pulled out his phone from his blue jeans and tapped to connect it to the car speakers.

Benson's voice boomed through the Jeep's closed interior. He was talking to Nancy Sullivan again. Something about cancelling a private jet from LAX airport.

"Was that my plane ride to Colombia you just cancelled?" Cody said.

"What makes you say that?" said Benson.

"There's a ten million dollar bounty to bring a drug dealer's wife home safe and sound. I'm obviously the bounty hunter. Figured that much out, Benson. What I can't figure out is why you didn't have me grab her right outside the Angel City Club. My Jeep was right there. Could've done it quick and clean. We'd be on that private jet to Medellin right now. You could be briefing me on the rest of the mission while I crunch on honey-smoked almonds from a crystal bowl and sip Perrier from a champagne flute."

Benson grunted. "It would've been peanuts in a bag and ginger ale from a can, Soldier. We aren't spending taxpayer money anymore. Gotta watch the budget."

Cody grinned. He leaned to his right and snapped open the glove box. The glint of black steel greeted him.

His grin widened as he retrieved his trusty Sig Sauer 9mm handgun and stuck it in his belt. Ordinarily he'd have had it on him, but it was too hot for a jacket and it would be too conspicuous on the street, even in LA.

"Speaking of money," Cody continued. "I'm guessing this isn't about the ten million dollar bounty. Darkwater's treasury is fatter than that old pig my dad refused to kill."

"Good guess."

Cody thought a moment. Lost the grin. "So it's an opportunistic mission, isn't it? Just popped up out of the blue and you pounced on it. You're figuring out the rest as we go along."

Benson was silent for a moment. "Something like that," he said finally. "Yes, the Cate Bonasera bounty was random coincidence, just dumb luck. I saw the chance and took it. Couple of ways to play it. Thought I'd think it over once you had her safe and secure."

Cody grunted. "Which I would have if you hadn't pulled me off. So we're back where we started. What changed?"

"I called Kaiser just to give him a heads-up. CIA actively maintains contacts with drug cartels and mafia organizations all over." He paused a breath. "Kaiser told me to hold off. There was something else coming through the underworld wires. Thought it might be related to the Cate thing. He's in a meeting. Said he'll call soon. I'm waiting for more info."

Cody knew Martin Kaiser was not just CIA Director but an old friend and colleague of Benson's. They didn't always see eye-to-eye—indeed, they'd clashed many times during the last mission with Bruiser and Brenna. But in the end Kaiser and Benson trusted each other in the strange way that liars and manipulators trust each other.

"Kaiser's running CIA operations with the Colombia Cartels?" Cody asked. Then he sighed. "Dumb question. CIA Director is running ops in every shadowy organization in the galaxy. What, he wants to take over the mission and turn it into a hit on Boro or something like that?"

Cody was almost hopeful. He pushed away the thought. It came back like a boomerang.

Then he found that switch and flipped it back to machine-mode. Cold steel in his eyes. All desire overruled by logic.

"No," said Benson. "Boro doesn't ship product to the United States anymore. Hasn't in ten years. That was the deal. DEA agreed to let him operate, just so long as he didn't operate in America. Our borders are closed to him. But Europe is fair game."

Cody narrowed his eyes. Inched the Jeep forward. Tapped the brake again.

"That's why he arranged to marry Cate," Cody said. "You told me that already. Her father gets Boro access to the Italian seaports. From there Boro just trucks sacks of cocaine all over the free-trade Eurozone without any border checks. The marriage was a business deal, a cross-border treaty."

Cody tried to push away a strange rush that burned up along his throat. He refused to consider that it might be the burn of envy. That for one dark moment Cody almost envied a rat like Boro for being handed a woman like Cate.

Cody wondered what it would have been like to spend the wedding night with Cate Bonasera. He wondered what it might be like to spend *any* night with Cate Bonasera.

But then Cody remembered that Boro was a murdering piece of shit drug smuggler, and Cate Bonasera had been married to him for a decade.

She sure as hell wasn't some innocent damsel. She was crooked and corrupt just like her damn husband. They were both criminals. They were both thugs. They were both a waste of space, a mis-allocation of oxygen, destined to burn in hell for the lives their white powder had no doubt destroyed.

"Why would the DEA cut a deal with a drug smuggler instead of just burning his ass along with his coca fields?" Cody asked coldly, pushing away an annoyingly warm image of Cate Bonasera with that single black rose. He imagined dragging it along her wicked curves, the tiny thorns tracing faint lines of dark red on her smooth brown skin.

Benson chuckled dryly. "They're always cutting deals,

just like the CIA. Drug Cartels are heavily connected to politics, military, and the local economy. Besides, you put one down and another pops up. Easier to play chess than whack-a-mole."

Cody nodded. Didn't surprise him one bit. SEALs worked on CIA-run missions all the time, and different three-letter agencies were always cutting deals with monsters, shaking hands with murderers.

Lesser evil. Greater good. So on and so forth.

It was how the game was played. They were all tricksters and gamblers, and the games sometimes felt like high-stakes poker crossed with high-wire twister. Or peek-a-boo with lives on the line.

"I get it, but what was the play with Boro specifically," said Cody with the bluntness of a soldier who clearly knew the difference between right and wrong, good and evil, friend and enemy. "Why let him live? The DEA was running those shock-and-awe missions on the drug fields back then, weren't they? Letting the bastards know we were taking the show on the road, bringing the fight to their countries instead to letting the drugs get close to our street corners and schoolyards."

Benson sighed. "It's complicated, Soldier."

Cody stared at the slow-moving lines of cars. "I got time."

"No, you don't," said Benson. "Look, at first I wanted you to hold off on taking her while Nancy arranged a private jet that wouldn't be linked back to any government agency. She wasn't sure if she could get you one at LAX or if you'd have to drive to Long Beach or Orange County."

Cody nodded. Made sense. Minimize the time he'd have to keep a woman captive in a car in the middle of a sunny day in LA.

He tried not to think of Cate Bonasera under his control in the backseat of his Jeep. He tried not to think of restraining her. Holding her down.

Maybe disciplining her.

Was it wrong to spank a drug dealer's criminally complicit wife? Cody didn't think so. Perhaps it was his duty.

Yeah, that sounded right.

It was his duty to spank that booty.

He smiled proudly at his masterful poetry. Is that a haiku, he wondered.

It's my damn duty
To spank that fine booty.

Nah. Not enough syllables for a haiku. He sighed and leaned to his right to check on Cate's car.

It was still six vehicles ahead. She was still in the back seat. He relaxed, was about to ask Benson to keep talking.

But then movement in his side-view mirror caught his eye. It was a tricked-out red Toyota Supra with the turbo-charged engine. It was racing along the freeway shoulder. Black tinted windows. Shining silver rims. He knew what it was.

Cody had spent some time in California while he was trying to get accepted to the SEALs. He'd hit the cop and military bars down near Laguna Beach on Thursday nights. One time he'd listened to an LA narcotics officer talk about how the local gangs liked to race those tricked-out Supra turbos in the middle of the night. They'd get hopped up on speed and angel-dust and shred the streets. Even the cops stayed out of their way most nights.

Cody adjusted his mirror, his body tightening as the car slowed down. It was still on the shoulder, which was wide open. No stalled vehicles or cops or ambulances. So if the Supra was slowing down, it was looking for something.

Or somebody.

"Looks like someone else is after that bounty," Cody murmured, snapping off his seatbelt and making sure his Sig Sauer was secure in his Texas-leather belt with a buckle the size of the full moon and twice as shiny. "Not sure how they found her, but I'll have to move on her now, Benson. Shouldn't take long. The bounty only gets paid if Cate gets home safe, so they won't risk a full-on shootout. Be right back."

"Wrong," said Benson sharply. "You'll stand down, Soldier. Mission is over. Team Darkwater is out. You're out, Cody."

Cody frowned as the Supra passed him on the shoulder. He could see four shadows behind the dark-tinted windows of the red car. It was a small car. Four men inside.

Which meant it was already full.

No place for a fifth.

They weren't here to take Cate home.

Not alive, at least.

"What's going on, Benson?" Cody growled.

"Kaiser just got back to me with the new underworld alert," Benson said with a nonchalance that pissed Cody off. "Turns out Cate Bonasera isn't some innocent, helpless woman escaping her nightmarish life. She's a killer just like her husband, Cody. She murdered her bodyguard in her hotel room suite late last night. Stabbed him in the eye."

Cody's finger hooked the door handle. He cracked the Jeep's door open, placed his big military boot on the runner. He was ready to go in hot. A SEAL is trained to take on multiple assailants and come out the winner.

And in this case Cody would be the damn assailant.

Those gangbangers weren't expecting him.

He was the wildcard, the joker, the phantom.

Cody shrugged. "I guess she really wanted to get out of that marriage. I'll ask her about her unresolved rage issues when I've got her trussed up in the backseat of my Jeep, Benson." He thought about the full-load of gangbangers. This was not a rescue mission. "Bodyguard was a local gangbanger, wasn't he?"

"Bingo," snapped Benson. "Boro hasn't had anyone on his payroll in California for a decade. He called an old contact with the Caliente Crew and asked him to put a guy on Cate. Instead of a thankyou, the guy gets a knife in the eyeball."

"Guess that's bad table manners?" Cody said, sliding out of the car and dropping to a crouch, body close against the black metal of his Jeep. His black tee shirt was enough camouflage. The red Supra was four cars ahead now, just seconds away from drawing level with Cate's taxi.

Sure enough, the Supra stopped almost perfectly in line with Cate's cab. It meant they had GPS coordinates. Taxi driver must be on the message-tree of the underground network. Probably got a broadcast alert to look out for a curvy Italian firecracker with eyes like dusk and lips like a sunrise.

Or maybe he got both alerts.

Cody already figured out what Benson was saying.

The Caliente Crew had just put out their own alert to avenge their dead brother.

So now there were two bounties on Cate.

One from Boro, to bring her back in one piece.

The other from the Caliente Crew, to leave her on the street in pieces.

And it was clear which bounty the taxi driver had chosen.

"Cody, you there?" came Benson's voice through the half-open Jeep door. "Stand down, Cody. We're aborting the mission. The Caliente Crew are top dogs in LA County. Nobody's gonna touch Boro's offer and go against the Crew. She's dead meat. We're not getting involved in this. I can't have a Darkwater man involved in a shootout on the LA freeway in the middle of the afternoon. Civilians might get killed. Hell, *you* might get killed. This mission isn't worth the risk. It's over. Stand down and pull out, Cody. You hear me, Soldier?"

Cody heard him just fine, but the words didn't register. His vision was locked in on the red Supra. It was a two-door coupe. He watched as the doors popped open.

Two men with red-patterned bandanas tied over their faces tumbled out. The seats sprung forward and two more guys rolled out.

They wore heavy blue flannel shirts and loose black jeans. Cody assessed their weapons situation. Each of them had a handgun tucked in their belts against their lower backs.

That wasn't the problem.

The problem was in their hands.

Machetes.

Long rope-handled blades designed to hack through Mexican underbrush and Central American jungle.

They were going to chop her to bits, right there on the freeway.

Benson's voice came through the speakers again. Louder this time, with a nervous edge to the tone. There were no traffic cameras in sight. Benson didn't have eyes on Cody right now.

He didn't have control over Cody either.

What happened next was Cody's call.

So what's the call, Cody?

Do you follow orders and stand down?

Or do you follow that strange other feeling and charge ahead?

The men were moving towards Cate's taxi. They stayed low against the other cars, ducking below side-view mirrors, scuttling around bumpers.

Some of the drivers and passengers had noticed the machetes. Cell-phones were being held up for some juicy footage. As usual, most people would post videos to shock their friends on Social Media before bothering to call 911.

Benson's orders rang out over the Jeep's speakers again.

The men were creeping closer to Cate. Time was running out. Cody had to decide. Stay or go. Forward or backward. Doing nothing was still a decision.

Doing nothing was not an option.

And so Cody reached into the Jeep and turned off Benson's voice. He flipped open the armrest-hutch and pulled out his eight-inch pigsticker with the serrated blade and a point sharper than a needle. Like all SEALs, Cody was deadly with a blade. And being a stealth guy, a recon specialist, the knife was his weapon of choice.

Smooth like butter.

Swift like the wind.

Silent like death.

The bandana-masked crew were halfway across the six-lane freeway, just two cars abreast of Cate. Cody swept his gaze across the sea of cars, saw hundreds of cell-phones being held up. He didn't have a bandana, but he had a shirt.

He whipped it off, tied it around his nose and mouth, made sure it was secure. Anyone who knew Cody would recognize him, but this was enough for plausible deniability. Just another masked man with a machete. Move along, folks. Nothing to see here. Just another day in the City of Angels.

And now Cody was moving, knife in his right hand, green eyes sharp like daggers, boots pounding the burning asphalt as he charged into battle like a sea-monster rising from the depths of the dark ocean.

Funny thing was, he didn't even question why he was doing it.

Why he was ignoring a direct order.

Taking a risk he knew was stupid.

Protecting a woman he knew was a criminal.

A killer.

Not worth the air she was breathing.

But he couldn't stop himself.

Couldn't get his cold logic to overrule his hot blood.

Couldn't get the soldier in him to overrule the man in him.

The man in him that was ancient and primal.

Driven by a force that was choosing to protect this woman.

Powered by an instinct that whispered yeah, she might be a criminal and a killer . . .

But maybe she's also something else.

Maybe she's yours.

3

"Maybe one of those motels near the airport?" Cate had told the taxi driver in her heavily accented English. "There are some near the airport, yes? I saw them on the way to town. Take me there."

The driver had glanced at her in the mirror, then adjusted it so she could no longer see his eyes as they drove. He was pockmarked and bearded. Judging from his accent, Cate guessed he spoke Spanish just fine. But she'd decided to only speak English now. She was in America now.

For years she'd streamed American shows and American movies, gone back and forth on Social Media, learned all the slang and abbreviations, euphemisms and exclamations. And of course she and Marya spoke English sometimes, just to practice.

Cate worried about Marya as the taxi pulled onto the highway and then immediately got stuck in traffic worse than the Medellin market square on Sunday after church.

Marya knew her way around Boro's compound better than Cate. She worked with the nurses and doctors in the infirmary, treating everything from accidental snakebites to purposeful mutilations ordered by Boro.

Everyone loved Marya for her shrill girlish laugh and her sweet smile that made her blue eyes light up. But still Cate worried.

Did Boro know Marya had warned Cate? Was Marya already just a reminder on Nico's knuckle? Marya had never wanted to be married, but she did wear a silver ring with a pretty red ruby on it.

"Oh, please let Marya be all right," she'd muttered anxiously to herself under the heavy backbeat thumping through the taxi's speakers. "Can you turn that down, please?" she called to the driver.

The driver looked up. He'd been tapping on his phone. He hadn't heard her. Cate sighed and shook her head. Leave it be, she thought. At least this way there is no danger of having to talk to the driver. I do not like how he looks at me. I do not like how he sweats at the neck. It reminds me of Boro.

So Cate looked out the window and tapped her fingernails on her Prada mini-pack. Her snub-nosed .38 was in there along with the cash she'd gotten for her ring at the pawn store. The rest of the cash was in her jeans, under her butt.

She shifted on the seat. The wad of cash felt uncomfortable. It put her off balance. She leaned forward slightly, raised her left buttcheek off the seat, slid her fingers into the pocket to smooth out the crumpled cash. She didn't want to pull it out in front of the driver.

Cate glanced across at the driver as she leaned forward. He was scrolling through his messages. She saw his phone screen. Some chat app she didn't recognize. A group chat, judging by the different user icons. Spanish. Her eyesight wasn't good enough to read the words.

But as he scrolled, somebody posted an image. It popped up in full color.

And Cate's face lost all its color.

It was an image of her.

Taken just three months ago, by Boro's photographer. They'd gotten it done for some official documents. It was clear and focused, which meant it was the original digital version. It could only have been sent by Boro.

Cate almost doubled over as a sickening pain ripped through her gut. She knew how criminal networks operated these days, especially in the world of drug gangs. There were hundreds of gangs all over the USA, smaller units within those gangs. Gang members all used encrypted chat apps, and they had various group chats setup for different purposes. They also had systems sort of like phone-trees to quickly send broadcasts and alerts up and down the line, even across gang lines.

Had Boro put out a hit on her?

Ordered her execution?

No, Cate decided as she slowly leaned back against the seat and tried to calm her breathing, slow her heart down. Boro would want her brought back to Colombia.

He would want to punish her betrayal in a way that saved his honor, reminded his men that nobody was above his law, nobody was safe from his twisted sense of justice. He would send the message that even his own wife was not immune from the most brutal of fates.

Now that sadness swelled in her breast again. A sinking feeling of resignation. A lonely realization that you reap what you sow, that a few hours of freedom was all that she deserved, that she was a fool if she thought she could escape her true fate.

The sadness was so deep she almost relaxed and just waited for whoever came for her. She felt foolish like a runaway child who gets no farther than the front yard before finding that the gate is locked and she has no key, is too small to jump the fence, has no wings to lift her to freedom.

On either side of her she could see people in other cars paying attention to something towards her left. She turned her head.

There was movement between the cars near the shoulder. She saw a man with a bandana wrapped around his face. Then another man. A third and then a fourth.

They were all masked with bandanas.

They all carried machetes.

Cate knew machetes very well. Boro's men carried them unsheathed in their sashes and belts. They were used to clear vines and shrubs. To slash the heads off vipers. To chop hands off at the wrist sometimes.

She'd seen it done. If one of Boro's men was caught stealing cocaine or cash, he lost a hand. If he was caught a second time, he lost the other hand. Without hands he could not harvest the crop or process the powder or bag the cash or protect his master.

Such men were not killed but simply relieved of their duties. They were fed and clothed, allowed to live in the barracks on the compound. They lived in shame. Reminders that a man who does not work is no man at all. They might as well be women, was the common taunt around Boro's compound.

Now Cate looked at her hands and frowned. It occurred to her that if she sat here helpless and gave up so soon then she truly *did* deserve her brutal fate. She would be like those disgraced men, handless and helpless.

She couldn't just give up.

Giving up was a choice.

Not everything in her life had been her choice, but if she gave up now, it would be her choice.

She felt the glimmer of hope in her breast.

Being born into a mafia family wasn't her choice, she thought. The wedding hadn't been her choice. Maybe she could even tell herself that staying with Boro a decade without slitting his throat or her own throat was forgivable.

But to sit here helpless and not choose a different fate could not be forgiven.

And so Cate reached into her Prada pack and pulled out that silver snub-nosed handgun. The driver's eyes went wide, and he yelled in Spanish and tumbled out of the taxi.

He scrambled to his feet and ran like Boro's starved, beaten watchdogs were after him. Cate wished she'd been ruthless enough to put a bullet in the back of his head for snitching on her. But a part of her was also relieved to know she wasn't that cold-blooded.

Still, this was not the time to be concerned about human lives other than her own. No doubt that photograph had been sent on Boro's orders, but surely he would not have ordered four men with machetes drawn if this was a simple matter of bringing her home to face Colombian justice.

Then who were they?

Why did they want her dead?

Were they Boro's enemies?

No, they were her enemies.

She thought of Ponytail and that teardrop tattoo. She remembered that he'd had contacts at the hotel, contacts who perhaps checked the room and found his body way before it had started to stink.

Which meant there was good news and there was bad news.

The good news was that she was not going to face Boro's jungle justice.

The bad news was that LA city justice was not looking much better.

For a moment she considered that using the .38 on herself might be the best option. Machetes were used more for their message than their efficiency. With four men, she would be held down and butchered starting from the ankles.

It would take less than thirty seconds to cut off all her limbs and open so many arteries that even if she were next door to a blood-bank there'd be no hope in hell. She'd die staring at her own fingers twitch on her severed hands like in the Addam's Family cartoon.

The machete-wielding men had risen from their low positions and were striding between the cars, their eyes focused dead on her. They seemed unconcerned about the cell phone cameras, and rightfully so.

Bandanas covered their hairstyles and their faces. Long sleeves covered any tattoos. They wore no rings. They knew what they were doing.

They had done it before.

Cate's hands trembled as she tightened her grip on the gun. She raised it and pointed it out the window.

Immediately the men split up. They moved quick like vipers in the dust.

Before Cate could react, they were approaching her from four directions at once.

She started to panic.

Her vision went blurry.

She pulled the trigger.

The back window of the taxi shattered explosively. She screamed, furious at herself for not realizing the window had been up. There was glass all over the seat, on her clothes, in her hair. The little square pieces sparkled like diamonds.

She looked out and saw that she'd hit one man in the chest. But he hadn't gone down.

He was leaning against a car. She knew the .38 was a small caliber gun. She should have emptied the gun into his chest. She should do it now.

The man took two gasping breaths, then raised his machete and came running at her.

Cate raised the gun and took aim.

But a big hand suddenly wrenched the gun out from her grasp.

A massive shirtless man sporting tanned muscles and wearing a black hood appeared like an angel of destruction at her window.

He shouted something at her. It was muffled through his hood, which Cate realized was a shirt wrapped around his face.

Capturing Cate

She stared into his eyes. They were green like the deep sea trenches off the coast of Colombia. He yelled something again, then shoved his hand through the taxi window.

She felt the base of his palm thump against her forehead so hard she was knocked flat on her back, landing hard on the backseat of the taxi.

Cate bounced back up, gasping for air.

She saw the shirtless man whirl his body away from her.

He slashed viciously at the air with a long shiny knife.

The clean silver metal of the blade was suddenly sprayed with fresh wet blood.

The machete-man she'd shot in the chest was on the street in a pool of dark blood that was getting larger from the cut on his neck.

Cate watched as the tall, heavily muscled man whipped his body around and kicked the second machete-man in the ribs.

Cate heard the crunch of bone, saw the gangster's body smash into the side of a blue minivan.

The black-hooded monster stabbed him twice in the gut, then slashed him across the throat so fast his hand was a blur. Blood streaked the blue minivan like graffiti.

The two remaining attackers now diverted their attention to this unknown maniac who'd just killed their buddies.

Cate exhaled, but took the next breath so fast she almost choked.

The black-hooded beast was dodging machete-swipes with a lazy quickness that looked like slow-motion to her frenzied mind. She stared at his massive chest gleaming bronze. He was sweating in the sunlight, the perspiration running rivers down the canyon-like grooves of his abdomen. His eyes were clear and focused, like he'd done this before too, done it so many times it was like a job to him.

A job he was damn good at.

He kicked the machete out of the third guy's hand, then grabbed the man's arm and whipped him towards his buddy like a weapon.

The two gangsters slammed into each other, and the black-hooded avenger swooped in and stuck both of them with two viciously precise stabs in their sides.

They went down gurgling as their lungs filled with blood. Cate watched with dark fascination as he cut their throats without any hesitation, like there was no doubt in his mind that they needed to die and he needed to kill them.

She could tell he took no pleasure in their deaths, but she suspected he wasn't going to mourn them either.

He'd killed before.

She knew it.

She saw it.

There was no remorse in his eyes, no doubt in his strikes, no hesitation in his moves.

"We need to move," he shouted to her as he wiped his blade on his jeans until it shone silver like the moon. "Get out of the damn car."

Cate fumbled for the door handle. She didn't know who he was or why he'd just saved her. She didn't think this was the time to ask. Would it matter what the answer was? He'd just killed four men in about twelve seconds. He'd also taken her gun. She wasn't going to club him to death with a pair of Carolina Herrera sunglasses.

The first thing that went through her mind was that if he wanted her dead, she'd be dead. The second thing was that he was just another thug, but this time responding to Boro's bounty to bring her to him alive.

Alive was better than dead.

At least for now.

While they were still in America.

While there was still a chance for escape.

Cate blinked as he strode over and stopped outside the taxi door. He was barely even breathing hard. His chest was like two bronze slabs of granite. An abdomen like a complex labyrinth of ridges and valleys.

His blue jeans hung low on his powerful hips, revealing a deadly V of muscle that disappeared beneath his waistband. He wore a heavy leather belt that looked like it had been through at least one World War.

Cate noticed that his oval belt buckle was very large and extremely shiny, with a proud bull snorting engraved puffs of smoke.

Perhaps he is a cowboy, she thought absentmindedly as the wailing of sirens rose up over the screams and gasps and shouts of the spectators.

The sirens snapped her back from the daze she'd slipped into while watching the black-hooded cowboy spatter the asphalt with the blood of her attackers.

It had been like a movie. A play. A scene so surreal it

must have been scripted, staged, made up by the mischievous trickster spirits that sometimes took the form of coyotes or wolves or serpents of the night.

"Damn it, *move!*" shouted the cowboy.

He yanked open her door, grabbed her arm just above the elbow, yanked her out of the taxi so hard that her head barreled into his abdomen.

"Ay!" she exclaimed, rubbing her forehead.

She didn't have time to exclaim again, because the cowboy was dragging her by the arm, leading her between the stopped cars towards the side of the highway.

People stayed out of their way, but cell-phone cameras were rolling. Cate covered her face like a movie star. She whipped her head forward so her long black hair flopped down and obscured her features. She stumbled as they weaved between the cars, but the cowboy's grip was firm and he didn't let her fall.

He led her across all six lanes to a red two-door car that was parked on the side of the road. It had black tinted windows. There was no one in it.

The cowboy pulled open the passenger-side door. The front seat was angled forward, clearing a path to the cramped back seat.

Before she could stop him, the cowboy had shoved her face-first into the backseat. He yanked the front seat back and locked it in place, trapping her in the back. The door slammed shut and Cate sat in the dark interior and blinked.

The sudden stillness and silence disoriented her. She blinked again, wondering if this was some scene made up by her brain because she was dying from blood loss.

Perhaps she'd already been chopped up and this was her brain going into death-spasms, releasing chemicals that formed the hallucination that she was alive. She had heard of such things.

She stared at the empty front seat. She peered through the front windshield. They were in the emergency lane. It was an open road ahead of her.

The cowboy was nowhere in sight. Cate stared at the steering wheel. She blinked three times like a butterfly testing its wings.

The steering wheel was covered in shiny red leather. She looked down at the driveshaft. The keys were in the ignition. The keychain was a tiny set of dice made of black leather. They swung gently back and forth like they were beckoning to her. Roll the dice, they seemed to whisper.

Cate blinked again.

She stared at the empty road ahead.

Then she sprang into action.

Or tried to, at least.

There were no rear doors, and she was too large to squeeze between the seats of the small car. She'd spent her whole life very happy with her big round Italian ass but now wished she had the slim hips of a prepubescent schoolgirl so she could slip between the bucket seats and take the wheel and speed off down the freeway like in that getaway movie playing through her mind.

She was jittery with anxiousness, but she tried to think calmly. Just incline the passenger seat forward, climb over, flop into the driver's seat, get yourself in position. Then turn the key, grab the wheel, and drive like a madwoman. Simple, no? Do it, you fool. Quick.

Cate found the lever and flipped the passenger seat forward. Then she tried to maneuver herself into the driver's seat from behind. It was not easy. She was not built for a car like this. Her hips were wide and her breasts were large. All sorts of objects poked and prodded her as she grunted and grumbled, contorted and complained.

And when the cowboy opened the driver's side door, Cate was bent forward, her elbows digging into the front seat cushion, lower back arched down, her big butt up in the air, those stretch jeans dangerously near the end of their range. Oh, please let my jeans not rip down the back seams, she thought feverishly.

"Hi," she said awkwardly, craning her neck up towards him. Her face was approximately level with his crotch. The bulge beneath that big buckle was equally big.

She gulped and moved her gaze upwards.

Bronze ridges of abdomen muscles like the rolling hills of El Salvador. She felt heat along her neck, tightness in her bra. He was sweating, and his bare torso glowed like wet granite in the sunlight.

She could smell his aroma. He smelled clean like the earth and very masculine. Not like Boro. Certainly not like Nico. His musk was strong and strangely appealing.

It invaded her senses and made her buttocks tighten. A warmth moved along the insides of her thighs. She felt some wetness under her black jeans. She told herself it was a trickle of perspiration.

"Get in the back," he ordered. His voice was deep, the

words somehow both calm and commanding. "Now, please."

He placed one very large leather laced boot into the seatwell and prepared to enter the car. His shadow blocked about eighty percent of the California sun.

Cate suddenly realized the cowboy wasn't going to wait for her to plan her retreat. He would sit on her face if she didn't move.

Cate scrambled backwards with the grace of a cat wearing gumboots. Her bottom hit the side of the passenger seat, which was still inclined forward. Getting from there into the backseat would make for a very awkward manipulation of her curves. Very unladylike.

Also very foolish to be worried about seeming unladylike, she told herself. Especially when police sirens were approaching, corpses were stiffening in the street, blood was drying on the freeway, and many groups of angry men apparently wanted her to suffer and eventually die screaming.

She brushed a strand of hair from her face and rolled herself into the backseat. She went face first, butt last. Blood rushed to her cheeks. She thought she saw the cowboy glance at her raised rump. More blood rushed to her cheeks.

Then she gasped when she felt his hands on her. Just one hand, actually. Palm flat on her bottom, pushing.

A quick, powerful, decisive push.

He was moving her ass out of the way so he could drive.

Cate righted herself in the backseat just as the cowboy started the car. She leaned forward between the seats, then was slammed back when the little red car shot forward like a rocket. She stared as the road came at her through the windscreen.

"Seatbelt," said the cowboy without taking his eyes off the road. "Now, please."

His voice oozed with authority, and the addition of the word *please* struck her as strange. It was clearly an order, but with an oddly formal politeness to it.

She looked at him. The shirt still covered his face. His eyes were dark green and very focused on the road. His shoulders were heavy with muscle, etched with scars. His triceps bulged as he operated the gearshift.

Cate glanced at his massive hands gripping the red leather-covered wheel. Fingers thick like lamb sausages. No rings at all. No tan lines where there might have been a ring.

She touched her face and wondered why it mattered. Perhaps it was years of seeing Nico parade his rings around the compound.

Or perhaps it was something else.

"You speak English?" said the cowboy. He reached towards his face and pulled the black shirt off his nose and mouth, tossed it towards the passenger seat.

The passenger seat was still folded forward, and the shirt slid down the back of the seat and landed by Cate's feet. She stared at it and blinked. Then she picked it up.

It was heavy American cotton. It smelled like him. She fought a strange desire to bring it to her nose and inhale his aroma.

Capturing Cate

"Shit, you don't speak English," he muttered, shooting a glance at her via the rearview mirror.

It was a quick glance at first, but then the cowboy's eyes flicked back for a second look.

He blinked, held the gaze, blinked again like he was surprised or something.

"I speak excellent English," she declared, blushing a little at her defensiveness. She was suddenly conscious of her accent.

The cowboy glanced at her again in the mirror. His green eyes smiled for a flash, then went hard. He nodded once.

"Good," he said. "Then put on your damn seatbelt, Senorita."

Cate looked left, then right. There were two seatbelts, not three. She'd have to pick a side and strap herself in

She slid her ass behind the passenger side, diagonally across from the cowboy. She reached behind her shoulder and pulled the strap over her bosom. She had to wriggle a bit and then adjust the strap to get it between her breasts.

She snapped in the buckle and looked up just in time to catch the cowboy's eyes hurriedly flick away from her.

This time he hadn't been looking at her face.

And this time the trickle of wetness she felt was perhaps not from the outside heat but from the kind of heat that warms you from the inside.

The kind of heat that only her own familiar fingers could bring out in Cate.

It surprised her. She absentmindedly straightened her loose hair as she looked down at herself and frowned. She could see the bold cut of her own cleavage down her V-neck. She saw her thighs looking thick on the seat.

She glanced up at the mirror again. The cowboy's eyes were back on the road. That hardness was still in there. It was not a cold hardness, though.

"Senora," she said to him.

"What?"

"You called me Senorita. That is incorrect. In Spanish culture a married woman is addressed as Senora."

His dark brows knitted together for an instant. "Well, I ain't Spanish. Senorita works just fine."

"It is rude," she said.

He shrugged those big shoulders. "Do I seem like I give a damn?"

She shrugged her own shoulders. "Actually, yes. You do."

The cowboy chuckled dryly. "You don't know shit about me, Lady."

"Calling me *lady* is even ruder. I have a name, you know."

"Yeah, I know."

"I know you know."

Now he turned his head and glanced at her. His hands were still firm on the wheel. Massive hands on a little red wheel. It was like a giant driving a toy car. A children's storybook picture, Cate thought.

She broke a giggle at the thought. Perhaps it was because for the first time all day Cate had felt safe. She knew she wasn't really safe, but her body was relaxing like it didn't know any better. Silly body.

"What is your name?" she asked, enunciating carefully in case her thick accent made it hard to understand. She wasn't sure if she was being condescending towards him or herself.

"You can call me Sir," he said with a touch of lazy amusement.

"No, thank you," she said curtly. She thought a moment. "I will call you Cowboy."

Those green eyes almost smiled. "You don't need to call me anything. We won't be talking much."

"Oh? Why is that?"

Cowboy grunted. He did not answer. Perhaps he was trying to prove his point.

Cate glanced at the profile of his face. He was certainly tanned like a cowboy. His stubble was thick and dark. His features were sharp and symmetrical, with a strong jaw above a neck thick like a tree. Perhaps some would call him handsome. She was not prepared to do so.

He made no attempt to put on his shirt. The air-conditioning was blowing strong from the center vents. The cool dry air brought his warm, heavy scent to her. She did not mind it.

The sirens were not following them, it appeared. The cowboy made no move to slow down. The traffic alongside was moving again. Soon the cowboy had merged back in with the flow.

He slowed to the speed of traffic, then took one hand off the wheel and pulled a sleek black phone out of his pocket. Cate did not see a brand name on it.

He tapped the screen, but then tapped it dead again like he had just reconsidered.

"You are a bounty hunter, yes?" she said.

He grunted. "I am now."

"Also before," she said flatly. "I saw you near the store that said Bail Bonds. You work for them?"

The cowboy glanced at her again, then shrugged. "Freelancer. Get paid by the job."

Cate smiled tightly. "And how much does this job pay?"

He was silent for a breath. "Ten million dollars is the bounty."

The number did not faze her. "Boro wants me alive, yes?"

"Alive is usually better than dead in my experience."

She smiled. "Then you have not experienced a man like Boro."

The cowboy did not respond. Cate was impressed. She thought perhaps he might counter that he had experienced men far worse than Boro. Perhaps his pride would be hurt and he would brag about the horrible men he had encountered.

Perhaps he is a horrible man himself, Cate told herself as the car's loud engine rumbled her body in a vaguely satisfying way. After all, he did not hesitate when killing four men. He also made sure each man was dead. He did it like it was his job.

"Why is a bounty hunter so good at killing people?" she asked. "A bounty hunter is paid to capture, not kill, yes?"

"I do just fine on the capture front too," he said coolly. "Case in point."

"Sorry?" she said, frowning at the expression.

He sighed, gestured towards her with his head. His eyes teased her, that hardness falling away for a fraction of a second.

"Oh," she said, understanding what he meant. She turned to the window and looked out the tiny triangle of window glass.

They were passing many cars, weaving through traffic but with a smoothness that told her the cowboy was as good behind the wheel as he might be on a saddle.

Still, she did not like sitting in the back of a two-door car. When she was sixteen they'd driven passed an overturned car on the way to Milan. It was a white Alfa Romeo. A two-door car. Cate saw streaks of dried blood on the little triangle of window-glass in the back. They looked like clawmarks. Like someone had been desperately trying to get out but couldn't because there was no door.

"I would like to sit in the front," she said.

The cowboy shook his head. "Nope."

He pressed down on the gas to overtake a pickup truck loaded with old wood boards that had chipped paint and bent nails like fingers saying come to me. Then the cowboy moved out of the fast lane, eased up on the gas, settled the car into a steady speed.

"Thought a woman like you would be used to riding in the back," he said after a little while.

She glanced up, partly amused, partly indignant. She settled down when she considered that the cowboy was correct. She was mostly driven places by men who worked for Boro. She always sat in the back. It was not appropriate to sit in the front with strange men.

So why had she just asked to sit in the front next to this man?

"Why do you say it like that?" she asked.

"Like what?"

"Like it disgusts you."

"Like what disgusts me?"

"Like I disgust you."

The man laughed once in surprise, shot a glance at her, shook his head and sped up again. "Look, forget I said anything, OK?"

She huffed out a breath. Straightened her neckline. Adjusted the seatbelt. "That will be easy. Considering you have said nothing interesting," she muttered.

The cowboy broke a crooked grin. "Didn't know I was being paid to keep you entertained."

"You are being paid to keep me alive, yes? So if I die of claustrophobia in the backseat of this little car, then no bounty for you. You will have killed four men for nothing."

"Not quite nothing," the cowboy said softly.

Cate's heart fluttered a bit and she felt her cheeks burn. It occurred to her that he'd killed four men not for nothing but for her.

Capturing Cate

She realized she hadn't even thanked him. Right now she would be fit only for the display window at a butcher shop if not for the cowboy.

She glanced at his profile again, her eyelids lowering as she dragged her gaze away from the sharp edges of his nose and chin, those dark red lips pressed tight together like they were holding back secrets.

There was something very proud about the way the cowboy was sitting. His back was straight and his jaw was set firm like a soldier at attention.

She wondered if he'd been a soldier before becoming a bounty hunter. Was that not a big step down? She wondered if he had done something bad, disobeyed orders, broken the rules. Perhaps he was not so different from her, yes?

"Thank you," she said stiffly, not really wanting to thank him because she was afraid it would make him believe she was in his debt.

Which she might have been if he'd chosen to protect her out of a moral code and not just greed.

"For killing those men," she added when the cowboy stayed silent.

"They needed killing," he said.

There was steel in his voice, almost like he meant it, like perhaps he did have a moral code. Of course, she knew that ten million dollars could instill a strong moral code in a mercenary too. "And I need the money," he added hastily.

She frowned inwardly at the last sentence. There was something in his tone that sounded forced, insincere.

"There is still a long way to go before you see any of that money," she said. Then she thought a moment. "In fact, you may not see any of that money even if you *do* manage to bring me to Boro," she said, hoping to put some doubt in the cowboy's mind.

It was already clear to Cate that her path to freedom went through the cowboy. The only question was how that path twisted and turned, how it wandered and weaved. She thought through it as logically as she could.

She certainly could not fight him.

She probably could not escape him.

But perhaps she could turn him.

Play him.

Break him.

Again that warmth tingled along the inside of her thighs. She touched her neck, looked away, stared out the window.

Her mind spun through her options. It was not as simple as offering herself to him in return for freedom. She was his captive and he was ten times as strong as she. She would not be offering something he could not take if he wanted.

She stole a glance at his proud, straight-backed posture. She tried to read him, to get some clear sign of what made this cowboy tick.

What were his chokepoints?

His vulnerabilities?

There must be buttons she could push.

Dials she could turn.

Levers she could pull.

Capturing Cate

"You know Boro is going to kill me," she said. Perhaps she could try pity. Perhaps the cowboy was the chivalrous sort.

The cowboy grunted. "Don't think so."

She huffed out a breath. "It is the truth."

"Why pay ten million to bring you back alive if he's going to kill you anyway? There were four machete-wielding madmen who were about to do it for free."

Cate huffed again. "You do not understand Boro."

The cowboy shrugged. "I don't need to understand Boro. He's your husband, not mine."

Cate looked at her hand. Studied her fingers. Touched the line on her ring finger that was a lighter shade of brown. She made a fist, digging her nails into her palm.

When she looked up, the cowboy's head turned back to the road.

He'd been looking at her.

What had he seen?

What had she shown him?

Had she been *trying* to show him something?

"He is not my husband anymore," she said. "I have left him."

The cowboy laughed. It was a full laugh, mouth open, strong white teeth flashing like a tiger's.

Cate did not like the laugh.

"You can laugh, but my blood will be on your hands." She spat the words out, not sure why she was bothered that he did not seem to give a damn about her. Why should he? He was a mercenary, a bounty hunter, a thug-for-hire looking for a payday.

"Nice try, lady," he said. "But it's not gonna work. You made your choice to marry the guy. Unless you're saying you had no idea who Boro was when you two got hitched."

Cate moved uncomfortably on the seat. She did not look at the cowboy.

"Thought as much," the cowboy said. There was an edge to his voice. A mix of triumph and something else.

She frowned as she tried to interpret his tone, the undercurrent of something he'd tried to hide but not well enough.

Disappointment.

She turned to face him now, fire in her dark eyes, hope burning in her heart. "I knew who he was. I married him not for love but for duty. Do you understand what duty means, Cowboy?"

He glanced up at the rearview mirror, directly into her eyes.

"Yeah, I know what duty means," he growled, his voice low and dangerous. There was fire in his eyes too now. That controlled coldness was gone.

Cate had pushed a button in him, she suddenly realized.

She'd found a chokepoint to squeeze.

A lever to pull.

A dial to turn.

And she was going to turn that dial all the way up.

Squeeze that chokepoint until she got under his skin.

Pull that lever until something snapped.

After all, she was a mafia princess by birth.

A brutal drug lord's woman by marriage.

A murderer and runaway by choice.

There was no moral code left for her to follow.

She'd passed the point of no return.

Committed herself to doing whatever it took to survive, to thrive, to break free from the cocoon of her life and flap her shiny black wings like the dark butterfly she knew she was inside.

4

It was hot inside the car, Cody thought as he glanced at the air-conditioner dial. It was turned to full blue, the fans blasting on high.

He was still shirtless. His sweat had dried. It was only when he felt the blood throbbing through that thick vein in his neck that he realized the heat was coming from inside him.

Maybe from inside *her*.

She's gotten under my skin, Cody thought.

He was pissed at himself. He'd guessed she would try every trick in the man-vs-woman book to get out of his clutches. He'd been ready for it.

What he hadn't been ready for was being so close to her body and feeling something very dangerous rise up in him. He'd felt a flash of it back there when he'd charged into battle and destroyed those four men with vicious precision and overwhelming force.

It was a strong protective instinct, no doubt about it.

Cody knew the difference between instinct and intent, and the need to protect Cate had bubbled up from the deepest part of his being, that place which was more animal than human.

Capturing Cate

Raw energy.
Deceptively simple.
Dangerously powerful.

Yeah, it was dangerous, Cody warned himself. SEALs are trained in interrogation and negotiation, to break enemy captives and extract information that can save lives or end lives—depending on the mission.

So Cody was no stranger to mind games and manipulation, to using any means necessary to win the battle. He knew damn well you gotta keep your head straight when you play those games.

But Cate Bonasera was already messing with his head.

Hell, she'd gotten to him before he even talked to the woman. He'd charged into a public knife-fight even though he knew better. Disobeyed Benson's order to stand down, even though he knew Benson was right to call the mission dead. Team Darkwater was bigger than one mission.

Bigger than one woman.

So Cody told himself to get his head straight. It didn't matter why Cate Bonasera was running. Didn't matter why she was desperate enough to murder a man and then start improvising like she didn't really have a plan, was making it up as she went along.

And it didn't matter that he saw something strange and powerful in those dark eyes of hers.

It *couldn't* matter.

Again he thought of a mustang that's almost been broken but then sees the gate swing open and makes a run for it. The mustang has lost some of its wildness, isn't entirely sure if it's been broken or not.

But still the creature runs.

She runs even though some part of her whispers that it's hopeless, that she'll be run down and brought back, that freedom isn't her fate.

But still she runs.

She runs because some little part of that wildness can never be broken.

Never be tamed.

Never be owned.

"Duty," came her voice through his swirling thoughts. "That is why you killed those men."

Cody shook his head. "Told you. I need you alive to claim the ten million from your husband."

"You were lying," Cate said, an annoying hint of smugness in her tone. "You said they needed killing. That was the truth, not what you said later about the money. You killed them because it was your duty."

Cody tried to laugh it off. "Sounds like we have different definitions of duty."

"Oh? What is duty to you, Cowboy?"

Cody shook his head. "We're done talking, Mrs. Bonasera."

"Fine. I'll go first," she said with a shrug.

Her breasts moved beneath her sweater as she shrugged. Cody saw it in the rearview mirror. He blinked and focused so hard back on the road that his head hurt. He almost crushed the steering wheel to powder. His heavy foot pressed down on the gas.

"To me duty is something that is above morality," Cate said from behind him. "It is something that must be done regardless of right or wrong." She took a breath. "What do you think of that, Cowboy?"

Cody took a long, slow breath. That was actually a damn good insight.

"I think nothing of it," he said gruffly. "I'm thinking about how long it'll take to count my ten million dollars."

Cate laughed once. "I advise you not to count it in Boro's presence," she said. "He will be insulted."

Cody shrugged. "Just business. He'll understand, I'm sure."

"I'm sure he won't."

"Doesn't he count the cash when he gets paid for a shipment?"

Cate shook her head. "Nobody steals from Boro. If anything, the distributers pay extra just in case they have counted wrong." She took a breath. "Boro would have the money counted in the early days after transferring his operations to Europe. Just to establish trust." She smiled, shook her head. "The first few deals were fine. Then, on a twenty million dollar deal, the distributor shorted him by almost a hundred thousand dollars. He insisted it was a mistake, that he would make it right in the next shipment."

Cody listened. Cate paused. Cody looked at the rearview mirror, searched for her eyes. She was waiting for him to look. Cody held her gaze. Her dark eyes were beautiful, he thought. And dangerous, he reminded himself.

But Cody didn't look away from her. He broadened his perspective so he could take in the road while he stared down her reflection. He understood that you don't give an inch when you're playing a game like this.

It was only when she blinked and looked down with the hint of a smile curling on her dark red lips did Cody wonder if she was reeling him into her story like Scheherazade weaving her web of tales, stalling for time, for her freedom, for her life.

Cate continued.

"Boro said the payment would have to be made on the spot or the deal was off and there would be no future deals," she said. "The distributer offered to take less product, since he did not have the cash. Boro said it was all or nothing." She paused. "Then Boro asked for his thumb."

Cody raised an eyebrow. "His *thumb?*"

This was interesting. A finger was one thing. Thumb was something else. A hand was pretty damn useless without a thumb.

Cate nodded, gazed out the window.

Cody watched her in the rearview mirror.

She wasn't lying, that was for damn sure. But that didn't mean she wasn't try to play him. Show him how Boro thought, how he acted, what he did to people who betrayed his trust.

Make him wonder what Boro would do to her.

Cody's phone buzzed in its spot near the gearshift. Caller was blocked, which meant it was Benson. Just a text. They couldn't talk right now without blowing Cody's cover. Without exposing Darkwater.

For a moment Cody wondered if a better cover would be the truth. Maybe she'd cooperate. A cooperative captive was a lot easier to handle.

But the moment didn't last. If she knew about Cody and Darkwater, she might betray him to Boro in exchange for her life. And anyway, Cody couldn't guarantee her safety once they were in Colombia, on Boro's turf.

Hell, Cody didn't even know the damn mission, had no what Benson wanted with Boro. It wasn't a wet job. Wasn't an assassination.

It might not even be a mission anymore, he reminded himself. Benson had ordered him to stand down, after all.

Cody drove in silence as he thought. Benson had said that Boro had cut a deal with the DEA. It wasn't a surprise. If anything, it would have been surprising if there *wasn't* something shady and secretive involving three-letter government agencies.

Cody knew all the details about Ax's and Bruiser's missions. Prince Rafiq had been working behind the scenes with the U.S. government. And Damyan Nagarev had been recruited by the damn CIA even though he was a monster.

So yeah, Cody couldn't offer Cate any guarantees. Whatever the mission was, it sure as hell wasn't going to be about protecting a druglord's runaway wife from the consequences of her own damn choices.

She was just a means to an end.

A ticket to the rodeo.

Just try not to get knocked off your horse before you even make it into the ring, Cowboy.

He stole another glance at Cate. She was looking out the window, lost in a thought, a memory, perhaps a dream.

Cody was reminded of what she'd said about duty, about how duty transcended right and wrong.

Was she wondering where she'd gone wrong?

Wondering what her life would have been like if she hadn't married Boro?

Was Cody wondering that too?

Benson had said Cate and Boro had been married for a decade. She would have been a young bride, still a teenager. Basically a kid.

Yeah, you're technically an adult at eighteen, but Cody remembered what it felt like to be that age. He'd made some pretty fucked up choices back then. Just because he'd been six foot five and built like a truck didn't mean he wasn't still a dumb, arrogant, overconfident kid who didn't know shit about the world.

"You got kids?" he asked, the question popping out before he could close the lid on that desire to know more about this mysterious woman.

She glanced towards him, color darkening her face. She shook her head quickly, turned back to the window. Clearly she didn't want to talk about that topic.

Which meant there was something there.

Cody made a mental note. If this was going to be a mind game, he might need some reserve ammo.

"What about you?" she asked softly after a minute. "You have a cowgirl on your ranch? Baby cow-kids learning how to break horses and rope cattle?"

Cody grinned. "What's with the cowboy fascination?"

Cate shrugged. A smile brightened her face. "I am Italian. You never heard of the spaghetti westerns? Many old American cowboy movies were made by Italians. And of course Latin America is also cowboy country, you know. There are horses on Boro's compound. I go riding sometimes." She laughed, her pretty red lips parting to show neat white teeth with a tiny gap between the front two incisors. "I would imagine I was in one of those spaghetti westerns."

Cody nodded. He loved those old westerns too.

He almost told her that but didn't. It was best to keep the chit-chat to the minimum, keep his mind on the mission, remember that in the end he'd probably be handing this woman back to her husband and nothing was going to change that.

Not a damn thing.

Didn't matter if it felt right or wrong.

Because duty transcended right or wrong.

She'd said so herself.

They drove in silence for a while, but Cody's thoughts were loud and chaotic. Nobody would accuse Cody of being a big talker. He was the stealth guy in the team. Silent as a rock. But he was itching to connect with her.

He was curious about the contrasts he could sense in this woman. She was interesting. Her energy was infectious. The way she'd brightened when mentioning those movies was genuine.

For a moment Cody thought he saw the innocence of that teenage girl in her. Life hadn't completely beaten it out of her.

He thought of Boro cutting off thumbs. Again Cody felt that raw need to protect Cate rise up like a snake about to strike.

And again he pushed it back down.

"What did you like about those movies?" he asked stiffly, unable to hold back from digging into what was behind those dark eyes that were sometimes sad and sometimes wild but right now were bright and smiling.

"I liked that the heroes were often the outlaws, the bad guys," she said. "It made me believe that perhaps the difference between good and bad is not so clear. That sometimes a bad person can become good. Or at least make up for the bad things. You know?"

Cody took a breath. "Yeah," he said softly. "I know."

She blinked at the reflection of his eyes. Cody wondered if he'd revealed too much. Let his guard down.

"How do you know?" she said, those dark eyes narrowing for a flash. "What bad things have you done, Cowboy?"

Cody adjusted the mirror away from her. He didn't want her looking into his eyes anymore. He kept his eyes on the road now. This wasn't the time for confession.

That time was long gone.

Some things couldn't be undone.

Some sins could never be absolved.

"That bad, eh, Cowboy?" she whispered from behind him.

Her voice was close to his ear. She'd leaned between the seats, moved close enough that Cody could smell her scent.

He thought he picked up the essence of that black rose on her skin. It sent a ripple of dark excitement through his hard body.

His hands gripped the wheel tight. His jaw went taut. He stayed silent.

Usually silence came easy.

Right now it was torture.

He heard Cate lean back again, felt the air move in the closed interior of the car. This woman was messing with him, playing with him.

Of course she was. She was fighting for her damn life here.

But there was still something alluringly innocent about her. An optimism in how she held on to that belief that a bad person might not be lost forever. That perhaps a bad person could make up for the bad things, pay back his debt, even the score with the universe.

That bad, eh, Cowboy?

Cody swerved into the fast lane as her words threatened to open up a part of him that had been locked away for years. No way she should have been able to affect him like that with just a few teasing words. She didn't know jack shit about him.

And she never would.

Because he was going to do what he did best.

Shut the fuck up.

And do his damn duty.

But Cody's mind started to roil as that raw primal energy hit him again like it had when he saw those men attack her.

It hit him like a fist to the face.

The energy in the car felt electric.

The tension in his body felt tight like a wire about to snap from the load.

Cody moved out of the fast lane to overtake a Benz that was probably doing at least eighty. He passed the

Benz, revved the turbo engine of his souped-up Supra, cut back into the fast lane and left the Benz in his dust.

He felt those teenage drag-racing instincts ignite like an abandoned oil well that still flamed in its depths.

The road was open for a bit. No cops in sight. No choppers looking for him.

He went a little faster. Felt his blood heat up.

Exhaled hard. Then slowed back down to the speed limit and moved over one lane.

Cody still loved speed, but he knew its dangers. He'd quit this kind of speed years ago. Sworn it off.

But Cody also knew that the need would always live in him like how even a recovered drug addict never forgets the high.

Now was not the time to slip into old habits, he warned himself.

Not the damn time.

Cody revved the high-powered turbo engine, annoyed that he'd let Cate get under his skin. She'd gotten to him enough for her to know she *could* get to him.

His mind spun ahead. He needed to connect with Benson, get briefed on the rest of the mission. Benson might be pissed, but he'd probably push forward with the mission.

Private jet to Colombia was probably the next step, Cody figured. After all, Darkwater had a war chest of three billion dollars in untraceable cryptocurrency now.

Again Cody was reminded that Benson had insisted on paying some of that money out to the team. He moved his neck side to side and frowned. He understood that even soldiers get paid, of course. He understood that compensation should match the skills you bring, the work you've put in, the risk you take. Still, it made him uncomfortable.

And so did she.

Cody took three long, slow breaths. The adrenaline from the fight still buzzed through his body. He tightened his grip on the wheel and tried to resist the urge to open up the turbo engine of the Supra.

He stayed put in the second lane.

Watched with a sigh as a wide-bottomed Mercury Grand Marquis cruised past him in the fast lane.

The dark blue Grand Marquis overtook him at a leisurely pace. Then it moved over, right in front of him.

It slowed down, which forced Cody to slow down.

He sighed again, but stayed behind the boat-sized car for a while. The Mercury Grand Marquis was the same car as the Ford Crown Victoria, just with different branding. A classic touring car. Average age of Grand Marquis owners was about seventy two.

The Marquis slowed down even more. Too slow now.

Cody flicked on his blinker, moved to the fast lane, sped up to overtake the elderly road warriors.

But the Grand Marquis cut into the fast lane, right in front of Cody.

Cody hit the brakes and flashed his high-beams. He respected his elders just fine—so long as they observed good lane discipline. Cutting in front of someone when they're trying to legally overtake you was not good discipline.

Cody flashed them again, closed in on their bumper. There was a sticker beneath the license plate. Cody couldn't read the text. Probably something about border collies or grumpy cats.

The car stayed where it was, drifting along like a damn riverboat on the Mississippi. Cody flashed his brights a third time, then moved close enough to read the fine print on the bumper sticker.

It said TO SERVE AND PROTECT YOUR DUMB ASS.

"Shit," Cody muttered, tapping the brake to slow down and let the car pull away from him. He hoped it was just a retired cop with a sense of humor.

He moved out of the fast lane.

The Grand Marquis moved over right in front of him again.

Cody slowed down some more.

The Grand Marquis slowed down too.

Cody felt dread rise up his spine. This was not good. The was probably the worst thing that could happen right now. If they were cops, he was screwed. Cody had no problem stabbing four machete-wielding gangbangers in the kidneys, but he sure as hell wasn't going to use his deadly training on his brothers in blue.

He saw two heads in the backseat of the Grand Marquis. The heads turned to look at him. They were not senior citizens wondering what the ruckus was.

They were hard looking men with buzz cuts and beards. If they were cops, they were SWAT guys. Cody and Dogg had run a training session for the San Diego SWAT units a few years earlier. SWAT guys were pretty darn close to military level bad-ass. Some of them were former military.

"Shit. Shit. *Shit*," Cody said again as one of the men grinned wickedly and shook his head. The other guy wagged a thick finger at him, then ran it along his throat and winked.

Cody grinned at them and shrugged his big shoulders. For a second he thought they might guess he was former military and let him off the hook.

The men turned their heads away from him. They were talking to the guys in the front.

They glanced back at him again. They weren't grinning anymore.

Now Cody realized he was still bare chested. No doubt that video of the freeway encounter was all over Social Media and on every damn news site right now. These guys must have made the connection.

One of the guys jacked his thumb towards the shoulder.

He mouthed the words PULL OVER, ASSHOLE.

Cody did nothing. He ran through his options with cool precision.

A quick glance at the fuel gauge told him that he could run but not far. He had a quarter-tank left, but this turbo engine chugged gas faster than frat boys downing beer before a home game.

Besides, although traffic was moving fast, there were a lot of cars on the freeway. Getting into an accident could cause a lot of collateral damage.

Been there.

Done that.

Not going there again.

Decision made by the process of elimination, Cody nodded and started to drift over towards the shoulder.

There were six lanes of freeway, and Cody took his time.

"Why are we slowing?" Cate asked from behind. There was fear in her voice. "Who are those men? Do you know them?"

Cody shook his head. "Relax. They're probably just cops. It'll be fine."

"How can it be fine? You killed four men. And I also killed a man. It was in my hotel room. My fingerprints are all over. I will be arrested and charged with murder. Do not stop. Outrun them. Drive faster."

Cody raised an eyebrow, held back his smile. "You've seen too many of those spaghetti westerns. Or maybe too many bad action flicks. Real life car chases do not end well. Not only are we likely to end up squished like bugs, but we might cause an accident that kills innocent folk."

"Since when do you care about killing innocent folks?" she snapped. "You are taking me back to be killed, are you not?"

Cody's eyes narrowed to green slits. "You aren't innocent," he said.

Cate's breath caught.

Cody knew the words hurt her.

He also knew they were true.

Nobody in this damn car was innocent.

It was bad people all the way down.

He swallowed hard, managed to control his anger. He wasn't sure if he was angry at himself or her.

Cody moved over another lane as the Grand Marquis slowed down, let him pass, then smoothly maneuvered

Capturing Cate

into place behind him. Cody glanced into the rearview mirror to get a look at the cops in the front of the Grand Marquis.

The driver matched up with the two guys in the back: Buzzed blonde hair, rough stubble on a square jaw.

But the front seat passenger did not match up.

It was a woman in a dark gray suit. She looked older. Gray hair styled perfectly like a helmet. A hard look about her, but a different kind of hard. She was not SWAT.

Cody had two lanes to go. He thought hard.

Sure, he could come clean about being former Navy, a SEAL for life. But he'd still need a story. He'd still need a plausible explanation for why a former SEAL who looked suspiciously like the hooded beast who'd stabbed and slashed his way through four men was driving a stolen car with a druglord's runaway wife in the backseat.

Oh, and she'd killed a gangster at the Beverly Hills Hotel this morning.

Yeah, no.

There was no good explanation for this carload of trouble.

He needed some divine intervention.

He needed Benson.

Decision made, Cody grabbed his phone. Tapped it twice. Called Benson.

"My boss at the bail bond place knows people in the LAPD," Cody said casually to Cate, keeping his voice calm, feeling an annoying need to make up for the earlier comment. "Besides, nobody's going to arrest you. The

Caliente Crew's man at the hotel must have found the body. He called his gang, not the police. They prefer to handle shit like that internally. They must have gotten rid of the body themselves. I bet no cops were involved." He wasn't certain about that, but it was probably true.

Cody glanced at the phone's screen. It was ringing. Benson wasn't answering. Had he cut Cody loose after that massacre on the freeway? Had Benson decided that Cody was too much of a loose cannon for Darkwater? Had Cody failed his first Darkwater mission before he even knew what the damn mission was?

Or did Cody already know what the mission was?

Did he already feel the mission staring at him with those dark eyes?

Eyes that were sad one moment, wild the next.

Hard one moment, vulnerable the next.

Innocent one moment, deadly the next.

5

I am dead either way, so what does it matter who kills me?

Cate watched the cowboy glance at his phone and then tap it dead. His boss did not answer. Perhaps it was a sign that her fate had arrived. Her destiny was here in the form of those hard looking policemen in that big car.

Cate turned in her seat as the cowboy slowed the car and then rolled to a stop on the side of the road. The dark blue car with the policemen stopped some distance behind them.

Three of the four doors opened. Three men got out. One person remained in the car.

It was a woman in a gray suit. She was very thin. She sat very still. Her hair was styled perfectly. It was shaped like a German Nazi helmet, Cate thought. Many Nazis had hidden in South America after the Second World War, she knew. Mostly Argentina and Venezuela, but Brazil and Colombia too.

The three men wore black cargo pants and dark tee shirts. Two gray shirts and one brown. The men had short hair, buzzed with clippers. One man was blonde, the others were dark-haired. They were all white men, but tanned. The woman was very white and not tanned at all. She must not like the sun. Perhaps she preferred the shadows, Cate thought.

She turned back to the cowboy. He had put on his shirt. He turned to her and offered a half-smile.

"Don't say a word," he said softly. "I'll handle it."

He let the half-smile widen all the way. It reassured her, but she did not smile back.

She was upset at what he'd said. What did he know about innocence and guilt? What did he know about her?

Nothing.

He knew nothing.

The three men were approaching. She could hear their boots crunch the gravel along the side of the road. She thought about what the cowboy had told her about the hotel and the gang.

Was it true? It must be true. Ponytail knew people at the hotel. He had gotten a keycard to her room. His contact must have found him and called it in to the crew.

So perhaps she was not a wanted woman. Not wanted by the police, at least.

And so perhaps she had a better chance with the police than with the cowboy. After all, if she was not wanted for murder, then she was a victim. She'd been kidnapped.

She should go with the police, she thought. It wouldn't mean she was free, but it would at least mean she wasn't on her way back to Boro.

The three men were close now. They smelled like tobacco. Cigar tobacco, but poor quality. Not Cuban but Dominican.

One man stopped behind the rear bumper, arms crossed over his chest. He wore sunglasses, the sporty wraparound kind with mirrored red lenses. She looked at his eyes and saw the reflection of her own face peering through the back window of the car. She looked tiny in his big red lenses.

The blonde man walked around to the front of the car and took up a position there. No sunglasses. His eyes looked very blue. His hand was flat against his right cargo flap. Cate guessed he had a gun in there.

The third man stopped a few feet away from the driver's side door. He wore glasses, but not for the sun. They had round wire rims with clear lenses. They looked small on his large square face.

He had a black handgun in his left hand. It was held diagonally across his abdomen, pointed at the ground. Cate knew enough about guns to know it was a Glock, the kind with no manual safety.

He made a winding motion with his free right hand.

The cowboy put down the tinted glass. He grinned wide, squinting in the late afternoon sun. Cate thought his smile was very symmetrical. His teeth were very clean.

The man with the gun did not grin back. "Step out of the car, please," he said.

The cowboy did not move. "Are you a police officer?" he asked. There was an edge in the cowboy's voice. A challenge.

"LAPD," said the man. His grip on the gun tightened, but he did not raise it. "Now step out of the car."

"Sure," said the cowboy cheerfully. "Just show me your badge and I'll step right out, Officer."

The man's jaw tightened. His Adam's apple bobbed as he swallowed. He glanced towards his car in the distance.

Cate whipped her head around just in time to see the woman in the front seat move her helmeted head.

She had nodded at the gunman.

Just one nod.

"Get down!" shouted the cowboy just then.

Cate jumped in her seat and then ducked down. She moved against the right side of the car just in time to avoid being squished by the cowboy reclining his seat all the way down with breathtaking speed.

At the same time she saw the man in glasses raise his gun.

He fired once, the bullet passing through empty space where the cowboy's head had been less than a second ago. It slammed into the side of the empty passenger front seat.

Cate saw the cowboy's right hand slide around to the small of his back. It emerged with a shiny black handgun. He fired twice through the car door.

Then, still reclined, he slammed the car into gear, rammed his boot into the accelerator, and smashed into the man in front of them.

The front guard had drawn his gun but was rolling over the roof of the car before he had a chance to pull the trigger. Cate stared wild-eyed out the back window as the man landed hard on the gravel, rolled over twice, then lay still.

The man behind them had drawn his gun. He pointed it right at her head. Cate felt that this was it. It was over.

Capturing Cate

Then the man lowered his aim. He fired three times in quick succession. Cate felt the bullets vibrate the car. She heard the tires explode. Felt the car swerve madly as the cowboy tried to steer blind from a reclining position.

"Hold on," he shouted as the car drove off the road into the dried scrubland past the gravel track. "Keep your head down, Cate."

The cowboy kept the car going. It was bumping and bucking over the rocks and hillocks like a wild bull at the rodeo. Finally it slammed into a mound of hard-packed dirt and stopped, its engine still running. The cowboy rolled over onto his stomach to aim out the back window.

The man with red sunglasses was running after them. The man hit by the car had gotten up and was running lopsided towards them. The first gunman was still by the road, on his knees, holding his shoulder, his face twisted in pain.

Now Cate felt the cowboy's big hand on her head. He pushed her down onto the seat. At the same time he fired through the back window glass. It shattered. Blunt squares of glass rained down on her.

The cowboy fired again.

Then there was silence.

Nobody was firing back.

"They want you alive," the cowboy muttered. "They were going to shoot me in the head and then take you and claim Boro's bounty. Must have gotten wind of the bounty through an informant in one of the LA gangs. Maybe from an undercover buddy in narcotics."

The cowboy took his palm off her head. She peeked

up over the seat, glass-squares falling out of her hair like tinsel. She saw the three men lying flat on the ground, taking cover behind hillocks of California scrubland.

Their guns were drawn, but they were not returning the cowboy's fire. She noticed that the cowboy had stopped firing too. Apparently he did not take it too personally that they'd tried to kill him.

"The woman," Cate said, remembering how the gunman had looked at the woman in the car for the go-ahead to fire. "She's the boss."

The cowboy shook his head. "She might be in charge, but this isn't her team. They're hired guns."

"How do you know?"

The cowboy nodded toward the blue car up by the road. The woman had shifted to the driver's seat. She'd started the engine.

"Because she's going to leave them out on the field, looks like," said the cowboy.

Cate watched the woman. The car started to move. Then it stopped with a bump, like the woman had hit the brakes hard. Cate saw her put a phone to her ear.

"She got a phone call," said Cate. "Perhaps she has a boss too."

The cowboy squinted into the distance.

"You got good eyes," he said.

Cate glanced at the cowboy's green eyes. "You too," she said, blinking when she felt the color rush to her face. She was still angry at what he'd said about her, but the rush of heat was not under her control.

Cate touched her hair and looked down. When she

dared look up into those green eyes again, she saw that the cowboy's face had darkened with color too. He looked away immediately, his jaw tightening.

He didn't like that she'd seen that. Cate smiled to herself. There was a flutter of warmth and excitement within her breast. Perhaps she was not that innocent after all. Perhaps she had been angry because the cowboy was right about her.

She smiled at him. He was studying the scene outside, his gun held very steady. He looked very macho, she thought inwardly. Very much like a cowboy.

She liked looking at him. She thought of how he'd moved his heavily muscled body with the grace of a tiger as he'd slashed and stabbed his way through to her. Yes, he'd only saved her for the bounty. But he had still saved her.

Still, what sort of man would go against four machetes even for ten million dollars? Perhaps no man would do that. Perhaps she was safer with him. Yes, perhaps she should ride with this cowboy for a little while. It was still a long way to Colombia.

And until she passed through the gates of Boro's compound, she was still free in a way, was she not?

For a moment Cate thought she was enjoying herself, living a scene from her dreams. She imagined they were cowboy outlaws on the run, caught in a standoff with the law in the badlands of New Mexico.

Their horses had been shot out from beneath them. The posse had them surrounded. They were out of options. The buzzards were circling overhead.

The sound of buzzing came through the air. Cate looked for a turkey vulture circling above the burning earth, waiting to pick her bones clean. But the sound was coming from the car. It was the cowboy's phone buzzing in the hard plastic cupholder.

The cowboy took a breath and looked at the phone. He glanced back out at the three men. They were still in their positions flat on the ground. The woman was still in the car. She had not left after all. The phone call had changed her mind.

"Hand me the phone," the cowboy said, keeping his eyes focused on the men.

"I can take a message," Cate asked earnestly, an almost slap-happy excitement bubbling up in her. "If it is your cowgirl wife, I will tell her we are just friends, not lovers."

The cowboy snorted a surprised laugh, his green eyes smiling at her for a flash before they focused back on his targets. But Cate saw that it took an act of will for him to turn away from her.

She felt the blood burn hot in her cheeks. Her heart thrummed with embarrassed delight at making a daring joke like that.

She was funny, she told herself with some pride. Nobody had gotten to see that side of her except Marya in real life and perhaps those who read her comments in the fake life you live online.

She handed the phone to the cowboy. His fingers closed on hers as he took it. His fingers were rough. The contact made her toes curl up in her white ankle-length socks.

"Better late than never, I guess," the cowboy growled into the phone. "We're in a situation here, Benson."

Cate tried to listen in. She could hear a man's voice from the other end, but she couldn't make out the words.

The cowboy grunted once. He shook his head twice. He rolled his eyes and let out a long exhale.

Then he tapped the phone and shoved it into the back pocket of his jeans. He sighed and stuck the gun into his belt.

"Stay here," he said.

Cate stared as the cowboy knocked out the last bits of the broken back window with the base of his palm. Then he crawled out of the car through the opening. He landed palms-first on the ground, did a quick forward-roll, and was up on his feet with surprising grace for a man that big.

Cate looked frantically at the three men whose guns were aimed at him. She held her breath, not sure what was happening.

The three men lowered their weapons. They clambered to their feet. Put their guns away. Cate still wasn't sure what was happening.

Then she saw the woman. She'd gotten out of the car. She was walking towards the cowboy. Her phone was in her left hand. She extended her right hand as the cowboy walked up to her.

"Cody Cartright? Margaret Malone. Drug Enforcement Agency. Call me Maggie," Cate heard her say to the cowboy. "Sorry about that. Almost got out of hand for a moment. Thought we could take her off your hands smoothly, but it got kinda messy. Doesn't matter. It'll end the same way for her."

The cowboy shook the woman's hand. He nodded at the three guys, two of whom were clearly in pain. Then the cowboy shot a glance over his shoulder at Cate before turning back to Maggie Malone.

"Kaiser gave you my phone's GPS location," said the cowboy whose name was Cody Cartright. "That double crossing son of a bitch."

6

"You double crossing son of a bitch," said John Benson through his teeth. He tossed his brown tweed jacket onto the chair against the wall of CIA Director Martin Kaiser's office. Then Benson strode to Kaiser's walnut desk and slammed both fists down, making the cigarette butts in the glass ashtray jump in panic.

"I'm the Director of the CIA. That's a compliment, John." Kaiser pushed his black leather swivel away from the desk somewhat hurriedly. Perhaps he was worried Benson might take a swing with those fists that could certainly still deliver a solid blow.

Benson took a long, slow breath. He felt his knuckles crack from the fury that had built up on the drive over to CIA Headquarters in Langley.

Benson lived twenty minutes away. The drive took six.

He'd screeched into the lot and parked sideways across three handicap spaces. He'd flung his ID at the security guard and only barely made it through the physical check without getting restrained or shot. Benson had a long history of being the coolest head in the room.

Not today.

This was different.

Darkwater was different.

"You sent in the damn DEA without giving me a chance to warn my guy first," Benson fumed. "You almost got a former Navy SEAL killed." He shook his head, ground his teeth. "We've crossed a lot of moral lines in the name of duty, Martin. But this is too much. I'll never trust you again after this, you son of a bitch."

Kaiser's clean shaven face paled, then clouded with color. He tried to shrug it off. "Malone is a major player at the DEA. She heard about the bounty. Then she saw the video of your SEAL stabbing people like it was a bad Hollywood out-take. Malone knew instantly he was former Special Forces. She figured it was some kind of CIA-sponsored black ops. She called me directly. Told me it was DEA turf. She's right. Had to give him up."

"You should have denied everything. Cody's face was covered," Benson said. "How'd she know he wasn't just an LA thug?"

"Hell, I did deny it at first." Kaiser shrugged again. "She wasn't buying it. Said it was obvious from the way he moved. Decisive strikes targeting major arteries and organs. No hesitation." He sighed. "Malone isn't a rookie, Benson. DEA and CIA work together often. She knows the CIA uses Special Forces all the time. She figured I'd sent him in."

"Well, you hadn't sent him in," Benson snapped. "You should have called me first."

"I might have—if you'd been honest with me on our call earlier," Kaiser shot back. "You only told me you were considering picking up this Cate Bonasera bounty thing, not that you'd already sent in a guy. You're damn lucky I recognized Cody after meeting him at Bruiser and Brenna's wedding. Or else I'd have cleared Malone to go in hot."

Benson grunted. "They'd all be dead if you had." He took a breath. Thought a moment. "Malone tracked Cody via his phone. Thought we had a deal that the Darkwater phones stay off the grid."

Kaiser shrugged. Said nothing.

"You should have called me before giving my guy up," said Benson again, his anger settling to a simmer. "Before giving my mission to the DEA."

Kaiser was unmoved. "What mission is that, John? Darkwater doesn't need the bounty money."

Benson grinned, but his gray eyes stayed cold. "When opportunity knocks, you know I answer."

Kaiser shook his head, laughed once. "You got the alert about the bounty. Jumped on it without really having a plan. You still don't have a plan. Why am I not surprised?"

"Because you've known me for thirty years," said Benson crisply. "I operate on instinct. Move first, then improvise."

"Well, clearly this move was a clusterfuck."

Benson shook his head. "The fight out in the open was a bit much, I agree. But in the end four gangbangers are dead and Cody got the Bonasera woman. That was the plan. It was working. I'd have figured out the rest. Hell, you should have called me first. Not after handing it off to Malone and the DEA. You know that, Martin."

"All I know is what I saw in that video," Kaiser said. "Your man was a damn maniac out there, Benson. Slashing and stabbing people like the Butcher of Highway 101."

Benson rubbed the back of his neck. He'd been pissed at Cody too, so he couldn't blame Kaiser for losing faith in Darkwater's ability to handle this clean. Still, Benson was going to stand up for his Team Darkwater man.

"In Cody's defense, he had the common sense not to use his gun. That shows he wasn't out of control, Martin. He's a SEAL. The best of the best." Benson paused, swallowed, took a breath. "And he was almost killed by Malone and her DEA grunts, Kaiser. You told her he was former SEALs, right? If she knew he was a good guy, then why all the action?"

Kaiser sighed. Blinked, looked down, then up again. He rubbed his jaw. "Malone said she wanted it to look real for Boro's wife. Maybe she tried to make it look like her guys were dirty too, freelance thugs or bad cops. She doesn't want Cate Bonasera finding out the DEA and CIA and every other damn agency is involved. Won't know for sure until she calls me back, though. Just tried her." He sighed again. "Anyway, you can't blame me—or Malone—for not trusting your man to just hand her over. He looked like a homicidal caveman protecting his woman in that video." He paused, thought a moment, narrowed his eyes at Benson. "Why did you send him in, anyway? Why is this throwaway mission even interesting to Darkwater?"

Benson deflected the question. "Why is this interesting to Malone?"

"Boro is a Colombian drug lord. Malone is a DEA player in the hunt to be Director. You put it together, John."

"I'm trying," said Benson. He paused, stroked his stubble. "Why is she so interested in Cate Bonasera?"

"That's Maggie Malone's business, not mine. Besides, I don't think she gives a shit about Cate. It's probably Boro she cares about. She was a big part of those operations and deals ten years ago with the major Colombian Cartels and the Mexican traffickers and all that."

Benson nodded. "She was a star on that operation, from what I hear. But there isn't much in the files by way of details."

Kaiser smiled. "DEA runs dark operations too, John. Anyway, Malone's very capable and she can handle her own operation. Maybe there's some unfinished business with Boro. Maybe she wants a bargaining chip for a new deal with the Cartels. Maybe she's just a concerned romantic who wants Boro and Cate to work out their marital issues." He shrugged. "I don't give a shit. It's DEA turf, John. Let it go. Pull Cody off and let Malone have the Bonasera woman. I don't see what Darkwater has to gain from a ten million dollar bounty anyway. After your last mission we agreed that Brenna's father's billions could move to the Darkwater treasury. Ten million isn't worth this mess of a mission."

Benson took a long look at his old friend and former boss. "It's not about the damn ten million."

"So what's it about, John?" Kaiser's voice took on that borderline mocking tone that Benson knew very well and disliked very much. "Fate? Destiny? Magic?"

Benson didn't take the bait. He stayed on point. "Why is Maggie Malone personally involved in this? It's way below her pay grade. You know that. You'd have been suspicious the moment she called." Benson shook his head, smiled tightly. "Malone must have told you something for you to give Cody up, to give me up. Now give it up, Kaiser. What did she tell you?"

Kaiser sighed. He stood, walked around the desk and across the thick carpet that blanketed the dark walnut floor with a faded CIA crest. He closed the door to his office and locked it, then turned and leaned against it.

"Ten years ago our media-conscious politicians had gotten the DEA to run that dog-and-pony show of burning South American coca fields and bombing warehouses. But of course the politicians don't *actually* want the drug trade to end. They just want to shift it around, depending on which Cartel is the flavor of the month. Which country needs to be starved and which needs to be fed. Who needs to be punished and who needs to be rewarded. Power games. You know the game well. You were one of the best at it."

Benson rubbed his eyes and nodded. It was a complicated web of give-and-take between the United States and countries where drugs were the cornerstone of the economy. Cocaine and Colombia. Heroin and Afghanistan. Marijuana and Mexico. He nodded again, waited for Kaiser to continue.

"Malone said she was the one who got Boro to stop shipping his product to the United States. Brokered the whole thing with the Bonasera European connection to make Boro agree. Now she's worried that if Cate isn't returned to Boro, the arrangement with the Bonaseras is dead."

Benson groaned. "Which means Boro might start shipping to the US again. Malone's deal unravels. Could ruin her chance to become Director. Is that what this is about?"

Kaiser exhaled. "Malone insists it's about keeping Boro's cocaine off America's streets. Which is true. So what if it also protects her reputation? So what if Malone wants to send a druglord's runaway wife back home just to stay on track to become Director? I have no problem with ruthless ambition. I've stepped on some toes to get where I am."

"That's the understatement of the century," Benson muttered, chuckling darkly. He nodded reluctantly. "I guess I can't argue too much with those motives. Boro is a druglord and Cate's his wife. They're criminals, plain and simple. Malone has history with Boro. Makes sense DEA takes it. OK, Kaiser. We'll back off."

"Thank you," said Kaiser pointedly. He stepped away from the door, like he was hoping Benson would leave.

Benson stayed where he was. Looked at Kaiser. "But still, Martin. Why didn't you just tell me all this before giving Malone the go-ahead? Why not have me just talk to Cody, get him to maybe lose the girl somewhere under some pretext so Malone could pick her up without all the good guys shooting at each other? Hell, maybe Malone could even use Cody along the way, just in case more gangbangers take their shot at either Cate's neck or the bounty. Why didn't you just bring me in on it, Martin?"

Kaiser's eyes narrowed. "Because I couldn't be certain you'd agree, John. I know how you work. I saw how you ran those last two Darkwater missions with those SEALs and those women. You were rolling the dice like I've never seen before. Extreme even for you." He took a breath, huffed out the air, rubbed his left eye. "You always had that weird mystical streak in you, John. Fate and destiny, unicorns galloping through rainbows, magic beanstalks and hell knows what else. But you had it more or less under control when you worked for me. Now . . . hell, now I don't know. After leaving the CIA and putting this Darkwater crap together, you've gone off the deep end. Couldn't be sure what you were thinking, sending Cody in to take that woman." He laughed now. "Hell, I *still* don't know why you sent Cody in on this Cate Bonasera thing. You've been evading the question. See what I mean? You've gone off the deep end, John."

Benson stayed composed. "We've been swimming in the deep end our entire lives, Martin. It's mostly worked out, hasn't it? You telling me you've suddenly lost faith in my instincts?"

Kaiser chuckled. "Yes, because you seem to have turned those instincts towards high-stakes matchmaking instead of running a serious operation." He laughed again. "Ax and Amy. Bruiser and Brenna." He held his arms out to the sides, widened his eyes mockingly. "And now it's Cate and Cody, isn't it? Fate and destiny at work again."

"That's not what this is," Benson said, somewhat defensively. He blinked and glanced past Kaiser toward the dark blue curtains shrouding the floor-to-ceiling window. "It was just an opportunistic mission, Martin. The Cate Bonasera thing popped up on my radar. Turned out Cody was already in California, helping out at Coronado Bay during Hell Week. You know I pay attention to coincidences like that. I always have."

"OK, I'll give you that," Kaiser said. "You have always been a seat-of-the-pants type operative. Figuring it out as you go along." He paused a beat. "But where were you going with this? It's not about the ten million. We've established that. And you insist it's not about Cody and that woman. So what's it about?"

"It's about the spy game," said Benson. "The game of shadowy deals. Give and take. I scratch your buttcrack, you tickle my balls. It's how we've operated for decades, Martin."

Kaiser laughed, then coughed a little. He cleared his throat, then looked up, his eyes shining. "So you wanted Boro to owe Team Darkwater a favor. You're just expanding the network of powerful but sketchy folks who are in your debt. Because that's how the spy game is played. The old CIA balance sheet. You're doing the same for Team Darkwater. Stacking the balance sheet with assets."

Benson grinned. "Exactly. Assets and liabilities. Assets are the bad guys who owe you favors. Liabilities are the assholes who want you dead." He shrugged. "On the

Amy mission we ended up with Abu Ziraak on the balance sheet as a Darkwater asset. On the Brenna mission we used Nagarev as an asset before discarding him." He shrugged. "I need to keep expanding my network. Boro commands a lot of respect and power in his world. He's a major player in the European raw uncut powder scene. Politicians on his payroll all across the white powder trail. Him owing Darkwater a big favor could come in handy someday. Gotta set up the players on the chessboard."

Kaiser took a long, hard look at Benson. It was a look of admiration. Recognition that perhaps Benson hadn't completely lost the plot. Was still a master of the game.

"So your plan was to have Cody deliver Cate to Boro. Refuse to accept the bounty. Say it was a gift from Team Darkwater, that now Boro owed them a favor." Kaiser's sharp eyes studied the lines on Benson's face. He was trying to read between them. Benson wouldn't let him. "Then Cody walks away?"

"That's right," Benson deadpanned.

Kaiser's lower lip twitched. "And you had no interest in watching whether Cody actually *did* walk away? This wasn't one of your games where you try to see if fate has some trickery going on?"

"I don't play games with people's lives," said Benson straight-faced.

"Oh, please, John." Kaiser almost choked himself on a laugh. "For one of the greatest liars I've ever known, you're losing your talent for bullshitting too," he said through an incredulous grin. "There, I see that mad glint in your eyes again, John. You've fucking lost it in your old age. This is your little private game again, isn't it? Hell, even their names match up. Ax and Amy. Brenna and Bruiser. Cate and Cody. What is this, a sick fairy tale? You're too damn ugly to be a fairy godmother, Benson."

Benson laughed. He'd noticed the weird connections with the names. It made sense to him in a playful, whimsical way. The universe liked to play childish games like that. Like how the CIA might use an alias like James Buns for a low risk mission just for fun. Fate liked to have fun too. Hard to get anyone else to understand that, though.

And hell, of course Kaiser wouldn't understand. Benson didn't really understand it either sometimes. It was best not to think too hard about it. It could drive you insane.

"I didn't *name* them, Martin," he said firmly. "Now you're the one talking crazy."

Benson watched as Kaiser strode to his desk and yanked open the top drawer. He snatched out a pack of Dunhill's and stuck one between his cracked lips. Lit it with that same old battered gold Zippo. Clinked the lighter shut and puffed.

Kaiser filled the room with gray, acrid smoke. Benson had to hold himself back from trying one more time to convince his hardened old friend that it wasn't magic and make-believe but science and quantum mechanics. Human choice and action could change the fabric of space and time.

Especially if those choices and actions were driven by deep emotion.

Driven by love.

"Those last two missions worked out, didn't they?" Benson said quickly, stopping his thoughts from getting away from him.

He'd seen that video of Cody fighting his way to the Bonasera woman like a possessed man, a mythical god of vengeance and destruction. It was wild and reckless, but also brutally beautiful.

Powerfully possessive.

"What's your point?" said Kaiser.

"That this mission was on its way to working out just like the last two. And then you let the DEA drive onto the scene with a clown car full of cowboys. You screwed this up, not me. Who the hell are those guys? Cody said one of them took a shot at him."

Kaiser frowned. "Nobody got killed, right?"

Benson shook his head. "Cody winged one guy. Rammed his car into another. They'll live. Cody could have killed them all, though. Good thing he's a SEAL who can control himself—and the situation."

Kaiser was pensive as he smoked. "DEA guys, I assume."

"Cody doesn't think so. Says something's off about the whole thing."

Kaiser's frown cut deeper. He clicked his jaw. Shot Benson a look. "Just tell him to give up the girl and get his ass out of there. I don't want any of us stepping on Maggie Malone's turf here. She's got history with Boro, and if there's something off, then all the more reason for us to stay clear of it. We've all pulled sketchy shit out there in the field. Things get messy sometimes. Let the DEA clean up their own shit. So just tell your guy Cody it's over. It's not his mission. It's not your mission. It's not even my mission. It's Maggie Malone's mission now. We clear on that?"

Benson thought a moment, considered his next words carefully.

He stood up off the chair. Picked up his jacket. Slung it over his arm.

Then he walked to the door, unlocked it to be sure he could make a quick exit in case Kaiser hurled the ashtray at his head.

"We'll see whose mission it is," Benson said quietly, his gray eyes shining, his lips tightening as he restrained his knowing smile.

Kaiser looked up, annoyed. "What the hell does that mean? I thought we agreed you were going to let it go. Don't mess with this, Benson. I don't have time for damage control if you fuck things up. You let it go, understood?"

Benson shrugged.

He stepped out the door.

Closed it behind him.

Walked down the empty hallway.

Benson got safely into his dark gray Crown Victoria, slowly drove down the winding road under the dark canopy of trees that had been planted during Roosevelt's time.

Only when the CIA buildings faded into the rearview mirror did Benson let the smile break full on his well-lined face.

Because he knew whose mission it really was.

He'd seen it in the raw protective fury of that SEAL.

Cody wasn't just a highly trained Special Forces weapon out there.

He was a man out there.

A man who'd found his fate.

A man who'd been delivered his destiny.

Which meant it was out of Benson's hands now.

Out of his control and into the grand arena where the universe played its wicked games.

Games that played out on the mystical dancefloor where the only moves were human choice and human action.

Choice driven by emotion.

Action powered by love.

7

The action was over, but Cody still felt on edge. He nodded tightly at the three men, who'd been introduced as Dan, Kevin, and Tim.

They didn't look like a Dan or a Kevin or a Tim, Cody thought as he glanced at Dan's shoulder wound.

The bullet had gone straight through the meaty part above the collar bone. He'd live. So would Tim, the blonde guy who'd been thrown over the Supra's red roof like a bad cowhand being bucked by a pissed off bull.

Cody didn't apologize. He wasn't sorry. Dan had taken a shot at him, he was sure of it.

Yeah, it had happened quick and maybe the guy was jumpy. But Dan's bullet was aimed right where Cody's head had been. The only regret Cody had was that the third guy, Kevin, was uninjured.

The guy pretending his name was Kevin took off his mirrored red sunglasses. His eyes were bloodshot and wide. He rubbed them and put his shades back on. "Dave needs a doctor," he said to Maggie Malone.

"Dan," Cody corrected.

Kevin gulped. Then he cracked a grin. His front incisor was chipped. "What'd I say?"

"You said enough," said Cody. He glanced at Malone.

She was in her fifties, with a lean, long face that hadn't seen much sun. Or much fun, Cody thought. "New team?" he asked.

She nodded tightly, smiled even tighter. Her eyes were pale blue and watery. "Took what I could get. They're DEA from San Pedro, down near the Mexican border."

"Explains the itchy trigger finger," Cody said coolly.

He flashed a dangerous look at Dan, then smiled at Malone. He was hyper aware of everyone's position. His gun was in his belt, cocked and ready. Cody was a fast draw. He grew up playing cowboy with real cowboys.

"What the hell is that supposed to mean?" said Dan. His wound was nice and red and swollen, just like Cody liked to see in a man who'd taken a shot at him.

Cody shrugged. "That wound looks painful, Dan." He paused. "Or was it Dave? Maybe Dick? Yeah, Dick sounds right."

All three fake-DEA men shifted on their feet. They shot glances at each other. Dan muttered something under his breath, shifted his shoes in the dirt.

Maggie Malone stepped in. She held her arms out and waved them like a referee signaling a dead ball. Her dark gray hair was styled so tight it didn't move.

"Let's dial down the testosterone, OK?" she said sharply. "We're all adults here."

Cody smiled. He hadn't shifted on his feet like the other guys. Hadn't adjusted his position.

Didn't need to, because Cody was trained to always be in position. He could see all three men clearly, and he also had a line of sight to Cate Bonasera.

Damn right his testosterone was jacked up.

Guns and women had that effect on Cody.

Cate was still in the backseat of the Supra. He noticed she'd turned off the engine. Smart woman. A stray bullet would turn the car into a bomb. Now at worst it would be a pleasant crackling fire of melting metal and gasoline fumes. Quarter tank of high-octane fuel. Gas tank was above the left rear wheel. It hadn't been hit. No leaks.

Cody glanced at the ripped black rubber on the back tires. Kevin had shot them out. There were no bullet holes in the bumper. Kevin didn't want to hit the gas tank.

Man knew how to shoot. These men had seen action. Sure, not at the level Cody had seen with SEAL Team Thirteen, but it still meant he needed to stay alert.

Because something was off here.

Some*one* was off here.

Maggie Malone glanced past Cody. She was looking at Cate Bonasera. Malone's lips twitched. The movement was barely perceptible, but Cody didn't miss it. He was a recon man. A details guy. He didn't miss much.

"Well, I guess we'll be on our way then," Malone said with a brisk head-nod. She looked at Kevin, then at Cody, finally back towards Cate in the car. "I'll escort Mrs. Bonasera over," she said, clearly deciding that it was best Cody stayed surrounded by the three guys. "She isn't armed, I presume?"

Cody didn't reply. He'd taken Cate's .38 at the scene of the machete madness. It was stuck in his boot now.

He scanned his memory for what might be available in the car. He hadn't checked the glovebox. The front seat had been inclined forward, blocking access to the glovebox.

He shook his head. Malone hesitated, then drew her weapon. It was on a belt holster with a button flap. A Glock 19. Black steel with a resin grip. Smaller than the 17 but just as deadly.

"I'll get her," Cody said, turning towards the car.

All three men stiffened. Kevin's right hand dropped down to his cargo flap.

Cody's eyes narrowed. He smiled. Held his arms out casually.

"Thought we were all friends now," he said coolly. His gaze met each man's eyes before focusing on Malone's drawn weapon. Then a blink and his gaze moved to her face. "Aren't we friends?"

Malone's mouth twitched again. Cody saw her grip tighten around the Glock. Her watery blue eyes were steady.

Cody tried to read her. She didn't make it easy. She was DEA but was good enough to be CIA if she wanted. She was damn good at being unreadable.

Then Malone's eyes flicked down to Cody's belt for a fraction of a second. She blinked twice.

Her grip on the gun relaxed. She nodded at Cody, gestured with her head towards the red Supra.

"Go ahead," she said.

Cody's gaze swept from Malone towards Cate, but his mind stayed with Malone.

What had he just seen?

What had Malone's tiny movements told him about her motives?

What was going on in her head?

Slowly he walked towards the red car, careful not to turn his back all the way. He wasn't a mind reader, but Cody got the distinct feeling that Malone had considered shooting him just then.

She'd been calculating her odds of putting a bullet between his eyes before he had a chance to draw. She'd glanced down at the gun stuck in his belt. She'd assessed whether she could do it clean, without it turning into a shootout that left dead bodies along the highway. She'd decided against it.

Good choice.

Of course, Cody didn't know any of that for sure. If the men hadn't worked with her or even each other before, it could explain the weird tension.

Men trying to prove themselves to each other and to their new boss. Two of the guys were hurt—and Cody had done the hurting. Yeah, it was logical folks would be tense and on their guard.

Especially when there was big money involved.

Yeah, Cody couldn't forget that Cate Bonasera was worth ten million dollars in cash. Even good men turned bad for that kind of money. Maybe Malone and her men were after the money. Or maybe they thought Cody was after the money. Hell, they were probably as suspicious of Cody as he was of them.

Cody got to the Supra without being shot in the back. He'd been prepared to drop down to the ground, roll to his left, draw and fire in one quick move. But this wasn't going to turn into Dodge City quite yet. Right now it was mind games more than war games.

"You all right?" Cody said to Cate through the broken back windshield.

Cate brushed a strand of hair from her pretty round face. She nodded and flashed a tiny smile. "Are you?"

Cody didn't answer. He walked to the front passenger door. Pulled it open.

The seatback had been snapped to the upright position.

Cody glanced at the glovebox.

It was closed.

Had it been opened?

He stroked the rough stubble on his chin. Glanced at Cate Bonasera. Reminded himself that he was in a strange position here.

The best course of action was by no means clear. There was a protective fire burning in him, and it was making it hard to think with a cool head.

But Cate was still an unknown. Just because he was attracted to her and intrigued by her and was starting to enjoy her company didn't mean she wasn't a druglord's wife who'd already killed a man today and probably wouldn't hesitate to kill another if it meant her freedom.

And right now, Cody was one of the men who stood in the way of Cate's freedom.

You're her captor, not her savior, he warned himself. Don't fall into the trap of being the gallant knight riding to the damsel's rescue.

There's a hardwired instinct in a man to protect a woman, and it's coming alive in you. But it's a dumb, simplistic instinct, blind to the complexities of the situation. It comes from two million years of evolution, when the most complex problem was a bear trying to eat your cavewoman.

It's just dumb instinct, Cody.

Instinct that might get you killed today.

So don't be a dumb-ass, Cody, he warned himself again as Cate touched her neck and shifted her ass in the seat. This woman is a mafia princess. A cartel queen. Yeah, she seems like she wants out of that life, but that isn't your damn business. Doesn't matter why she was running from her husband. SEALs didn't train you to be a marriage counselor. Mind your own damn business.

And make the right damn choices.

"Time to go," Cody said, snapping the front seatback forward again and gesturing for Cate to get out.

Cate leaned forward from the backseat. Her sweater was slightly out of position, and her neckline opened up as she clambered out of the small two-door car.

Cody got a glimpse of smooth brown curves that pretty much guaranteed his testosterone was staying jacked up the rest of this mission.

He stood back as she straightened up. Blood rushed up his neck. He was glad of his deep tan.

Cody glanced over at Malone and the triplets. He saw Kevin's sunglasses-shielded head move slightly as Cate straightened her sweater and dusted some red California dirt off her tight black jeans.

Her thick thighs moved like rolling thunder as she smacked the sides of her hips, sending red clouds of dust into the golden sunbeams coming from the west.

Kevin touched his shades, licked his lips, touched his shades again.

Cody swallowed hard, his fists clenching until all his knuckles cracked like walnuts.

He imagined ramming those red sunglasses down

Kevin's gullet, then driving him feet-first into the dirt like a nail for the coyotes to finish off. He imagined the wily coyotes eating Kevin's cheeks first. Then the buzzards would swoop in for the leftovers.

"What is going to happen, Cody?" Cate said, uncertainty in her voice.

She said his name with a halting lilt between syllables. Coh-dee. It didn't help regulate his testosterone-fueled protective madness.

It took a moment for Cody to push away the thought of destroying Kevin in a jealous rage.

He looked at her, left eyebrow raised.

Coh-dee, he heard her say in his mind.

She was looking up into his eyes. Cody did his best not to hold her gaze. He turned sideways, gestured towards Malone with his head.

"You're going with them," he said gruffly. "You'll be safe with them."

Cate didn't move. "So they will not take me back to Colombia?"

Cody kept looking away. He could feel her dark eyes on him.

"Not sure what their plan is," he said. "But they're government agents. At least you'll be safe from any more machete-wielding bandana-boys from the Caliente Crew."

"I am already safe from the gang with you," she said quietly. "I will stay with you, please." She paused. "Please," she said again, her voice soft and wavering.

She was still looking at him. He could damn well feel it. It was doing something to him. He couldn't let it do that to him.

"It's not a choice," he said harshly.

"Why not?" she said stubbornly.

"Because you're a captive, and captives don't get to choose their captors."

"But I thought I was *your* captive, not theirs."

"Things have changed."

"So they have captured me from you?"

Cody sighed. "Something like that."

"Or are you giving me to them," she said, her voice hardening slightly. "Like my parents gave me to Boro."

Cody whipped his head towards her, his eyebrows raised. She was smiling.

"It is a joke," she said through that smile which had a touch of sadness to it. "Marya and I watch many soap operas in Spanish. We joke and laugh about the crazy situations. If you watched Spanish soap operas you would see the humor. Melodrama. You understand?"

Cody's throat felt thick as he stared at this strange creature who was sad but smiling, who could make a joke about her own sorrow and laugh at it too.

Then for a moment he thought there was hope for this woman, that perhaps she deserved her shot at freedom, a chance to break free from the prison-cell constructed from a tragic mix of circumstance and choice.

After all, Cody had been given a shot to break free from the prison of his own bad choices, hadn't he?

And he hadn't turned out so bad. He turned that speed-loving youth-fire into patriotism. Made it through BUD/S and found his place in the world standing proud next to his brothers in SEAL Team Thirteen.

He'd kicked ass that needed to be kicked. Done his duty. Faced the enemy on behalf of his country. Fought beside his brothers.

What would have happened if the SEALs had told him that he could never make up for those bad choices made early in life? Where would he be if nobody had given him a hand when he was alone and lost, running away from his past? Where would he be if he hadn't learned that you can't run from your past.

You gotta stand your ground and face your past. Acknowledge your sins and forgive yourself for them.

Even if they were unforgivable.

"Nah, no Spanish soap operas," Cody said with a half-grin. "I'm more of the action-adventure type."

Cate nodded. She took a step forward. Another step. They began to make their way towards Malone and the men.

There was a strange melancholy to the moment. Cody felt like they were only just getting started on this adventure and it was already over. Felt like unfinished business. A mission not yet accomplished.

"It was a good adventure with you," Cate said as they walked as slow as possible. "I do not want it to end so soon, Cody Cartright."

Cody glanced at her. "You heard Malone say my last name," he said. "What else did you overhear?"

Cate shrugged, then moved her shoulders playfully, like a teenage girl with a secret. "CIA. DEA. Special Forces. Drama. Conspiracy. Danger."

Cody grinned. "Sounds like one of your Spanish soaps."

Cate giggled. She glanced towards Malone. The DEA men had walked back to the Grand Marquis. The back door was open. The trunk was popped.

Kevin had a medical kit open and was cleaning off Dan's gunshot wound. Dan's round spectacles had bloody fingerprints on the lenses. Tim was standing watch. His knee was crooked. Cody didn't feel guilty about ramming him with a car. Didn't feel guilty at all.

"She nodded at him, you know," said Cate softly.

Cody frowned quizzically.

"The woman. Malone. She nodded. When the man with the clear glasses looked at her," Cate explained. "Before he tried to kill you. She approved it. She gave the order."

Cody stopped. Malone was leaning against the front door of the Grand Marquis. She was watching them. She'd put her gun away.

"It happened fast," Cody said slowly. "I reacted. He fired. It happened too fast to be sure."

"I am sure," said Cate firmly. Her dark eyes burned through him. "I know what it looks like when someone gives the order to kill."

Cody glanced into her eyes. She didn't look away. That sadness was gone. That helplessness was hidden. This woman had seen violence before. It was in her blood, just like it was in his. How often do you meet a woman like that?

"Believe what you want," he said. "But they want you alive, so either way you're safe with them. Besides, they may offer you a deal. Maybe they won't hand you back to your dear loving husband."

"Maybe you won't either. Maybe we can make some deal too, yes?"

Cody chuckled. Said nothing. This woman was unbelievable. She was negotiating for her life, but with a sense of play that was getting to him. She was teasing him even as she challenged him. It almost looked like she was having fun. Enjoying it like it really was an adventure.

Maybe it was her first taste of freedom. After all, she'd been married off when she was still a teenager, then locked away in a Colombian drug compound for a decade. What does that do to a person?

Cody had no idea, but he was curious to find out.

"What was your mission with me?" she asked.

"That's confidential."

"She will tell me anyway," Cate said, looking at Malone and then back at Cody.

"Then why ask me?"

Cate smiled. "To check if *you* know."

She lifted her shoulders in a slow, triumphant shrug. Her breasts moved up too. They were round and heavy and would fit damn well in Cody's bear-sized paws.

Cody looked away. There was a giddy excitement rolling through him. His head buzzed like a teenager in heat. He tried not to get pulled in by her infectious charm. His attempt failed.

"Well, do I know?" he drawled, unable to hold back his grin. He was also curious to see how well she could read a man.

How well she could read *this* man.

She shook her head. "I think your boss or commander told you to capture me and then wait for instructions. I saw you look at your phone when we were driving, before these people found us. You wanted to call your boss but decided to wait. You did not want to reveal yourself."

Cody couldn't hold back the smile of admiration. This woman was sharp. An eye for detail. A mind that could put together clues and draw the right conclusion.

His type of woman.

"And now I've been revealed to you?" he said softly.

She nodded earnestly. "Very much so. Now you have been revealed as a soldier. And that means you cannot give me up."

Cody stopped in his tracks. "Why not?"

"Because it would mean you have given up on your mission. A good soldier always finishes his mission, yes?"

Cody shrugged. "Maybe I ain't a good soldier."

Cate looked him up and down like she was evaluating him. Then she shrugged.

"Maybe," she said. She thought a moment. "But then maybe you can *become* a good soldier, Cody Cartright. All you have to do is finish your mission successfully. Your cowgirl wife will be very proud, yes?"

Cody laughed. Damn, she was fun.

Crazy? Yes.

Baffling? Yup.

Dangerous? For damn sure.

But fun. Fun as hell.

And she could play the game in a way Cody couldn't help but admire. He thought of Ax and Amy, Bruiser and Brenna. Two of his SEAL brothers had been thrown together with women who matched up with them like it had been designed by some mischievous matchmaker.

Yeah, Ax and Bruiser had found women who challenged them. Women who got under their skin, messed with their heads, fucked with their damn minds.

Both Amy and Brenna were women who'd been brought face to face with violence and danger. And they'd refused to be broken. When the violence came for them, they didn't run. They turned to face it, knowing that they had SEALs protecting and defending them. They'd both stepped up and stood their ground, trusting that their men would have their backs.

Challenging their men to have their backs.

Because in the end that's where a man's deepest duty lies, doesn't it?

Just like a soldier is sworn to defend his country, a man is bound to defend his woman.

And just like the need to protect your tribe comes from an ancient place in a man's psyche, the instinct to protect his mate comes from a deep place in a man's soul.

For one strange moment Cody let his mind drift. Earlier that year the four SEALs had talked long and hard over beers back at Ax's ranch.

It was two months after Bruiser and Brenna got married in Chicago. Ax and Amy had just had their twins. Bruiser and Brenna were expecting soon. Things had changed for the former SEAL Team Thirteen.

Changed for two of them, at least.

The four of them were sitting on the wooden porch facing the barn. The Georgia night was hot. The grill was smoldering from the evening's ribeye steaks. The longneck beers were sitting in a steel tub of melted ice. They were eight beers into the night when Bruiser finally blurted out what was on all the men's minds.

Or at least on Cody and Dogg's minds.

"You guys are next," Bruiser had said, his loud voice carrying over the dark fields, making the horses stir in the blackness. "Cody and Dogg. The only question is which one of you gets hit first. Does fate fuck with Cody first? Or is it Dogg's turn next. Hard to say."

"Marriage seems to have softened your brain, Bruiser," Cody said.

"It's called dad-brain," said Dogg.

Cody reached out and fist-bumped Dogg, who was grinning wide in the dark.

"Fate's coming for you, brother," whispered Bruiser tauntingly. He pointed his beer bottle at Dogg and then Cody, then took a long sip, his eyes still on them.

Cody had been about to let loose with a wisecrack that would stampede the horses, but he held back when he saw the expression on Ax's face. Their Team Leader had been mostly silent the past few minutes.

"Bruiser might be right," Ax had said, taking a long swig from his drink. His eyes were shining in the dark. They were clear, despite the beer. "John Benson's a sly motherfucker, but there just might be something to this whole fate and destiny thing. Amy believes it. Brenna does too. And the way shit happened on those last two missions . . . hell, it makes you wonder."

"Wait, so you two actually *believe* that hokey bullshit?" Cody asked with a half-laugh. He glanced at Bruiser, then looked back at Ax.

Ax and Bruiser shared a look. They each took a long drag from their bottles. Neither of them answered.

There'd followed a strange moment of dead silence

in the night. The horses moved about in the dark pasture far beyond the cattle barn. The guys finished their beers and then sat quietly for some time, each of them lost in thought, in that strange mental place where you think you see something in the patterns of events, see a hidden order in the way things play out.

Dogg finally broke the eerie silence. He slammed his empty bottle on the wooden porch railing, then got noisily to his feet.

"Ax and Amy. Bruiser and Brenna," he said, stretching his heavy body, twisting out the stiffness. Then he thumped Cody on the shoulder. "So if Benson sets you up on a mission involving some chick whose name starts with C, then you better tuck your balls between your legs and run like the wind, motherfucker."

All four of them had roared like lions at the watering hole, hooting and hollering until finally Amy leaned out the ranch-house window and announced that the twins were awake, so thank you very much. That scattered the troops, but that odd feeling had stuck with Cody.

And that feeling came back to Cody again now.

It came back hard.

Flanked him like a jungle ambush.

Pulled him out to sea like a Hawaiian riptide.

Was Cody losing his mind?

Losing it over a woman who was playing him? A curvy Italian goddess shaking her hips and getting him turned around like he had balls for brains, making him believe in fate when it was just dumb coincidence?

Cody looked at Cate staring up at him. He glanced over at Maggie Malone watching them.

Capturing Cate

He tried to think logically, use reason and common sense instead of emotion and instinct. After all, he reasoned, there were millions of women whose names started with C. Didn't mean a damn thing.

Besides, the whole Ax and Amy thing didn't match up with the names. Ax's real name was Jake. There was no mystical pattern here. This wasn't a damn soap opera.

But then he looked at Cate Bonasera again.

The feeling was still there.

He thought of that conversation in the Georgia night.

Thought of what Ax had said about how Benson viewed fate and destiny as simple science, pure physics, a system of probabilities just like quantum mechanics. A wave of possibilities that were affected by human choice.

And when Cody looked at Cate again he saw her for what she really was.

She was a choice standing there in front of him.

A choice that made him want to trust in fate.

Made him want to believe in destiny.

Made him want to finish the mission.

Because maybe . . .

Just maybe . . .

She was the damn mission.

8

"Finish your mission," Cate whispered to him as she looked into his green eyes.

That electric tingle rippled down her spine again. She felt a desperate urgency to stay with this man. She'd felt a protective fire burning in him, and she'd been drawn to it like a butterfly to candlelight.

She'd only just found out he was a soldier not a cowboy, but somehow the two archetypes merged in her mind.

There was something about this man that hearkened back to the age of chivalry and knights, honor and duty, when the only law in the land was a man's word, the only safety to be found was in his powerful arms.

Cate almost laughed at herself for the thoughts. The madness of the day must have shaken something loose, she decided.

She'd killed a man, was running from Boro, breaking from the only life she'd ever known. Perhaps it had caused a psychotic break. She'd read of such things, where people believe they are living in delusional worlds created by their broken brains.

Except it felt so real, this delusional world.

She gazed at Cody Cartright's handsome face, the dark stubble on his jutting chin, the veins running like tree-vines down the tree-trunk of his neck. She was attracted to him in a way that frightened her.

The blood-soaked images of him slashing and spearing those men were still vivid in her mind. She could see his muscles tighten and release with every strike.

The sun made his tanned body gleam and glisten like a gladiator oiled for the arena. The black mask added an air of mystery that made her warm and wet beneath her clothes, affected some part of her that was buried deep in the private recesses of her mind, places that she'd gotten glimpses of when alone with just her fantasies and her fingers.

"You two finished saying your goodbyes?"

The woman called Maggie Malone was still leaning against the dark blue car's front door. She wore a pantsuit that was charcoal gray and tailored to perfection. Cate was not certain if America had such fine tailors these days. Perhaps they did. America was supposed to have the best of everything.

Cody stepped in front of Cate and stopped. She stopped too. His shadow was broad enough to shield her. She stayed in his shade.

"Been thinking, Malone," he said. "Maybe we can work together on this. I got nothing else going on. Was just messing around with the new class of SEALs at Hell Week when Benson called." He shrugged those massive shoulders. "It's my first mission in this new outfit. Kinda want to see it through, you know?"

"It's not your mission anymore," said Malone.

She pushed her hips off the blue metal, stood up straight, touched her helmet-shaped hair, then crossed her arms over her chest.

Cate could see no wedding ring. She wondered if DEA agents wore wedding rings while on duty.

Then she wondered if soldiers wore wedding rings while on duty. If cowboys wore wedding rings on the range.

"Get in the car, Mrs. Bonasera," said Malone. "You'll sit up front with me. We've got a lot to talk about."

"Bonasera is my maiden name," said Cate. She stepped out from behind Cody to face Malone. "So it is incorrect to call me Mrs. Bonasera."

"Nice try," said Malone with a tight smile. "But you've always been Mrs. Bonasera. Boro instructed you to keep your maiden name so nobody forgets you come from the Bonasera Family of Sicily. Besides, Boro doesn't use a last name." She rolled her blue eyes in a strange way. "Like Madonna. Or Prince."

Cody frowned. "That's what Benson told me too. Is it true?" he asked Cate.

She nodded. "He is an orphan. Nobody knows if there was a last name. Perhaps Nico does."

"Who's Nico?" said Cody.

"This isn't your mission anymore," snapped Malone. Her eyes were glassy blue and narrowed. She turned to one of the three men. The one who'd stood behind the car. Red mirror sports-shades. "Escort Mrs. Bonasera over, please."

The man grunted. His head turned towards Cody.

He touched his shades, then placed his palm on his right cargo flap.

"Stay right there, Kev," said Cody. He looked at Malone. "I need to clear it with Benson before I hand her over. Need to get the formal go-ahead. Procedure and all."

Malone shook her head. "John Benson isn't with the Agency anymore. And I don't give a rat's ass what he's got going on the side. Kaiser's cleared me to take over, and that's the only clearance that matters. Now step aside, please."

Cody did not step aside.

He grinned at Kevin, then glanced pointedly at the two other men who were in various states of disrepair.

"Your operation isn't gonna make it past the San Fernando valley with these guys. You can use me, Malone. I won't step on your toes. Won't steal your thunder or your glory. Everybody wins."

Malone laughed once. It was a shrill sound, like a hawk shrieking in surprise. "You're on every damn newsfeed right now, you idiot. A loose cannon who isn't capable of understanding what's going on here. I have a lot of respect for the SEALs, but we don't need your skillset on this operation, soldier. We won't have a need for any more over-the-top public massacres. Those can stay in Hollywood. And so can you."

A murmur of laughter rose from the three men. Cate sensed Cody's body tighten. She imagined the ridges of muscle on his torso harden as he took a long breath and exhaled slowly.

He stayed absolutely still. His big boots did not shift an inch on the gravel.

Those slow breaths were to control his anger, Cate realized when she saw how calm Cody's expression was right then. He was looking at Malone with a slightly trancelike gaze, sort of like how you must relax your focus when you look at those pictures which have patterns hidden in the chaotic design.

Cate followed his gaze towards Malone. Her long, lean face was tight and serious. But she was not angry. She was very much in control of herself.

Cate wondered if she'd deliberately insulted Cody just to get a rise out of him. Perhaps she wanted to make Cody lose his temper, provoke him to draw his weapon. Give her an excuse to order him shot.

The thought scared her. She knew about the DEA and the CIA, just like every organized crime group from South America to the South Pole knew about such agencies.

The DEA had worked with Pablo Escobar's old Medellin Cartel. They'd made deals with the Cali Cartel, double-crossing Escobar and starting a brutal Cartel war.

The CIA had been rumored to work with the Russian Bratva and the Italian Mafia just as they might work with Britain's MI-6 or Israel's Mossad.

After all, organized crime played pivotal roles in the politics and economics of almost every country. Boro paid millions every year to Colombian politicians and army generals and police chiefs. In turn those millions trickled down to underlings, who spent the money at village taverns and city whorehouses.

Capturing Cate

In the end everyone got a little piece of the pie. Nobody was fully innocent. Nobody was squeaky clean. Besides, in the shadows nobody can tell who is good and who is bad. Nobody even cares, yes?

And which are you, Cody Cartright, she wondered as she tried to read his mind.

Good or bad?

Saint or sinner?

Captor or protector?

"Hey, so is it true that a few years ago the DEA was exposed for running drugs and guns just to finance some of their black ops down in South America?" Cody said suddenly, his voice earnest but with an edge. "This got something to do with that?"

Malone's blue eyes stayed calm. Her cheekbones moved up slightly, then down again. "Is it true that a few years ago a high school kid in Texas got a girl killed because he was a hot-headed dumbass? This got something to do with that?"

Now Cody's boots moved in the dirt. His breath caught in his throat. He said nothing.

Malone took a step forward. "There are no secrets in the post 911 world." She shrugged her shoulder-pads. "I read your file on the way over. Now you understand why I don't want you near this mission. Why I don't want you near this woman. Don't want you thinking you can save someone to make up for what you did."

Cody let out the breath that had caught in his throat. He turned his head sideways, glancing at Cate through the corner of his eye. He looked back at Malone.

And then he moved.

Moved like a whip.

So fast you feel the lash before you hear the crack.

Before Cate could blink again Cody was behind her. His arm slid around the front of her waist, pulling her into him with violent force. She felt his big belt buckle dig into her lower back.

Her buttocks were pressed tight against him. His scent was warm and heavy and overwhelming. Her heart was thumping behind her breastbone. Her breath came in short bursts.

She was very aware of her soft bottom pressing into his front. His body felt firm like a concrete wall behind her. Sweat beaded on her forehead.

Then she felt cold metal against her temple.

"What're you, crazy?" said Malone, her eyes widening. She held up her hand to stop her men from drawing their weapons. "Put down the gun, Soldier. You aren't going to shoot."

"I might," said Cody. "But you won't. You need her alive."

Malone carefully ran the back of her thumb across her eyebrow like she was smoothing it out. She blinked several times, then she shook her head and sighed.

"You won't shoot her," she said again. "That's part of the damn reason I don't want you on the mission. I saw the video of you going all knight-in-shining-armor on those guys when they attacked her. I know about your past." She sighed again. "Simple behavioral psychology. You're a textbook case, Cody. I know you won't give her up to Boro in the end. That's why I can't let you have her. She needs to be returned to her husband, and my gut tells me that will be a problem for you."

Cate stared at Malone. She felt Cody stiffen, then relax again with that masterful control over himself. For a moment Cate wished Cody hadn't calmed down so quick.

"Maybe it would be a problem for me. Maybe it wouldn't," Cody said with a cool nonchalance that made Cate's heart sink a little. "Question is, why would it even matter to you so much, Malone?"

Malone's sharp features twisted. She glanced at Cate, then bit her thin lower lip until it turned white. She looked at Cody again. Sighed.

"Because marrying Cate Bonasera was Boro's passport to the European drug market," Malone said. Her expression was pained, like she was explaining something to a toddler. "If Cate leaves him, then Boro loses his privileges at the Italian seaports. Which means he can't sell his product in Europe. Which means he turns his attention back to the United States. Which means ten years of complicated deals that the DEA has made with the other Colombian cartels and the Mexican traffickers go to shit." She shook her head again. "And that's a big problem. Big like you wouldn't understand. Big like I have neither time nor patience nor clearance to explain right now. Especially to a man who isn't part of an official government agency." She whooshed out a breath and blinked twice in annoyance. "And even if you were still military, this is way the hell above your pay grade, Soldier. Not to mention above your IQ grade."

Cody grunted. "I passed second grade math. That's

all I need to put two and two together and see it doesn't add up."

Malone frowned. "What doesn't add up?"

Cody's grip around Cate's waist tightened. "Wish I had time to explain, but I don't. So here's what we're going to do." He pressed the gun barrel tight against Cate's head. It hurt. She felt a chill run through her. It was fear this time. "Now, you were right when you said I won't shoot her. Call me old-fashioned, but I prefer not to execute unarmed women in cold blood. But I know you need Cate alive, so you won't risk her getting shot."

"We can shoot you if you don't stand down," Malone said quietly.

Cody's breathing stayed calm. "Not with my gun to Cate's head. Even if you nail me between the eyes you can't guarantee my finger won't spasm and blow her brains out. Unless one of you has the confidence to draw and fire and hit me in that tiny place in the brain stem that will freeze my motor functions and guarantee my finger won't spasm and kill Mrs. Cate Bonasera."

Nobody said a word. Malone's frown cut deeper.

"Thought so," said Cody. "Now place your cell phones and weapons in the backseat of the Grand Marquis. One by one. Slowly, but not too slow."

"You're an idiot," Malone growled. "People are going to die because of the choices you're making."

"I'm a SEAL, Malone. People die from my choices every time I pull the trigger or draw my blade," Cody drawled. "Now do it. Guns and phones in the backseat. Move, please."

Cate winced from the pressure of the gun against her head. Cody's grip around her waist was so tight it was difficult to breathe. The tingling excitement she'd felt earlier had morphed into fear and dread.

Suddenly she wasn't sure of this cowboy after all. She wasn't certain if he was a soldier or a mercenary. Malone had said Cody was no longer military. But then Cody said he was a SEAL. Present tense.

It was very confusing. Cate was flustered. Her throat was dry. The hope that had kept her energy up was fading. She was fading too.

Her vision went in and out as Cody pushed her towards the large car. He kicked the back door closed, then dragged her around to the front passenger side.

She blinked from the sunlight in her eyes. The sun was moving low in the West. Malone and the three men had been ordered to back away. They were standing near the red car with the torn tires. The men were muttering and grumbling. Maggie Malone's thin face was tight. Her eyes were a vicious blue.

"You'll never get her to Colombia," Malone said to Cody. "We're going to be looking for you. So will every gangster, thug, and freelancer in LA County looking for either a payday or to make good with the Caliente Crew." Her voice sounded thin in the gentle breeze. "But even if you make it out of California, this bitch will slit your throat first chance she gets. And she'll get her chance. I see it in your eyes, Cody. You're being played like a dickhead with a hard-on for brains. She's a mafia princess married to a drug lord, you fool. If you just want some curvy ass, you're better off hitting the whorehouses in Puerto Vallarta instead of playing her game. She's not some innocent victim, Cody."

"Nobody here is innocent," Cody said coolly from behind Cate. "I'm just finishing my mission. That's all. If my final orders are to put a bullet in her head, I'll do it and never think about her again. Not even when I swing by Puerto Vallarta on my way to my next mission."

Cate's heart almost burst as the last shred of hope tore its way out of her. Cody's cocky, unruffled nonchalance wasn't an act. It was real, and it was ruthless.

He didn't care about her.

He never would care about her.

He was a machine. Not a man.

He would take her back to Boro. She was certain of it now.

He pushed her roughly into the front seat, pulled the seatbelt across her chest, snapped it into place. Then he leaned his body across hers and popped open the glovebox.

He rummaged inside and came up with some plastic ties. They were long and black, that hard plastic that Cate knew was unbreakable without a knife.

She didn't struggle as Cody bound her wrists tight without a word. He slammed the glovebox shut, kicked the door closed, then strode around the car and got behind the wheel.

Cate stared out the window with glazed eyes as Cody drove them away. He merged into traffic and sped up.

The plastic ties were cutting into her wrists, but she

didn't care. She glanced at the glovebox, then thought of the glovebox in the red car.

She looked down at her wrists, then dragged her gaze up past her neckline. She could feel the coolness of stainless steel between her bare breasts.

The three-inch switchblade she'd found in the red car was secure inside her bra. It wouldn't slip out. That was one of the many good things about having breasts that both men and women would kill for.

Or die for, she thought as she rested her head against the seatback and closed her eyes. She needed some rest.

After all, she would be on the run again very soon.

Free again very soon.

Alone again very soon.

Alone again forever.

9
EIGHTY MILES OUTSIDE MEDELLIN COLOMBIAN JUNGLE

"He is alone?" said Boro, stroking his goatee that was short and thick, like many parts of his body. He glanced inquiringly at Nico, who sat to his left.

Nico always sat to Boro's left. Long ago Boro had taken issue with the term "right hand man." Boro was left-handed, and so his top man should sit at his left.

Nico nodded his big head. He was taller than Boro by a foot, but although a large man, was still narrower than the thickset drug lord. Nico wore dark green cargo pants and the sleeveless flak jacket that many South American guerillas wore in the jungles. It had many pockets and loops and hooks.

It was utilitarian, not symbolic. Nico had never been a guerilla. He was too much of a loner to join with other men in some grand effort to overthrow a brutal regime and replace it with another that would soon be corrupted by power and turn equally brutal.

"It appears he is alone, Boro." Nico punched a key on the silver laptop resting on the round teakwood table that usually held Boro's morning coffee.

The video of a man with a black shirt tied around his face played once more. They had watched it twelve times. Studied closeups of the surrounding cars. Looked for signs that the spectators were like extras in a movie, planted there in a scripted scene. Any evidence that it was a ruse, just actors on a stage, an elaborate setup orchestrated to trick Boro. Perhaps orchestrated by Cate herself.

But twelve viewings had revealed no evidence of staging.

The kills were genuine.

The fight was real.

So the thirteenth time Boro watched the man doing the killing. He stroked his goatee and pursed his lips out and in as was his habit. Then he grinned, showing his two gold front teeth. "He fights well."

"Too well," said Nico. "He has been trained. But more than just training. He has seen action."

"Military?"

Nico nodded. "Special Forces would be my guess. Army Ranger. Perhaps Navy SEAL. They are trained with knives."

Boro arched his thick neck, stroked the clean shaved skin above his collarbone. He prided himself on being well groomed even though he lived hidden in the jungle like an animal.

But he was not an animal. He was a man. A great man. So what if he could not trace his lineage back ten generations like the Escobars of the world.

Like the Bonaseras of the world.

Now Boro took a rumbling breath and stood from the green velvet cushion held firm against the teakwood bench by smooth studs of carbon-blackened steel. He strolled to the open balcony and gazed out over his estate.

Below him the green waters of a decorative pool rippled as the warm breeze blew across it. The stone estate walls gleamed white in the distance, shining in the unforgiving sun. Beyond the walls was a stretch of clearing. And beyond that lay the jungle.

Dense. Impenetrable. Lethal.

"What does Romero Bonasera say when you tell him of his daughter?" came Nico's question.

Boro did not turn. "He says what I expected him to say." Boro turned quickly, gazed upon Nico, saw something in the man's sullen brown eyes. "He agrees that when a woman marries, she belongs to her husband not her father. But he says that so long as Renata Bonasera lives, he cannot allow Cate to be hurt. He agrees that I should bring her back to Colombia, whether she wants to come or not. But he forbids me to punish her in the way I believe is necessary. Not while her mother is alive, he says."

Nico looked down to hide his scowl. He raised his right arm and reached around to caress his pony tail that was streaked with gray, perhaps some of it dirt. The diamonds on his fingers caught the light. The stench from the damp cave of his armpit caught the breeze.

It was ungodly. Inhuman. A torture device on its own. Nico did not care about grooming. He was much closer to a jungle creature than Boro liked. But he was loyal. And useful. He deserved to be rewarded.

And Cate deserved to be punished.

"How long have you wanted her ring on your finger?" Boro asked quietly as Nico stroked his ponytail like a pet python.

Fear flashed through Nico's brown eyes. He blinked, brought his hand back down, straightened up. "Boro, I never . . . never even considered it."

Boro grinned, flicking his tongue against the back of his gold teeth. They had been knocked out by one of the nuns at the San Rafael Orphanage outside Bogota. Sister Francesca. May her wretched soul rot in hell. Boro had made sure it would do just that.

He'd returned to the San Rafael Orphanage years later. He'd made sure Sister Francesca was violated and soiled while her soul still lingered in her broken body. He wanted her to know where she was headed before he allowed her to leave.

"How long have we known each other, eh, Nico?" Boro strolled up close, patted Nico's pock-marked cheek that was etched with scars and stubbled like a battlefield. "I see how you look at my wife. You have wanted to wear her ring as your prize for years, Nico. Admit it to me. Trust me with the truth of your heart, Nico."

That fear tore through Nico's eyes again. Boro liked to see it. He stood in silence. Let Nico squirm. Then he chuckled low in his throat.

"Relax," Boro said, his voice still low in his throat. "It is not a betrayal to have such thoughts. In fact, to have thoughts like that and restrain them for so many years is a show of loyalty." He took a breath and sighed it out. "And fate has rewarded your loyalty, old friend. You will indeed wear her ring, Nico. When Cate returns, she will be given to you."

Nico blinked profusely, his sullen eyes lighting up in a way that Boro had not seen in years. Had not seen ever, perhaps.

"It is strange how attraction works," Boro said thoughtfully. "Strange how fate itself works."

"How so?

Boro shrugged with his face. "You lusted after Cate for years, your eyes always following her with a wild hunger as she walked through these hallways." He sighed, cracked his short neck to the left. "But for me she was physically uninteresting. Ah, if only the Bonaseras had been Northern Italians instead of Sicilians. I have always had a fancy for tall, thin, fair-skinned women. Everything I am not. Everything Cate is not." He laughed.

Nico laughed too. Partly in relief, Boro sensed.

"Like that DEA woman, yes?" said Boro. "I recall her being tall and thin and very white."

"White like a vampire," Boro said, his eyes sparkling as he poked at his gold teeth again. "She used to burn red like fire in the heat of the jungle. No wonder she was so quick to close the deal."

Nico laughed like a hyena being throttled. "Perhaps you should have negotiated something more with her back then, eh? Like the old days, yes?"

Boro's eyes narrowed at the memory. Not of ten years ago, but many years before that. He smiled. Nodded tightly. Said nothing.

There was silence in the large, open room. The warm breeze flowed in through the balcony, carrying the pungent scent of fresh green coca pods with it.

You could not see the fields from the mansion, but you could smell them clearly. Boro had cleared vast tracts of the Colombian jungle and planted his coca in the clearings. It had been backbreaking work, but the fields were dispersed in many different areas and hard to access without helicopters and aircraft.

It would take considerable time, expense, and resources to find them all. And destroying them with firebombs or pesticides would demolish half the jungle with it, which would no doubt anger the environmentalists who appeared to have surprising clout within the new world governments.

Yes, Boro's coca fields were mostly untouchable now. And a decade of supplying premium product to Europe had made Boro wealthy beyond any reasonable measure.

So by external measures Boro was a great success.

But inside Boro still hurt.

Yes, it still hurt Boro that he had been driven out

of the American market like a beaten dog. He could imagine the leaders of the big Colombian cartels clinking champagne glasses in five-star hotel rooftops in Bogota and Medellin. He imagined them discussing their pure bloodlines. He imagined them laughing at Boro, the beast without a bloodline, an animal who had been sent back to the jungle, a second-rate operation who had been forced to ship his product to Europe, which was considered a step down from the American market.

"And perhaps fate is smiling on not just you but me as well, Nico," he said as the aroma of those coca pods filled his senses as the breeze picked up. "Perhaps Cate choosing to run is a sign that it is time to forget about the Bonaseras, to forget about the European market. I hated how Romero Bonasera gave me his daughter like he was forced to do it, forced to accept my money to pay back his European bankers who had him by the balls. He is just like the big Colombian cartel dons, proud of their bloodlines and family trees and all that bullshit. Family means nothing to me. In fact I am relieved Cate bore me no children. I find the idea of inheritance by virtue of birth disgusting. A king should earn his kingdom, not be born into it."

"Agreed," said Nico.

He folded his arms across his chest. The buckles on his flak jacket tinkled like ornaments. He carried no weapons when in Boro's private chambers, of course. Boro trusted Nico more than any other man, but he trusted in self-interest above all else. After all, Nico would take over the operation if Boro was found with a bullet in the head or a knife in the eyeball.

Capturing Cate

Boro's mind snapped back to the situation at hand. "Though I am pleasantly surprised that Cate stabbed a man in the eye to make her escape," said Boro. He grinned. "Careful with her, Nico. You may gain a new ring but lose an eyeball."

Nico grinned. He had all his teeth. They were surprisingly white given his generally poor levels of personal hygiene. There was a dentist on the estate, of course. Along with doctors, nurses, a small but fully equipped infirmary, and a well-stocked pharmacy. There was also a state-of-the-art laboratory for testing the purity of his product and synthesizing new strains of coca plant genetics.

Boro walked to the high bar topped with black glass. He flipped open a wooden cigar case and pulled out a large Cuban. He clipped the end, stuck it in his teeth, then strolled back to the balcony to light it.

He blew out the first puff of smoke and watched it curl like black tendrils. He marveled at how things were playing out for him. In a strange way, losing Cate had freed Boro too, had it not?

Now he was forced to choose between letting Cate's betrayal go unpunished or breaking with Romero Bonasera.

If he gave Cate to Nico, then his European privileges would be revoked. Boro would have no choice but to turn back to America, the greatest cocaine market on earth. From Wall Street in New York to Rodeo Drive in Beverly Hills, Boro's new strains of potent product would powder every nose.

Every businessman wanted to play in the big leagues. Every king wanted to rule the world.

"What should we do about the man who has Cate?"

Nico said from behind him. "Give me the word and I will track him down in America, kill him, and bring Cate back myself."

Boro took a smoky breath and held it inside until his lungs burned. He exhaled in a rush, feeling the tobacco send a buzz through his brain.

"No," he said, turning towards Boro. "I want you to go to Italy."

Nico's frown did his grizzled, hollowed out face no favors. "Que?" he said.

Boro nodded, doubling his resolve. Once he gave the order, there would be no turning back. It was a one way street.

"Romero Bonasera wishes that his daughter stay unharmed so long as her mother still lives," Boro said thoughtfully. "I should honor my father in law's wishes, don't you think?"

Nico's frown disappeared. There was a glint of light in his eyes again. Twice today, Boro thought as he glanced at Nico's hands. Four rings on each hand. Just those big knobbed thumbs left to fill.

Two thumbs.

Two more rings.

"You will go to Italy," Boro said as he gave the order. "And you will return with Renata Bonasera's diamond on your left thumb."

Nico stared. He blinked, licked his lips, then nodded quickly. There was silence for a moment.

Boro continued. "Also, that Italian maidservant of Cate's. What is her name?"

"Marya."

"Yes, Marya. Sweet girl. The mansion staff love her. She helps out in the infirmary sometimes. Friendly with the medical people. Gentle touch, they say of her. The lab people say she is smart too." He rubbed the back of his neck, which had been sunburned so often it was like aged leather. "When Cate is back, you will give the maid Marya to the troops. Have Cate watch. Make sure Cate counts how many men her sweet maid Marya can take before the lights go out on her gentle soul." He grinned, licked his gold incisors as he did it. "Of course, you can take Marya too if you like. But she is unmarried, and I know women without rings are of no interest to Nico, yes?"

Nico shrugged like he did not care much either way. "The men will enjoy her," he said with a grunt. He thought a moment. "But what of the man who has captured Cate? Should I arrange for a team to find him, take her from him?"

Boro smiled. "Are you afraid he will get a taste of her before you? Am I to play referee between the hordes of men who wish to take my wife as their private whore?" He laughed with open-mouthed glee, shook his thick head and laughed again. "Anyway, I am not certain a team will be successful against that masked man who fights like a machine of war. Besides, he protected her from the Caliente Crew's hit squad. She will be safer with him. Let him bring her to me. We will see what he wants."

Nico exhaled noisily. "He might be CIA. They use Special Forces. It could be dangerous. A trap. Some kind of operation to get close to you."

Boro took a breath and nodded. "All the more reason to let him come to me." He chuckled, thumped Nico on the arm. "Have you learned nothing about the CIA and DEA and all the other three-letter agencies of America? They could wipe out every Colombian cartel by pushing a few buttons on some fancy bomber-drones or whatever they have these days. If he is CIA Black Ops, then he is coming to negotiate something or perhaps just hand Cate over as a gift in lieu of future favors. If he is working alone, then he just wants the ten million, which is no problem. Either way, he is just one man, Nico." Boro's face darkened at the implication that he might not be able to handle the man without Nico around. "Just one damn man."

10

"Just one room," Cody said to the guy at the motel desk.

He was a lanky Arizona hipster with stoned out eyes and a droopy lower lip. He barely glanced up from his phone when Cody handed over eighty dollars in twenties.

Cody took the large key and looked at the shoehorn-sized plastic keyplate. The number was 69. He raised an eyebrow, glanced at Droopy. The guy looked up from his phone. He had no clue what was happening outside of his little screen.

Cody sighed and walked to the glass double doors. They hadn't been cleaned in years. There were probably fingerprints on there from the 1960s. He peered through.

The Grand Marquis was parked face-in right outside the door. Cate was still inside. She was asleep. She'd been snoring gently like a lioness cub most of the way here.

Cody had considered ditching the Grand Marquis when they crossed over into Arizona, but he didn't want to wake Cate. It was better for his state of mind that she stay in the dream world.

But now the real world was knocking, and Cody needed to face the facts.

He'd fucked up.

He'd disobeyed his boss Benson.

He'd ignored the CIA Director's directives.

He'd overruled a high-ranking DEA operative at gunpoint.

And he'd taken a druglord's runaway wife as his captive.

For a moment Cody wanted to laugh. Howl like a mad dog. Pound on the thick glass doors and smash them to bits just to work off some of the wild energy that had been pouring through his bloodstream all the way across California.

Malone hadn't called the cops. Cody knew this because he'd passed two California black-and-whites when he pulled off the freeway for gas. Then he'd zipped past a State Trooper parked nose-out in the median. Cody had been going fifteen over the speed limit, but the State Trooper didn't bother with him.

That told him a lot.

It told him his instincts were still good.

Malone was dirty.

Or at least she wasn't on the level.

Cody took a long, lingering look at Cate sprawled out in the front seat. The motel's red neon lit her up like a billboard from the Twilight Zone. The lights cast dark red shadows on her white sweater. Her curves were highlighted in a way that made Cody uncomfortable.

Testosterone does two things in a man, Cody knew.

Brings out the fight in him.

Brings out the fuck in him.

And the fighting was done for now.

Cody clenched his jaw and rubbed his eyes. For one

dark moment he wished he were a bad man, wished he could let himself do what the animal inside wanted.

But Cody had been trained to face the beast that lives inside every man. He'd learned that the animal spirits that live inside are beyond judgment. The animal wants what it wants and doesn't give a damn about the morals of the human.

It took training to learn how to use the animal inside.

To control its raw power instead of letting it control you.

To make it serve you instead of enslaving you.

You unleash the animal when you need to hurt the enemy.

You rein it in when you need to protect what's precious.

Cody calmed down. He smiled. He was a SEAL, a man of discipline and honor. He knew where the line was, and he knew how to stand his ground and never step over that line.

Cate stirred in the front seat. Her eyelids flickered open. Her lips parted. Tongue slithered out and curled upwards for a moment. She turned on her side. Her eyelids closed.

Cody looked at his watch. The battered black Fossil Chrono said it was 2300 hours. That was long enough for Benson to cool off.

Cody had tossed all the phones—his included—out the window about two hundred miles ago. He needed one now.

He looked around the motel lobby. There was an old cigarette machine with handles like you see on a foosball table. There was a Coke machine with a faded logo from back when there was no Coca Cola Classic because it was just Coke. And in the corner by the window was another relic of decades past:

A pay phone.

Cody grinned, dug into his jeans, came up with some coins. He carried them in case he needed to unscrew a bolt. Or short-circuit a fusebox. Or, he supposed, make a phone call.

"How are you, Benson?" he said into the round black perforated plastic mouthpiece.

Cody had memorized Benson's number. He assumed Benson would now have Cody's location from the caller ID. He also assumed that the location would stay private.

He sure hoped it would. Cody could stay awake fifty hours before he started to hallucinate, but he would rather not do it on this mission. Life was already dangerously surreal and only getting weirder.

"Oh, I'm good," came Benson's pat reply. "About to call in a drone-strike on the Desert Motel in Beechwood, Arizona. I can take your confession over the phone if you like. Maybe you'll get into heaven."

"Nah, there are folks keeping my place in hell toasty and warm for when I get there," Cody drawled through a grin.

He leaned on the wall, turning so he could keep an eye on Cate. And on the night sky in case Benson really did send some drones in for a quick kill.

Cody and the guys had done a training session where they'd learned how to take out drones with handguns. About a thirty-percent chance of winning, Ax had informed them matter-of-factly. Bruiser, Ax, and Cody had shrugged. Sounded about right. They'd all turned thirty-percent odds into one-hundred-percent wins on the battlefield countless times. It was called SEAL math. It only made sense to madmen like Navy SEALs.

"You're a damn madman," Benson muttered into the phone. "Kaiser wants you in a cage. Maybe at the zoo. Malone wants you . . . hell, I don't know what Malone wants."

Cody glanced at his watch and sighed. "I gave you eight hours of alone-time and you couldn't extract that intel from your shadowy contacts? What's your job at Darkwater anyway, Benson?"

Benson chuckled coldly. "It's not that simple. DEA's taken a page out of the CIA playbook when it comes to keeping records of their Dark Ops."

Cody sighed. "Let me guess. They don't keep any." He sighed again. "What about Malone's personal history? Got anything useful on her?"

Benson was silent. Cody heard him breathe. Finally he spoke. "You don't seem to understand the situation, Cody," he said slowly. "Malone doesn't matter anymore. Neither does this mission. Darkwater is off the case, buddy. It's bigger and more complicated than I thought when I sent you in."

"What *did* you think when you sent me in?" Cody said, glancing at Cate, tightening his jaw, heat rising up his neck. "What was the end game, Benson? You never told me that."

"It was a straight up capture-and-deliver job," said Benson. "Darkwater delivers the package back to its rightful owner. Darkwater collects its reward in the form of a future favor. Give and take. Reciprocity. The oldest trade system in the universe."

Cody thought for a second. He'd been around the block a few times with the CIA when he was still a SEAL. He knew how the spooks liked to collect favors, stack up the debt owed to them by various sketchy motherfuckers.

Boro would qualify as a sketchy motherfucker.

It would have been a fairly clean mission if not for the Caliente Crew sending out a damn hit squad, Cody realized. Hell, with a private plane waiting at LAX, Cody might already be on his way home from Colombia. Maybe with time to squeeze in a stopover at Puerto Vallarta.

Cody rubbed the back of his neck. "Puerto Vallarta," he said without thinking.

Benson was quiet. Cody swore he heard the man's breath catch. He pushed harder.

"Malone's been there," he said.

"So have I," said Benson quickly. "Along with about a million tourists a year. What's your point?"

"It's meaningful to Malone," said Cody. "Dig into it."

Benson sighed. Cody sensed he was shaking his head. "Look, it's over, Cody. This is no longer a Darkwater mission."

Cody's eyes flashed as he looked at Cate in the surreal red neon. "Doesn't look that way to me."

"Then you're looking at it wrong."

"Doesn't feel wrong."

"Your feelings aren't relevant here, Soldier."

Cody took a breath. Nodded. "So what now?"

"Where is she?"

"Outside in the car."

"Alone?"

"Asleep."

Benson was quiet. "Leave her there. Walk away. I'll call Malone, give her Cate's location."

Cody didn't reply. He watched Cate's nose wriggle. For a moment he thought he saw the innocence of that child she once was, a princess born to a life she didn't choose.

Now she was choosing to run, and Cody had stopped her. Cody was taking her back to her prison. He was stealing her chance at freedom.

It didn't feel right.

But sometimes duty trumped right and wrong, didn't it?

So what was Cody's duty here?

Whose duty was calling to him in darkness?

Was it the soldier in him?

Or was it the man in him.

The part of his essence that was ancient and hidden.

The part that was instinct, not intelligence.

Animal, not human.

The need to protect a mate.

Protect her with his life.

"Get your damn head in the game, Soldier," barked Benson over the phone. "I know what you're thinking, and you're dead wrong on this. You can't force it, Cody."

"Force what?" Cody said.

The words came out with violent force, the air whistling through his gritted teeth. He could feel the soldier in him charging forth in the battle for his damn soul.

He knew it was insane to think there could be anything meaningful with a runaway druglord's wife. This was just his cock trying to punch above its weight. Even a strong man can be brought to his knees by the raw lust of the animal inside.

Remember, he warned himself. The animal doesn't give a damn about right and wrong. Instinct doesn't care about intelligence. An elite warrior has to balance those forces inside him. That's the only way he can bend the world to his will.

The greatest enemy the elite warrior must conquer is the one that whispers in the darkness of every man's heart.

A whisper that wants one thing.

One thing only.

Wants it now.

"Look, you want to fuck her, go ahead," said Benson sharply. "Maybe if you get your rocks off it'll clear the fog and you'll be able to think like a rational man with a shred of common sense." He paused a breath. "But don't try to force something that isn't there, Cody. Something that can never be there. Not with a woman who comes from the place she does. A place that's going to take her back, no matter what you do." He sighed. "It's partly my fault, I know. All that talk about fate and destiny with Ax and Bruiser was a bad move on my part. Shouldn't have done it. I get carried away sometimes, and it's possible that I'm not thinking straight either." He took a shuddering breath. "Maybe losing Sally on that first mission . . . maybe it broke something inside me."

Cody listened, a frown creasing his brow. He knew that Benson had been secretly married to Sally Norton,

Amy's boss at the State Department. Sally had been poisoned by Prince Rafiq's assassin during that crazy mission with Ax.

Everyone at Darkwater knew that Benson had lived his entire life as a shadowy loner. He had nobody close to him other than Sally Norton. Losing her couldn't have been easy. Maybe it had indeed broken something inside him.

Cody stayed silent for what seemed like a long time. He looked at Cate, then scanned the lamp-lit streets of the little Arizona town.

No cars screeching around the corner. No drones swooping down from above. No distant rumble of an approaching Nighthawk chopper with Maggie Malone in the sniper's seat.

Benson hadn't called it in yet.

Benson was waiting.

Waiting for Cody to decide.

Waiting for Cody to choose.

The soldier or the man?

Whose duty comes first?

"Yeah, something's definitely broken inside you, Benson," he said finally. "But I think it's always been broken. Don't blame the dead for your shortcomings, old man. You're bullshitting me, aren't you? Bruiser told me how you fucked with his head on that mission. You want to see if I take the bait. Choose the woman over common sense."

Benson huffed out an exasperated breath. "Look, all that seems meaningful after the fact, but it's just dumb luck that it worked out for Bruiser and Brenna. Anyway, you need more than dumb luck. You've got the entire damn world against you, including me. Hell, even if I don't call Malone, she'll find you soon enough. You can't just drive around the continent in stolen cars with a druglord's runaway wife as your captive. This thing is a dead end, Cody. You try to force fate's hand, it'll blow your damn engines, send you down in flames like a million other tough guys who thought they saw the future and reached for something that wasn't meant to be."

Cody listened in silence. He looked at Cate again. Then he blinked and nodded.

"I'm not that far gone, Benson. I'm not an idiot, despite being called that a couple of times today and maybe even acting like it for a spell. Anyway, you can relax, OK? I've no intention of eloping with a druglord's wife. And I sure as hell don't plan to fuck her."

He swallowed hard, told himself that was the truth. If he let his mind go there, he was in real danger. She'd play him like a football. Spike his dumb ass in the endzone and do a touchdown-dance on his grave.

"I'm just following my instincts on this mission. Something's off with Maggie Malone. You know it too. So come on, Benson. You love the game, don't you? The game of cat and mouse, smoke and shadows, deception and danger. Hell, SEALs love the game too. Let it play out. Come on. Play it out."

Cody straightened his lean, hard body as the words fired up his blood, reminded him that the times he felt most alive were when he was knee deep in the blood of his enemies, planning the next battle with his brother SEALs. He knew Benson would get it. He knew Benson was close to breaking.

He pushed on. "Look, my head is straight, Benson. I got no illusions about Cate Bonasera. She's got blood on her fingernails, cocaine on her lips. She's just like Boro, just like her Sicilian family."

Benson exhaled. "So what do you propose?"

Cody blinked twice. "I'll finish the mission. The original mission. It's still a useful mission for Darkwater, isn't it?"

Benson was silent a beat. "So you'll deliver her to Boro. Make the connection. Get his name in the Darkwater account ledger as someone who owes us his gratitude. Let him know that one day Team Darkwater will call in the favor."

"Just like in the Godfather," said Cody. "You suck my dick today, I'll finger your butthole tomorrow. Everybody wins."

"Did they do a remake of the Godfather?" Benson deadpanned. "I need to see that new one. Might learn some new tricks."

Cody grinned, rubbed his stubble, stretched some of the tension out of his neck. That motel room was calling. Cody hoped Droopy had given him two double beds like he'd asked. He didn't want to have to change rooms after he got Cate upstairs without anyone noticing her wrists were tied. Didn't want to sleep on the couch either. If it was one bed, he was taking the prime position.

He went over some details with Benson, then hung up and walked to the car. Pulled open the door. Cate almost rolled out because she was leaning against it.

Cody caught her. She opened one eye and stared up at him like an upside down cat. He tried not to smile. Tried not to let that warmth invade his heart, weaken his resolve.

Cody warned himself that his dick wasn't in control, but the tingling warmth flowed through his heart, not his balls.

Well, maybe his balls too, he thought as he pushed her upright and caught a glimpse down her neckline. Those dark brown globes looked warm and full in the red shadows of the neon sign. Cody imagined the earthy scent of the secret perspiration hiding between those lush boobs.

He looked away, then stole another glance just because he was a shameless dog.

And then he frowned.

There was something tucked in there.

Snug between her breasts.

Something metal and shiny.

Cody exhaled slowly as his blood rose hot up his neck. Instantly he thought of the glovebox in the red Supra.

He should have searched her earlier.

He should search her now.

Search her hard and rough. Tie those bound wrists to her ankles until she screamed in pain. Gag that treacherous mouth with her own panties. Toss her in the damn trunk.

She could spend the night in the darkness. Maybe

Malone's guys would find her while Cody was snug and snoring in the comfy motel bed. Maybe they'd take her and make it easy for him. Then Cody wouldn't need to decide a damn thing. Fate would solve his problem.

Benson was right the first time, Cody thought as the blood roared behind his ears. He felt like a fool. A damn idiot. Yeah, Benson was right the first time. Cody had been influenced by the sentimental bullshit Ax and Bruiser and their pregnant wives had been gushing about.

Fate could go fuck itself.

Destiny could go die in hell.

His head was straight now.

Damn right his head was straight.

Cody watched with burning eyes as Cate arched back against the slightly reclined seat, stretched her neck, raised her arms straight up and out.

Her wrists were still bound. The plastic ties had cut into the flesh. She was bleeding a little.

Cody swallowed hard, tried to think cool. He glanced through the glass doors at Droopy behind the desk. He was drinking a big tumbler of green juice. Perhaps he was alert now. Perhaps he'd notice that the big guy who'd just checked in was escorting a Latin-looking woman whose wrists were tied and bleeding.

Cody sighed. He pulled out his knife. Wiped it on his jeans in case there were any remains of the machete warriors on the blade.

Then he grabbed her hands, slipped the tip of the blade under the plastic ties, cut them clean.

"If I get tetanus and die then you will not get your

bounty," she said, frowning at her wrists and then glaring at him.

"Tetanus takes a few days to kill you," Cody said coldly. "You get lockjaw first. I'll just knock out your front teeth and feed you with a straw if that happens. Should be fine."

Cate kept her glare on his face, but there was the hint of an amused smile. She looked at the faint lines of blood on her wrists, then up at him again, her eyes wide, a slight frown starting to crinkle her smooth brown forehead.

"Boro had his front teeth knocked out by a nun at the San Rafael Orphanage," she said.

"Boro had lockjaw?"

"No, silly. He bit her."

"What happened to Thou Shalt Not Bite Nuns?" Cody almost bit his lip for the wisecrack. Stop flirting with her, you dumb shit, he told himself.

Cate's little smile flashed again. She blinked and kept her gaze on Cody. "Years later, Boro and Nico sought out the nun for revenge. She was eighty three years old."

"So she had a nice, full life," said Cody with a shrug. He couldn't resist. Battlefield humor.

Cate laughed, arching her head back, opening her mouth, smiling with her dark eyes.

Cody kept his eyes down. Regained his composure. Flipped his internal switch from humor to hardness.

He snapped off her seatbelt and gestured for her to get out. His expression stayed cold and unreadable. A stone wall.

He knew what Cate was doing. He wasn't going to let

Capturing Cate

her horrify him with tales of Boro's viciousness. Cody had seen worse.

Hell, Cody had done worse. No nuns in his kill count yet, but he was still active. Still in the game.

Cody stepped back as Cate got out. He glanced at her chest. Couldn't see the outline of what she had hidden in there. Might be a switchblade, judging by the size and where she must have found it.

It was secure between her breasts. He imagined searching her. Ripping off her bra. Spreading those heavy globes. Examining every soft inch of smooth skin. Sniffing her like a damn bloodhound.

Then he'd find her secret.

Punish her transgression.

Punish her hard.

Now Cody's cock hardened. He gritted his teeth and willed himself to stand down. But seeing Cate in all her curvy beauty was not conducive to standing down. The red neon made her look dark and deadly. Dangerously sexy.

"Won't they be searching for the car?" Cate asked.

Cody shook his head. "Malone didn't call the cops. There's no GPS in this model. It's safer than switching cars. I steal someone's minivan and it gets called in. The Grand Marquis is safer. Nobody's called it in."

He glanced at the intersection past the blinking traffic lights. There were no cameras up there. But no doubt there'd been cameras at the gas stations and rest stops. There were cameras at major highway interchanges.

Cody knew that surveillance tech was like science fiction these days. If you had access to the right systems, you could have Artificial Intelligence programs search traffic camera footage for all sorts of stuff. There was face recognition. Number recognition. If Malone had that kind of access, it would only take a few hours to narrow it down to a small enough radius to search.

Still, Benson had Cody's back for now. Benson's phone was off the grid, so nobody could trace the call to the motel phone. And Benson said he'd call in a favor with the CIA tech group to monitor the surveillance requests. Anyone looking for Cody or Cate's particulars or the Grand Marquis' plate would get blocked. Then Benson would call the front desk. Ask for Room 69.

"Room 69?" Cate said when they made it up the stairs without incident and stopped outside the metal door painted pink like Pepto Bismol. "Ooh, la la."

"Shut up and get inside," Cody managed to say while stifling a laugh.

He rammed the key into the lock, turned it so hard it almost broke off in the keyhole.

Then he kicked open the door, shoved her into the room with more force than he'd intended.

Cate stumbled in the darkness as Cody pulled the door closed and slid the deadbolt in place. He clawed at the wall. Flipped on the lights.

Fuck you, fate.

Damn you, destiny.

There was just one bed.

11

"I told that stoned out airhead I wanted two double-beds," growled Cody.

He glared at the queen-sized bed like it was a badly behaved child, then marched across the rough carpet and yanked the pink plastic phone off the cradle.

Cate stood there in the middle of the room and watched the big SEAL punch buttons on the phone. The pink plastic phone looked like a toy next to Cody's big hands, she thought.

She touched her sore wrists and winced. Pain did not bother her much. If anything, physical pain made her feel alive in a weirdly appealing way.

When she was younger she would pinch herself alone in her bedroom. Pinch herself all over. Hard, until red welts rose up on her arms and thighs. Until her nipples throbbed and turned dark red as she pulled on them.

Cate touched her hair and blinked away the heat she was feeling inside. She'd slept long and hard, she realized. Her mind was alert. Her vision was clear. She felt bright and fresh, like it was a new day.

Her clothes, however, were not bright and fresh. She could smell her armpits without even raising her arms and sniffing like she sometimes did when no one was looking. She glanced at the closed pink door that must be the restroom.

She used it quickly while Cody was on the phone. It was clean and small, with a white porcelain tub and a stainless steel shower like a little hook with a smiley face at the end. She imagined hot water with powerful pressure. She sighed at the tiny pink hotel soaps and cute bottles of green apple shampoo.

Then she heard Cody slam down the phone.

She hurried out.

"He said the housekeeper didn't show today and there aren't any clean rooms with two beds," Cody grumbled.

The phone was back in the cradle. It was on the bedside table. Cody glared at it, then looked over at her. Cate thought he looked red in the face. Like he was hot inside.

Cody glanced at the thermostat, then walked over and turned it all the way to blue. He pulled the curtains open. The room turned red from the neon. The sign was right outside the window.

Cate giggled as Cody cursed and pulled the curtains closed again. She looked at the bed.

The bedspread was thick and looked heavy. It had turquoise flowers set on a black background. The turquoise was very bright.

Cate blinked and looked around the room. There was a small wooden desk in the corner. One straight-backed chair. One wood-framed armchair with blue upholstery that looked prickly. There was a floor-lamp with a cream shade.

Capturing Cate

There was no couch.

"You take the bed," Cate offered. "I have slept well. I will be fine in the chair." She glanced at the bathroom door. She was certain Cody could smell her from across the room. "Perhaps I will shower first, yes?"

"You will do no such thing," said Cody gruffly.

She looked up, annoyed at first, then immediately confused. Cody was unbuckling that thick leather belt with the big buckle that had a bull on it.

"Are . . . are you going to whip me?" she stammered.

Cody's green eyes went wide. Then he looked at the belt and understood. He shook his head. Gestured towards the metal radiator near the wall.

"Sit there with your back against the grill," he ordered.

His voice was cold again.

He was a machine again.

A soldier following orders.

Not a man following his heart.

Cate felt indignation heat up her cheeks. He was going to tie her to the radiator like she was a dog.

She shot a fiery look at his face. He did not look at her. Just stood there with the belt.

It was very long and very thick. It would sting her bottom very much if he used it that way.

Stop it, she thought furiously. He does not want you, just how even an animal like Boro never seemed to want you. With Boro you were thankful, but with the cowboy you are disappointed. You are a sick girl. You always were twisted. You deserve what is coming. You deserve it all.

Remember, this man is not your friend. He is not

your protector. Not your damn savior. He is your captor.

He is not a path to freedom but a wall stopping you from being free. You must see him as a machine, not a man.

Yes, you have seen him glance at you sometimes like he wants you. But never forget that if he wants you, he can take you. You have nothing to offer that he cannot take anyway.

He can tie you, take you, then deliver you to Boro and walk away without looking back. Without ever thinking of you again. Did he not say that to Maggie Malone?

Yes, he said he could put a bullet in me if those are his orders, Cate thought as that familiar sadness rose up again like mist over a swamp. He said he would do it and never think about me again. Do not overestimate the value of your round ass and bouncy breasts. They have not done a thing for you in your miserable life.

But perhaps they can help me just enough this one time, Cate thought as she nodded meekly and made her way towards the radiator. Help me just long enough that I can strike out to freedom.

She could feel the cool switchblade between her breasts. Once her hands were tied again she would not be able to use the knife. Her chance was slipping away with every step she took.

Cate stole another glance at Cody's eyes. They were green and cold, dead like that swamp in her soul.

He had switched off.

She saw it.

She felt it.

Good.

Because that would make it easier to kill him.

She played it out in her mind. Then she stopped a few feet from the radiator.

She needed to get the knife out of her bra. Open it up.

She wished she had thought of it in the bathroom. If she could go there again she would return with it behind her back. She'd be like a viper coming out of its hole. Poised and ready to strike.

And she had to strike.

Cody had saved her life, but he was also taking her to certain death. He was the last obstacle to freedom.

With him dead she would have a gun and a car. He had money too. Cash and cards. She'd seen his wallet when he paid for gasoline. It was brown leather and very full. It would be enough to get her going.

Then she would have to find a way to earn a living. Perhaps after all this practice she could just stab people for money, eh? Why not. What did she have to lose now. She was never getting into heaven anyway.

"If you will not let me shower, at least may I use the facilities?" she asked sweetly, wondering if it was too sweet, like one of those Spanish soap opera scenes where you know the woman is an evil schemer.

Cody shook his head. "Do it on the carpet. I don't give a damn."

She stared at him. "Why have you become such an asshole suddenly?"

"I was always an asshole," he snapped. "I was being unnaturally nice earlier."

"You were never *nice*," she countered. "But at least you were not an asshole."

"Well, I am now. So do what I say."

"Or what?" she said firmly, even though it was absolutely the wrong thing to do. She needed to get to the bathroom and prepare her attack. "You cannot kill me. So what will you do, hah? You are a big bully, you know that? Ordering people about like you own everyone."

Cody squared off towards her. The belt hung down by his side. His eyes narrowed to green slits. "I don't own everyone," he growled. "Just you. Now do what I say, Cate."

Cate stared up at him. He looked massive in the small room. Like a giant in a dollhouse. She wasn't going to out-bully this monster, she realized. She needed to change her approach.

"Why can I not just sit in the armchair while you sleep?" she asked, lowering her voice. "Why must you treat me like a dog?"

Cody's expression stayed cold and hard. "I treat my dogs much better than this, actually," he said. "Because they do what I say, when I say."

"Earlier you were joking with me," she said, not sure if she was acting or if it was real emotion bubbling up in her. "Now you are a mean asshole."

"That's the third time you called me an asshole."

"How many times do other women call you asshole?"

Cody took a long breath that rumbled out like thunder. Cate saw him curl the belt around his hand. She could feel the air crackle and pop like those volcanoes in El Salvador, the calderas bubbling up and boiling over.

She didn't know what was happening, but she couldn't stop it.

It was like a cosmic tidal wave, sweeping them both along in its deadly froth, swirling them around in a whirlpool of stardust, drowning them in the depths of their own destiny.

"How many times before you use that belt, you big bully," she taunted as she felt her life running away from her, felt that wave sweeping her farther out to sea.

That knife felt cold against her beating heart. She moved her body a little, felt the switchblade start to slide down between her boobs. She sucked in her belly, shimmied her midsection as subtly as she could.

Now she felt the knife get beneath her bra's underwire. Cold excitement rushed up her spine. With one quick movement she could reach under her sweater and whip out the knife. Quicker than reaching down her neckline. She might just be able to pull this off.

She had to pull it off.

"You're not gonna be able to pull it off, little girl," Cody whispered, his own tone now full of taunt. "I'm not that stupid. Not that blind. Not that foolish."

He took a long, heavy breath, flashed a deadly glance at her chest, then looked directly into her eyes. "And not that damn forgiving."

For a moment she thought she saw hurt in those eyes.

A flash of emotion.

A fleeting moment of vulnerability.

Then he blinked and it was gone.

Nothing but cold ruthlessness again.

The eyes of a man trained to kill.

To kill and walk away.

She saw that he had it in him.

The ability to do exactly what he said he could do.

Kill her. Walk away. Never think about her again.

"You almost had me," he whispered in that deadly calm voice. "You were this close to making me think you deserved a chance at freedom, deserved a shot at running from that life. But you are what Malone said you are, Cate. A druglord's wife who will slit my throat the first chance she gets."

Now time froze for Cate.

Dread slithered down her spine, curled around her navel, crawled back up to her throat.

He knows, she thought as the sickness took her breath and almost took her vision. He knows about the knife. He knows who I am inside. Sees the emptiness in my heart. The darkness in my soul.

For a moment she felt naked, exposed, torn open and put on display.

Her eyes flashed with both shame and anger.

Her heart pumped hard with blood hot like that volcano.

Then her feet moved on the carpet.

Her body twisted like a snake.

She felt the knife slide down her naked belly.

She reached under her sweater and caught it clean.

Snapped the blade open like she'd learned back in Colombia.

And leapt at his throat with the wildness of a beast.

12

Cody saw her coming in slow motion.

Her eyes were like black fire.

Her hair like snakes in a storm.

She looks deadly beautiful, he thought as he watched her come at him with every part of her soul laid bare. He'd seen the anger in her eyes. Heard the shame in her cry.

She hated that he could see into her heart, her mind, her damn soul. That he'd seen she would kill him even though he'd saved her life. That her desire to be free had overridden everything else, swept away all sense of give and take, right and wrong.

This was pure instinct, raw as a fresh wound, sharp as a new razor.

It was beautiful to see.

Mesmerizing to experience.

Breathtaking to witness.

And Cody knew he was done for.

She'd gotten to him.

Not with the knife, but with everything else.

Now the sound and fury of the scene came rushing

back to Cody. His own instincts burst forth like a panther on the pounce.

With moves practiced a thousand times Cody sidestepped her. He turned his body and grabbed her wrist. He twisted sharply.

She screamed in pain, dropped the knife, tried to whip her body around and hit him in the face with her free hand.

The move was quick, and Cody took the punch on the side of his mouth.

It burst his lip, and Cody roared in surprise.

The taste of blood drove him wild. He roared again, spun Cate around by her trapped wrist, then hurled her face-first onto the black bedspread.

She bounced off it and turned, immediately kicking at his face with all the power she could generate from her thick thighs.

Cody was blind with adrenaline now, and he parried her kicks with his palms, tried furiously to grab her ankles and hold her down.

"*Dannazione te*," she screamed in Italian. She kicked him in the face with her pink-laced sneakers. Drew her leg back and tried to get him again. Got him on his broken lip and made him bleed. "*Dannazione all'inferno*," she snarled viciously.

Cody shouted something in no language at all. He spat more blood, then grabbed one of her ankles.

She lashed out again, but Cody wasn't playing anymore. He got the other ankle. He had her now.

Cody yanked her towards him. She screamed and

clawed at the bedspread, ripping the heavy cover along with her as Cody dragged her towards him like a shark pulling its thrashing victim down for the kill.

He flipped her around like she was a doll. His vision was hot red like lava. His head thundered like a stampede of bulls in heat. His heart pounded like ten thousand insane drummers. The metallic taste of blood was strong in his mouth.

And her scent was heavy in the air.

Her scent was everywhere.

Calling to him like a drug.

Ripping away the last of the soldier's discipline.

Tearing through the last of the man's self control.

Leaving nothing but the animal.

That alpha beast driven by raw instinct.

The taste of blood on its lips.

The scent of its mate in the air.

Cate was trying to turn her body, but Cody was holding her ankles and she couldn't twist all the way. He grinned wickedly at her, licked his bloody lips, spat onto the bed.

Her head was turned, her eyes wild like his. She spat back at him, called him something else in Italian, spat again and called him a fucking asshole, a filthy dog, told him to go to hell and rot there, die there, suffer there forever.

"You're coming with me to hell," he roared, pulling one hand off her ankle to wipe her saliva from his face.

Cate immediately broke loose and kicked at his face again. He smacked away her kick easily.

She tried again. Cody cracked a bloody grin, jammed his knees into the mattress, kept parrying her vicious kicks with lazy left-right swipes, like a bear toying with a honeycomb before going in for that sweet sticky prize.

Cody was grinning like a maniac, breathing hard and heavy, inhaling her scent. He inched closer towards her on his knees, slapping away her legs as she was forced to bend her knees more and more to get a kick in.

Soon Cate understood she couldn't get a kick in, and she desperately tried to turn and crawl away from him to the side of the bed.

But Cody grabbed her by the waistband of her jeans, yanked her hard towards him.

Still holding her by the waistband, fingers tucked against her lower back, he tossed her back to the center of the bed like a ragdoll.

She shrieked and bounced on the mattress, face down, ass up.

And Cody brought the flat of his right palm down hard on her ass.

Right on the meatiest part of her thick right buttcheek.

Cate shrieked as the sound ricocheted through the room. She tried to turn, but Cody shoved her back into the mattress.

Her face slammed into a mountain of pillows. Cody grabbed her hips and raised them, then grabbed the elastic waistband of her stretch jeans and yanked them down.

Her pink satin panties came down with the force of his fingers. Cody's head, balls, and cock almost exploded all at once when his blood-red gaze fell upon the expanse of smooth skin, two perfect, round globes separated by a long dark crease that beckoned like a bear trap. The kind of trap where the bear sees its own destruction but barrels forward anyway.

Cody rammed his face between her buttcheeks, roughly pulling her jeans and panties down her thighs.

With urgent need he got her jeans down to her knees and shoved his hand between her thighs from behind and beneath.

He cupped his palm upwards, forcing her tight thighs apart. She was so damn wet it was all over her inner thighs, sticky like sap, sweet like honey.

Her jeans started to rip as her knees moved apart. Cody reached for her obscenely stretched jeans and panties, pulled them all the way off.

Her sneakers popped off as he did it. He hurled the shoes at the wall, tossed the tangled mass of jeans and panties over his shoulder.

Cate tried to crawl away again, but Cody grabbed her wide hips and dragged her back. He shoved her face into the pillows and spanked her nice and hard, twice on each cheek.

She yelped, gasped, then moaned.

He spanked her again.

Three times on each side.

Hard.

With authority.

The sound of his big palms smacking her smooth skin was loud as rifles on the range. Cody was so far gone he could barely see straight.

Didn't need to see, though. Her scent was guiding him. It was beautiful and strong.

Cody rammed his nose and mouth between her thighs from behind, pushing her ass up, spreading her legs.

His tongue did a desperate recon mission for ground zero, and when he felt her thick, dark nether lips open and release their magic potion, Cody groaned so loud the bed rumbled in resonance.

Now he realized Cate had stopped moving.

She'd stopped thrashing.

No more kicking.

No more crawling.

Her face was buried in the pillow. She was making little sounds, like a small animal.

Cody opened his mouth wide against her wet pussy. Dragged his lips along her slit. Slid his tongue inside and tasted her.

She shuddered. Wetness oozed out of her cunt. She was so warm, so wet, so damn sweet.

He kneaded her ass with his big palms, ran his tongue up along her rear crack, squeezed her thighs and breathed in her musk again.

He wanted her like a dying man wanted another day alive, would give anything to feel the sun on his skin, the wind in his hair, the ground beneath his feet.

But the ground was nowhere in sight. Cody felt like he was flying as he kissed her lower back, slid his hands beneath her, caressed her lovely round belly, then grasped her breasts firmly through her sweater and squeezed.

She moaned out loud now, murmured something into the pillow.

Cody raised his head, eyes glazed with need, her wetness on his lips.

"Kiss me," she mumbled into the mountain of pillows. She turned her head to the side, curled those red lips up at the sides, fluttered those butterfly-wing lashes. "Kiss me, Coh-dee," she whispered.

Cody moved back so she could turn to him. She turned onto her back, hands down by her sides, face half covered with hair wild like a hurricane had just passed through town.

Her sweater was crooked, bra cups askew, cleavage winking at him. Her thighs were open, and Cody's heart hammered against his chest when his gaze rested on her trimmed triangle of deep black curls.

Her slit was a delicate line of dark red, glistening with her thick oil. Cody was completely spellbound, taken in by the sights and sounds and scent of this woman.

That wild rage had slowed to a simmer now. Cody was hard and thick inside his jeans. The blood on his lips was crusting over. Her tang on his tongue was sweet and salty. Strong like sangria. Crazy like cocaine.

He thought for a moment he'd been wrong about her and right about her, all at the same time. Not everything in her life had been forced upon her, but not all of it had been her choice either.

She was trapped between things she chose and things she was born into, married into, perhaps sold into. But she'd chosen to run, hadn't she? That was a choice too, wasn't it? It meant something, didn't it?

And hell, she'd chosen not just to run but to fight, Cody thought as he gazed at the invitation on her lips, saw a hint of shyness in her eyes, saw the shadow of submission in her smile. Of course, not a great idea to try and stab a SEAL, but you gotta admire her guts.

At least she's learned the hierarchy, Cody thought as his eyes narrowed and his cock throbbed.

The image of her nice round buttocks shuddering as he spanked them made it hard to breathe, hard to even see straight. The need to dominate this feisty firecracker had ripped to the surface when she'd taken a shot at him, got him in the face, kicked him a few times too. He couldn't think of one damn person who'd hit him in the face and was still alive.

"Come closer," she whispered, nestling her head into the pillow.

Cody dragged his gaze away from between her legs.

He leaned forward to kiss her.

Then he saw her arm move up from near her hip.

Saw the flash of steel against the sheets.

And felt her plunge the knife right into his chest.

13

A streak of sadness plunged through Cate's heart as she backed away from Cody on the bed.

She watched him jerk back, go up on his knees, frown as if he was confused.

Cate covered her mouth, felt tears roll down her face and fingers as she watched the sharp edges of Cody's handsome face twist into a grimace.

But it wasn't the knife that had cut the deepest, she knew.

"I'm . . . I'm sorry," she whispered as the look in his green eyes broke her from the inside, left no doubt in her heart that she was as twisted and forsaken as she'd feared in even her darkest moments.

She was still wet from his touch, still hot from her need, very aware that she'd wanted him in her deep, wanted him to hold her down and take her hard, make her his.

And maybe that's why she'd done it.

It made no sense, but she was certain of it.

"I'm sorry, Cody," she said again, her voice barely making it to her own ears.

She stared as Cody finally tore his green gaze away from her face. He glanced down at the knife.

Cate had stabbed him in the left pectoral. It was heavy muscle, thicker than her thighs. The knife was a short switchblade. Three or four inches long. Cate prayed to anyone listening that the blade was not long enough to make it to his proud heart, that her darkness was not strong enough to pierce his powerful soul.

With barely a grunt Cody pulled the knife out. He wiped the blade on his black shirt, then snapped the blade back into the handle and slipped the knife into his pocket.

Without looking at her again he got off the bed.

Stood and stretched. Took off his shirt and dropped it onto the carpet.

Cody turned his back on her and strode to the bathroom. He pulled open the door and left it open. Turned on the tap in the sink. Cleaned the wound thoroughly with water.

Then he picked up one of the little bottles lined up on the shelf above the sink. He squinted at the label. Grunted and put it back on the shelf. Picked up another bottle. It had a thin blue liquid in it. Mouthwash, Cate guessed.

She winced as Cody poured the mouthwash on his wound. He rubbed it in to let the alcohol kill any microbes. Then he grabbed a clean white towel and pressed it against the wound. Finally he stepped out of the bathroom.

"Get on the floor," he said. His voice was steady, low,

and cold as death. It made Cate want to cry. "Now, please. Don't make me tell you again."

His eyes were like molten emeralds, and Cate clambered off the bed and stood on the floor.

She was naked from the waist down. She could feel her own wetness sticky in her curls. She could smell herself. It was not perspiration like before. It was a different smell.

The smell of her need. It made her hot. She thought of all those times alone in her room. So many thoughts that mixed sex and violence into a potent potion that tasted like pure sin, smelled like how it smelled right now.

Cate glanced at Cody's eyes to see where he was looking. He was looking directly at her face. Nowhere else.

Not the slightest twitch of any muscles on his face. Not the smallest sign of the out-of-control animal who'd stripped her bare and spanked her raw. Almost fucked her blind. Almost made her his.

Until she'd asked him to kiss her.

She blinked, then stole a glance at his lips. They were dark with his own blood. She imagined his blood mixing with her wetness.

Her pussy tightened. She pulled at the edges of her sweater, stretched the cashmere down as far as she could.

"Over there." said Cody. He nodded towards the radiator. It was black metal and grotesque like an iron sculpture. "Sit cross legged and face the radiator."

Cate padded over to the radiator in her socks. She did what he said. She couldn't understand what she was feeling in her heart.

It was a dreadful sinking feeling. It was more than just losing her chance to break free. It was so much worse. She hated the feeling. She wanted it to go away. She was certain it would not go away until she died. Perhaps she would die tonight.

She stared at the black pipes as Cody leaned over her from above. He took her wrists and looped that leather belt around them. He pulled the belt so tight she winced. The big buckle was pokey and uncomfortable against her wrists. It hurt where those plastic ties had made her bleed earlier.

"Cody, I am sorry," she said for the third time. "Please. Say something. Will you say something?"

Silently Cody slipped the other end of the belt through the heavy black iron structure. He looped it through again, then twisted it into a knot. Cate saw his triceps bulge as he pulled the knot tight. She wouldn't be able to wrench or wriggle her way loose.

Cody still hadn't said a single word to her. Cate craned her neck to look for him. She was sitting cross-legged on her bare bottom on the rough carpet. It was hard to see the rest of the room.

She sighed and stared at the wall in front of her. He'd tied her facing the radiator so she could lie down on her side and sleep if she wanted.

"What was I supposed to do, Cody?" she said after several long minutes of silence so loud it almost made her scream. "What was I supposed to think? What, hah? You tell me, Cody. Answer me, OK?"

Cody said nothing. She heard the mattress sink noisily

as he sat on the bed. She heard him take off his boots. They fell on the carpet one by one. Thud. Thud.

She heard Cody unzip his jeans. The sound of heavy denim against skin was followed by a whooshing of air as he tossed the jeans onto the armchair.

There were clinks of metal. Two knives and one gun, Cate knew. Plus keys and a wallet. He had thrown all the other weapons away. They'd stopped in a deserted spot on the highway and she'd watched him dismantle the guns and toss them into the woods.

Cody's barefoot steps moved past her. He went into the bathroom again. She craned her head towards the open door and gasped.

He was naked, his back to her. The yellow light highlighted contoured muscles like she had never seen on a man. His thighs were like tree trunks, hamstrings like tree-vines, buttocks like a bull's haunches.

She stared in wonder at this magnificent man with a body like a god. That dreadful sinking feeling stabbed through her heart again. She did not want to know what it was. It was not a useful feeling. Nothing good could come of it.

Cate started to look away, but Cody turned to close the bathroom door just then. She caught a glimpse of him from the front. It made her breath catch, made her thighs tighten, made a heavy drop of nectar drip from her secret place onto the carpet.

"*Madre di dio*," she muttered.

He was enormous. Thicker than the pillars of her mansion. Long like the trunk of a wild elephant. He was not fully erect but very filled out. His cockhead was big and dark red and shined with his oil. Behind Cody's thick shaft his balls were heavy like a bull's in peak season.

The door closed with a thud.

The shower came on with a hiss.

Cate sat alone in silence.

14

Cody's silence broke in the hiss and steam of the shower.

He shouted at the walls, slammed his palm into the tiles, curled his toes against the porcelain floor. Dried blood mixed with the dirt of the day made the swirling water look like red mud around his bare feet. He watched the soap suds chase everything down the drain.

"Twice," he growled as the steam rose around him like mist. "She got you twice. You're a dumb shit, Cody. If the guys could see this, they'd laugh their way to the grave, die happy just from the sight of you turning into a walking cockhead with balls for brains."

His cock throbbed in the warm jets like it objected to the implication. Cody grinned and shook his head, wiped shampoo-sweet water from his face. The knife wound throbbed, but Cody welcomed the pain. Served his dumb ass right.

What was I supposed to do? she'd said to him.

He'd barely listened to what Cate had been saying after she stabbed him. The blood had been hammering away in his head, making it hard to think straight.

The wound itself was nothing. He'd dealt with worse

just during SEAL training. A puny switchblade wasn't getting through inches of hard muscle and a sternum like a stone wall.

But somehow Cate had struck a blow to his heart anyway.

And so Cody yelled into the steam once again.

He yelled because this was more than just a man thinking with his cock.

It was hundred times worse.

A million times more dangerous.

"You were supposed to trust me," he muttered into the hot water. "That's what you were supposed to do, Cate. You were supposed to fucking trust me."

Again that sickening feeling invaded his heart, made it feel like something was wrenching at him from the inside.

He knew what it was.

He'd let all that talk of fate and destiny get to him. Let himself believe he was feeling something real for this woman, that maybe they'd been thrown together like how Ax and Amy had been forced to fight for their fate, like Bruiser and Brenna had battled their way to their destiny.

"Get your head straight, Soldier," he told himself as he turned from the shower and let the hot jets pound against his back. "Get your damn *heart* straight too."

Cody finished up and toweled off and pulled open the door. Steam flowed out into the room, swirling around the furniture like white tendrils.

He glanced at Cate. She was exactly as he'd left her. Sitting cross-legged like a punished schoolgirl.

She looked at him as he strode through the room, towel around his waist.

"Shower must have been nice," she said, a flash of hope in her eyes.

Cody ignored her.

"You cannot blame me for it," she said, something else flashing in those eyes. She had clearly progressed beyond apologizing. "You said you would shoot me in the head and never think of me again."

Cody stopped at the bed. He arranged the pillows in a big stack. Turned down the comforter.

Cate went on. "You are taking me back to Boro. He will give me to Nico. I will be killed in a way no one can imagine. It was reasonable for me to attack you."

Cody climbed into bed. The mattress caved in at the center from his weight. The stack of pillows collapsed on his face.

He punched most of them away, kept one under his head. Pulled the comforter up past his hard stomach. Reached under the covers and yanked out the wet towel.

He tossed it without looking.

It landed on the carpet near Cate.

"Ah, that smells so nice," Cate said pleadingly. "Green apple shampoo."

Cody reached out with his left hand. Flicked off the light. The room went full dark.

"Asshole," Cate said under her breath.

Cody turned noisily on his side. Cleared his throat. Closed his eyes tight.

"I will not let you sleep," she declared.

Cody sighed. Stayed silent.

"You will have to kill me if you want to sleep," she announced.

Cody slammed a pillow over his ears. It smelled like her hair. His cock moved under the covers.

"Malone said she did not think you would give me back to Boro," Cate said after a while. "Was she correct?"

Cody turned onto his other side. Pulled the covers up over his ear.

"Malone said you killed a girl once," Cate said. "So it should be no problem to kill me if you want to sleep."

Cody's eyes flicked open. It occurred to him that Cate hadn't actually asked about the girl. She just pivoted off it to continue her weirdly childish game of keeping him awake. Like an annoying little girl who knows she can get under anyone's skin and loves to do it.

Still, it affected Cody that Cate didn't seem to care whether or not he'd killed some girl. There was no judgment in her voice. She said it plain and simple, like it had no bearing on her opinion of him, one way or another.

"Are you asleep?" she asked cheekily. "If you are asleep, then wake up and tell me you are asleep so I can wake you again."

Cody felt a smile break in the darkness. He stayed silent, but his eyes were wide open now.

His head was buzzing. His heart was doing that embarrassingly exciting thing again where it thumped like he was a teenager on a first date with his major crush.

"I can sing you a lullaby if you are still awake," she said. "Actually, I do not know any lullabies. But I will make one up just for you, Cody."

Cody buried his face into the pillow to stifle a laugh. He managed to do it.

"Lull-a-bye Coh-dee, on the tree top," she sang in her strange accent that was Italian and Spanish and YouTube all mixed up. "If the belt breaks, his trousers will drop."

Now Cody couldn't stop the snort, and the moment he let one through, he turned into a shuddering, rumbling mess of laughter on the bed. His heart felt so full of pure delight that he almost cried.

This woman was amazing. She'd gone from fighting for her life to singing for her life.

Cody just listened to her madness in the dark. Her voice was sweet like syrup, thick and full. The words were mostly nonsense, but it didn't matter.

She'd already won.

She'd broken Cody

She'd broken him with this strange childish innocence that was so real and genuine that no one could doubt there was beauty and goodness inside her along with the darkness and the violence.

She was his, Cody decided in the darkness as she sang to him like a wild bird of paradise, sweetness and sadness all mixing together in a song that was hitting him harder than a hammer, digging deeper than a spear.

She was his.

She had to be his.

He didn't know how or why or when or where or who or what or whether or not.

He just knew she was his.

And so as she sang in the darkness, her voice wavering

at the high notes, like she was fighting to keep her wits, struggling to keep her strength, battling to stay sane, Cody slipped off the bed under cover of night.

Then with the stealth of the greatest recon-artist the SEALs had ever produced, Cody moved across the floor without a sound.

He tracked her by her voice.

Hunted her by her scent.

And claimed her with his heart.

15

Cate's heart almost burst when she felt his big warm body settle in behind her on the floor. She hadn't heard him come to her, and her silly song caught in her throat as she gasped from the heat that ripped through her body.

"You're mine," he whispered into her hair. His breath moved through her wild unkempt locks like wildfire through the underbrush. They were the first words he'd spoken since she'd stabbed him in the heart. She almost cried as she felt those words stab right back. "You hear me, Cate? You're mine. You were mine before we even met. And you'll be mine even if we never make it to our happy ending. Even if we go down in flames together."

Cate's heart burst now, and a wrenching sob erupted from her chest. She caught herself before she completely lost it, and she took a gulping breath so she wouldn't bawl like a little girl from the release of what felt like a lifetime's worth of tension concentrated in one crazy day.

She nodded as the tears rolled down her face. They were very salty. Cody kissed her neck and held her so close and so tight and so hard that she felt safe like she was back in the womb, protected like she was the world's greatest treasure, loved like a child's favorite teddy bear.

Cate told herself the feeling couldn't be real, but in the heavy darkness it felt more real than everything else in her life. In the dark she could be anyone. She could be anything. She could do anything.

And all she wanted right now was to be his.

Even if it was just for this moment.

Even if it was just make-believe.

An illusion in the darkness.

A fairy-tale in the night.

Cody kissed her neck again, moved his hands down along her arms to where his leather belt was knotted stiff and tight around her wrists. She turned her head sideways as he placed his hands over hers.

He didn't undo the knot.

She'd tried to stab him twice.

Perhaps it was better for both of them this way.

The darkness was absolute, but she knew he was grinning as his fingers teased her tied-up hands. She turned her head sideways again.

And he found her lips and kissed them.

The kiss was overwhelming in the pitch black room. Vision was useless, making Cate's other senses vivid and outsized.

Cody's natural aroma had already chased away the hints of soap and shampoo, and she was flooded by his taste and smell and touch and heat.

He kissed her hungrily. He kissed her deep. His right hand stayed firm against her cheek, holding her in place as he leaned over her shoulder from behind.

They kissed long and slow, but it was the slowness

of a tidal wave coming in from miles off the shore. It looked lazy and serene from afar, but beneath the surface was ten thousand tons of raw power that would destroy anything that dared stand in its way.

Cody broke from the kiss, his grizzly stubble grazing her cheek and making her tremble. He stroked her cheek, then the side of her neck, finally sliding his hand down around her front and caressing her right breast.

The nipple perked up instantly, and Cate moaned as he pinched her gently between his fingers. She moaned again, pushed back against Cody's chest, arched her neck back as he grasped both her boobs firmly and pressed hard.

He plucked and pinched her nubs through her sweater and bra, and Cate felt hot along her neck and wet under her arms. She was very warm beneath her sweater, and her bra was itchy and needed to come off.

Cody appeared to feel the same way about it, but in a moment it was clear that the belt-and-radiator situation made it hard to undress her.

She waited for him to undo the leather knot, even though there was something darkly erotic about that cowboy-leather binding her to a metal pipe, the heavy brass buckle hard and cool against her wrists.

"Be right back," said Cody with a kiss to the neck.

She frowned in the dark, shivering slightly as his warmth left her. She smiled when she felt his protective heat behind her again.

Then she lost the smile when she felt cold steel against her front, just below her neck.

"Hold still," he whispered wickedly into her hair.

Cate gasped as she felt the point of Cody's big SEAL knife slide down the front of her sweater. It traced its way between her boobs, then lodged itself at the base of her bra.

With a quick upward thrust Cody cut through the underwire like it was a thread. Then with devilish precision he slit her cashmere sweater right up her center line, the cold steel grazing her bare skin and raising a line of goosebumps that made Cate shiver.

With a series of blindingly fast slashes, Cody sliced and diced her sweater and bra in the darkness. The cloth fell off her shoulders and arms like ribbons.

"Well," Cate gasped after she got over the shock of Cody's speed and skill. "At least one of us can be trusted with a knife, yes?"

"Thanks for reminding me," Cody whispered against her cheek. "I'd better keep this out of reach."

Cate giggled. She felt Cody back away.

Then she gasped at the chilling sound of a knife whipping through the air. She heard it stick deep into the wooden headboard behind the bed with a loud *thwang*.

Cody was behind her again now. His bare muscles felt huge and hard on her naked back. She shivered as he pushed her forward and ran his fingers down her spine. Then she groaned when he reached around her and grasped her naked breasts full in his big hands.

Cate leaned back against his body as his strong hands explored every inch of her front in the darkness. Her nipples were so hard and pert they ached. They throbbed from his increasingly rough pinches.

She moved and moaned as Cody's hands slithered down her stomach, circling her belly button, then proceeding below sea level.

When his fingers got below decks her pussy was already shamelessly dripping onto the carpet. And when he pressed two fingers lengthwise against her slit and pushed down hard, she almost came all over his hand.

"Oh, Cody," she muttered as his fingers moved through her curls. The darkness was adding to the arousal, waking up her imagination since vision was useless.

Cate had spent many years alone with just fingers and fantasy. She smiled in the dark. Her tongue curled up over her top lip.

She moaned again, then gasped when Cody's thumb found her little hood, pulled it back, and touched her clit.

She came with a gasping, gurgling, heaving violence. Her body bucked forward and then jerked back. Cody fingered her rough and deep, grinding his thumb into her bean and making her spurt all over herself and his hand and the carpet.

He slid one thick finger so far up her cunt it felt a mile deep. He kept it inside her as she thrashed her way through that choking orgasm that came out of nowhere but seemed here to stay.

"Damn," Cody whispered against her cheek from behind. "You're beautiful when you come, you know that?"

She felt a blush flood her cheeks with blood. This was the first man who had ever seen her come. She wanted to tell him but kept it to herself.

"It is too dark to see me," she said softly. "Perhaps I

look horrible when it happens. Like a goblin dying of suffocation."

"Sounds hot," Cody said. His finger curled inside her. Her breath caught. He kissed her on the neck, then slowly took his finger out of her.

"Why did you do that?" she whispered. "Leave it inside."

"I'm a team player," he said. "Like to give all the boys a taste."

She gasped as Cody slid a different finger past her slick entrance. He curled it up and moved it around with an expertise that rivaled his other skills. She felt her wetness flow like a river.

That climax which had worked its way through her had been on the way out.

Now it turned its head around like it was being summoned back by this SEAL's dangerous fingers.

Cate closed her eyes and relaxed against Cody's broad, naked body as he worked each of his fingers into her with stealth and precision.

After three fingers she was breathing heavy again.

When he moved to the other hand she was writhing against his ridged torso.

And by the time he pulled out his pinky and then jammed his thumb into her, she was a howling, thrashing mess of a woman.

She came hard again, convulsing in the darkness, uncrossing her legs and spreading them wide as she leaned back against Cody's hard body.

She moaned and whimpered against him as he worked

her through the orgasm and brought her breathing back down to normal. She let out a shuddering gasp and rested against him for a wonderful moment of peaceful bliss.

Her breathing was slowing, but Cate felt Cody's chest moving as he took bigger, heavier breaths. He went up on his knees behind her, and she felt his cockhead slap against her back. It was wet and heavy. There was a sticky patch where it touched her back.

"I cannot turn," she said, tugging at her wrists as she sensed Cody's need. She moved her head in the darkness, trying to figure out where he was.

Then she felt him in front of her.

He'd sat down on the flat top of the long radiator. His feet were planted flat on the carpet on either side of her thighs.

Her hands were tied dead center beneath where he was sitting.

Cate couldn't see a thing except in her mind. She imagined Cody big and erect in front of her, his cock standing straight up like a tower.

She thought of his huge cockhead, imagined it oozing a thick bead of his natural lubricant. His shaft would be glistening and shiny. His balls would be hanging heavy and free.

The image made her so wet she wondered if she'd come again without being touched. She leaned her head forward, swaying side to side like a cobra as she sought him out.

The darkness took away any sense of self-consciousness or shame, and Cate felt safer than even when it was just her alone with her solitary thoughts, her lonely touch.

"I saved your life twice, and you tried to kill me twice in return," came Cody's whisper in the darkness. He paused. She could tell he was grinning but with an edge to his smile. Joking but not completely. "Now I made you come twice. What do I get in return? Don't know if I should trust you."

"I do not know either," she whispered back. Then she gasped when something very big and very hard and quite wet and sticky brushed against her cheek. "Do you want to get your knife?" she asked innocently. "Keep me honest?"

Cody laughed, then groaned when Cate pushed her head forward and rubbed her cheek against his thick, throbbing shaft. She felt him flex, sensed him get more erect. Even in the darkness she was certain he was full hard, close to exploding, at the edge of his control.

Cody didn't answer. He had gripped his shaft and was teasing her lips with his cockhead, coating her with his clean masculine oil.

She kept her eyes closed, held her mouth open. She could see it all in her mind. Vivid color. More real than the real world could ever be.

Now Cate's breath caught as she felt Cody's fingers slide into her hair, dig down close to the roots, hold firm and tight.

Her hands were bound. She felt the leather rough against her skin. It burned in a way that made her hotter.

She imagined Cody's knife at her throat, the blade

delicate and deadly, keeping her honest, keeping her clean, keeping her his.

She tugged at her bindings, tested the strength of Cody's grip. She was completely under his control.

Then he pushed himself past her open lips, into her warm, wet mouth.

And as she felt his monstrous girth force her lips wide apart, Cate realized that he was now under her control too. He'd trusted himself to her in this little game. He was giving her a third chance to prove herself worthy of his trust.

She teased his throbbing cock with her teeth, then gasped when Cody's grip tightened in her hair. Her roots burned with that good kind of pain.

She eased up with her teeth.

Cody's grip eased up in her hair.

"Careful," came his voice in a growling whisper that reverberated through his hard cock and made her head buzz.

He stroked the back of her neck roughly with his free hand, then dragged his fingertips against her throat. His hand moved down her neck, and he squeezed each breast with breathtaking force, pinched each nipple until she whimpered like the bound and gagged captive she was right now.

Her head was buzzing with images, swirling with fantasies that were dark but strangely safe. She couldn't move her head or her body, but she felt oddly safe in the darkness with this man who was powerful enough to break her neck with a simple twist of his grip on her hair.

The realization made her wetter, and she started to suck Cody hard and deep in the darkness. She understood that she'd gone at him twice with a knife, stabbed him three inches deep once. If he wanted to break her neck she'd already be dead in a ditch somewhere.

That's why Cate felt safer than she'd ever felt even in her walled mansion in Italy. She felt more protected than in her Colombian castle surrounded by a hundred guards.

And although she was tied up and held down, naked and vulnerable, Cate felt more free than she'd believed was possible.

Cody groaned from deep in his chest as she opened her throat for him. He was so big in her mouth that the sides of her jaw hurt. She could feel his balls slapping against her chin as he moved inside her, pushing so deep down her throat her eyes bulged like they were going to pop.

"Fuck, I'm losing my mind, Cate," he muttered, pulling her hair and fucking her harder in the mouth. "This is insane. I'm losing my damn mind."

Me too, Cate thought as she felt him flex inside her. She felt her pussy drip onto the carpet, and she was desperate to be touched there.

She pulled on the belt, yearning to break free to touch herself. She couldn't, and it made her wetter, hotter, more hungry to be touched, more desperate to be fucked.

Cody was grunting hard now, and he'd gotten up off the radiator and was hunching over her as she sucked him. She could feel the climax building in his panting breaths, sense it in the urgency of his thrusts.

Then suddenly he pulled out of her.

Cate screamed and spat, her eyes flicking wide open in the darkness. She felt the air swirl around her as Cody's body moved.

Then she felt him behind her again. He grabbed her hips, pulled her towards him, arched her ass up, smacked it twice.

She felt him spread her cheeks and run his fingers down her crack. His thumb pressed on her asshole, and she groaned and almost choked from a sudden burst of the most filthy arousal.

He pushed his thumb inside for a moment, then popped it out and smacked her hard on each buttcheek.

And then he was inside her from below.

It happened so fast she was stunned into silence.

Her mouth opened wide as Cody's cockhead opened her up and drove deep into her like a torpedo slipping into the darkness of a night-sea.

"*Inferno di sangue così profondo*," she muttered as the curve of his cock touched parts of her inner wall and lit them up like gasoline lines bursting into flames. "*Così grande e profondo*, Cody."

"You're mine, Cate," came his rasping whisper, thick with arousal, peaked with passion. He pulled back and plunged deep, his powerful hips slamming against her rear cushion in the most wonderful way.

The radiator began to rattle as Cody pounded into her from behind. His breath was heavy. It came out in bursting snorts as he pumped.

Cate thought of that bull on his belt buckle. She

screamed as she imagined Cody as a half-man, half-bull like from some ancient myth. In the dark it seemed like anything was possible, everything was possible, nothing was off limits, nothing was taboo.

Nobody can see you and nobody can stop you and nobody can judge you, Cate thought as she felt the cowboy take her hard and dirty, imagined the soldier enjoying the spoils of war, pictured a dragon with the head of a bull snorting and grunting behind her as it claimed her flesh, her womb, her soul.

The fantasies were too much, and Cate arched her neck back and screamed like a banshee being strangled. She howled as a violent climax ripped through her like a cannonball, bursting her mind into a million pieces of stardust, scattering the splinters of her soul all over the universe.

The darkness was all-consuming and she stuck her tongue out and screamed with the shrillness of some unknown bird as Cody rammed into her twice more and then exploded into her depths like that torpedo finally hitting home.

Images of home flooded Cate's mind as Cody flooded her with his seed. The images were splintered and shredded. They were hurtling away from her. Getting smaller as they whipped through the air like shrapnel from an explosion.

She watched them shrink into tiny dots and then disappear like an old television going dead. She spat onto the invisible floor, then smiled to herself as the comforting blackness closed in on her like a blanket.

Those images of other homes were gone.

This is my home now, Cate decided.

It is not a place in the world, but a place inside me, she told herself.

A place where there is just me and him, she thought as Cody's strong hands pressed against her bare back, reached up and massaged her aching shoulders, then moved around her front and held her breasts firmly and securely, like their body parts had been designed to fit one another perfectly.

Yes, this is home, Cate told herself as she pushed back a sudden burst of panic that when the lights came on all of this would mean nothing.

Please let this be home, she pleaded with the darkness. This place inside me where there is just me and him. I want that to be my home now.

"You're never going home, Cate," came his voice in the dark. "Don't know how I'm gonna pull it off, but your place is with me now. You're mine. I captured you fair and square. Those are the rules of war. I captured this territory, and now it's mine. To hell with anyone who tries to take you from me. Nobody's taking you from me, Cate."

Cody squeezed her breasts again. She nodded in the dark as that panic was chased away by his confident claim that she was his property now.

The soldier had planted his flag on disputed territory.

The cowboy had put up the fence around his range.

The alpha beast had marked the borders of his domain.

"This is the best home I have ever had," she said softly.

Cody chuckled, kissed her back, then reached along her arms, undid the belt, set her free. "You grew up in an Italian mafia mansion. In Colombia you've got a castle. And being tied to a radiator at the Beechwood Motel in Arizona is the best home you've ever had?"

"Yes," she said matter-of-factly, rubbing her sore wrists. She leaned back and he caught her in his arms, pulled her into his chest, pressed his face into her hair. "My home is in your arms, Cody. It can be anywhere. As long as you are there, my new home can go anywhere with me."

Cody's breath was warm in her hair. "Where would you like to go?" he whispered.

Cate was quiet. "I . . . I don't know."

"I do," said Cody. There was something in his voice that made her sit up and listen. "We have to go back. You know it. I know it. There's no escaping it."

She whipped her body around, tried to look into his eyes, see that he was joking. It was too dark.

She scrambled away from him, pulled the thick curtains open. Red neon and yellow lamplight flooded into the room.

Cody was sitting on the carpet, gazing at her with that coolness she loved and hated at the same time.

"You'll never be safe so long as Boro is alive," he said.

His voice was low.

Steady.

Deadly.

She understood what he meant.

She nodded and looked at him.

His eyes burned with a possessive green fire that

warmed Cate as much as it made her cold with fear. She thought of Boro with his gold teeth and thick leathery neck. She imagined Nico fitting a new ring on his ugly thumb. She thought of the legions of armed men on Boro's compound.

Cate swallowed hard, sat down, hugged her knees, rocked back and forth in the red-yellow light. Cody pulled her into him again, and they sat together and looked through the window glass.

The night sky was gray and overcast. The street lights cast a dark gold glow on the cloud cover.

"I need to kill him," said Cody with the calmness of a man ordering a cup of coffee. "You won't be safe with him still breathing the same air." He took a slow breath, rumbled it out. "Besides, it's only right I give him the chance to fight it out with the man who's stolen his wife."

Cate laughed nervously. "Boro will not fight you," she said. "He is not stupid. You will not get close enough to hurt him."

"Don't need to get too close. You see me throw that knife across the room?" Cody grinned behind her.

"You will not get close enough even for a rifle," she said. "The estate walls are miles from the mansion. Cameras all over. Guards patrolling in Jeeps outside the walls. More guards inside. There are dogs too."

Cody grunted. "I like dogs."

She giggled. "These are wild dogs. Fed very little. Beaten regularly. Boro says it keeps them hungry and angry."

"OK, now I'm *definitely* killing the bastard. Can't treat an animal that way. Not right."

Cate arched her head back like a cat and looked up at his face upside down. "Um, you just tied me to a radiator and told me to pee on the floor."

"Did you?" Cody asked innocently. He pressed his palm to the carpet where she'd been sitting while he did things to her with his fingers. All his fingers. "It's still quite wet. Here. Taste my fingers and tell me if it's salty."

She squealed and slapped his hand away. He laughed and pulled her into him before she could get away.

"You are dirty, filthy, gross, and disgusting," she declared.

"Comes with the territory," he growled against her ear. "SEALs are trained to spend days buried in the mud on a recon mission. Where do you think we pee?"

"OK, I do *not* want to think about filthy men covered in gross things," she said, clambering to her feet and walking towards the bathroom. "Anyway, I assume I am free to shower now?"

She felt Cody's eyes following her ass as she walked. Her legs were stiff. Her thighs were tender. His semen was sticky between her legs. She loved it.

She got to the restroom and flipped on the lights. It hurt her eyes and she closed her eyelids. She stood there in the light for a moment, then peeked to see if Cody was looking at her.

He was very much looking at her.

Looking at her like she was his.

"Leave the door open," he said, his eyes steady and sharp.

She saw that he was getting erect again just from

looking at her. She blinked and nodded. Padded into the bathroom.

Got into the shower and turned it on. She groaned in pleasure as the hot jets hit her cheeks, the water streamed down between her breasts, rushed along her curves, warmed her and wet her and made her feel so nice she almost cried

Cate peed standing up like a girl outside in the rain, smiling and wrinkling up her nose when she thought of how gross Cody was. She peeked out past the shower curtain to see if he was coming in after her.

No sign of the SEAL through the steam.

She sighed.

She let her thoughts drift.

Soon she understood more why Cody wanted to kill Boro.

It wasn't just possessiveness—though that was a big part of it.

It wasn't just so she'd feel safe—though that was a bigger part of it.

It was for himself too.

For the soldier in him.

The part of him that had a duty to something other than just his woman.

Cody knew that if Boro was alive, he'd never feel comfortable leaving Cate alone.

Never feel comfortable going on the next mission.

Being the soldier that he was.

The SEAL that he was.

"I'll have to share him, won't I?" she whispered to the

spirits in the steam. "Share him with this other world of soldiers and spies and whatever else calls to his sense of duty. Share him with his SEAL brothers. Share him with that boss or commander or whatever." She lathered up her hair and sighed again. "Share him with that man he calls Benson."

16

"Benson," said Cody with a sigh. He glanced at his watch on the bedside table near the pink phone. "How much time do we have before Malone gets here?"

"Oh, so it's *we* now?" came Benson's taunt. "Did you two sweethearts get married in the hotel lobby? That hipster at the front desk has been ordained by an online church, you know. According to my intel, he performed the wedding ceremony of two gender-neutral hamsters last week."

"You'll be gender neutralized when my foot connects with your balls, Benson," Cody muttered. "Especially if you've been spying on us, you sick bastard."

"We. Us. These pronouns are quite concerning, Soldier," Benson said.

"How about concerning yourself with organizing that private jet to Colombia," said Cody. He carried the pink handset with him to the window. Glanced down. Things were quiet. He figured if Malone were on the way, Benson would have told him by now.

"Malone's already on her way," said Benson.

Cody snapped to attention. Glanced at the steamed up bathroom. The shower was still on.

Then he saw her tattered clothes on the carpet. He'd turned her sweater and bra into ribbons like he was the knife-artist in a damn circus. Great planning, Mister Navy SEAL Elite Warrior, Conqueror of Captured Women. Now you'll have to wrap your squeaky-clean woman in a bunch of towels or bedsheets.

"On her way to Colombia, that is," Benson added like it was the punchline to a bad joke. "She may have figured out that she can't track you without alerting me. And she's smart enough to know that if you have a head start, she'll never find a recon SEAL who doesn't want to be found. My guess is she's going to position her men at Bogota and Medellin airports in case you show up there with Cate."

Cody grunted. "Any word on who those guys are?"

"Ex-DEA."

"Ex. Not former."

"Yeah," said Benson. "They did not end their careers clean."

"And Malone is dirty too?"

"Not necessarily," said Benson. He sighed. "Look, you know how it is in all these agencies. DEA. CIA. FBI. NSA. DHS. IRS. You name it. We all make compromises with bad people for the greater good—or what we believe is the greater good. From what I can tell, she brokered the deal with Boro ten years ago. Got him to pull out of the U.S. drug trade and ship his stuff to Europe. It made her a star in the DEA. She's on track to be Director of the DEA. Politics at the federal level after that. She's ambitious, and I got no problem with ambition. I get it. She doesn't want her flagship deal from ten years ago unraveling now." He sighed. "Sure, maybe there are some skeletons in Malone's closet from that deal. And yeah, that's why she's using ex-DEA thugs to keep it off the books. She wants to keep those skeletons locked away until she's too powerful to be damaged by bad publicity. But that's the game. Anybody looks in my closet, they'll run away screaming."

Cody took a slow breath. "So she's trying to protect the deal that made her a star. Wants to make sure the bodies stay buried."

"Yes." He took a breath. "But she's probably figured that your body isn't gonna be one of them. I doubt she expects you to show up at Boro's compound. It'll be hard to find you and get Cate back, so Malone's cutting her losses, playing it as if Cate is gone. She's moving to her next option. Damage control with Boro. She'll leave her guys watching for you in case you do show up, but my gut says Malone herself is going directly to Boro. She'll try to salvage her old deal, maybe work out a new one."

"Fine," said Cody. "Greater good and all. I'm cool with that. So long as Malone and her thugs don't get in the way of *my* greater good."

Benson was silent for a breath. "You're going to kill Boro," he said flatly. Not a question.

Cody nodded. Didn't say a word. Didn't need to.

"Are you absolutely certain you want this, Cody?" Benson said slowly, softly, his tone taking on a surprising warmth. "You dead sure this is real? That you aren't being played?"

Cody glanced towards the steamy white shower. Cate was singing. He smiled and shook his head. "She isn't playing me. Not anymore."

"I didn't mean Cate," said Benson coolly. "I meant you, Cody. Are you absolutely sure you aren't playing *yourself?*"

Cody frowned, wondering if Benson was talking in circles to stall him while he sent in Malone or maybe those drones. He flipped off the overhead light, glanced out the window again. No movement.

"The only person playing me is you, Benson."

"It's my job to play you," snapped Benson. "Now listen up. I need to know you're sure about this woman, Cody. I've never met her. Don't have eyes or ears on you guys. Can't make a call on this."

"It's not your call to make," said Cody smoothly.

Benson was quiet. "All right," he said after a moment. Something in his voice sounded different.

Cody got the feeling the old bastard was grinning ear to ear like the wicked wolf he was. Was he testing Cody? Trying to see if the SEAL would crack? Making sure Cody was damn sure. No second guessing. No turning back.

"All right, Cody," Benson said again. "But it's going to be messy. You kill Boro and a lot of dominoes start falling. He's running a massive cocaine operation. It's not clear who takes over if he's killed. Could be chaos. The other Cartels will move in like vultures. Could upset years of negotiations between the DEA and the Colombians. It would affect our relations with not just Colombia but perhaps Mexico too." He was quiet a moment, thinking. "Shit, then maybe Malone blames Martin Kaiser and the CIA for the hit on Boro. Brings down Kaiser as her own career goes down in flames." He blew out some air. "Maybe Darkwater gets blown in the process too. Hell, Cody, I'm going to have to do a lot of damage control here. Don't know if I can pull it off."

Cody shifted on his feet. He rubbed his jaw. "Then don't," he said. "Cut me loose. Tell Kaiser I'm on my own now. Call Malone and tell her that too. Give up my location. Tell her I'm heading to Colombia to kill Boro. Tell her if she tries to stop me, I can't guarantee she won't be one of the bodies that gets buried in the jungle."

Cody paused, took a breath, realized that he was stepping off the damn ledge here, jumping from the plane without a parachute, diving deep without oxygen. There was nothing backing up his decision but the feeling in his heart.

He glanced at the open bathroom door. He could smell shampoo and soap. He could hear Cate humming like a happy little bird.

Was it worth destroying half the world so this hummingbird could keep singing? So this butterfly could spread her dark wings and fly by his side, ride by his side, maybe die by his side?

Fuck it, Cody thought as his jaw set tight. Nothing's ever felt like this. So if I'm wrong, then I'll go down in flames too. Ax and Bruiser and Dogg will understand.

And other than that, nobody else's opinion matters one damn bit.

So fuck it, Cody thought again as his determination hardened. He saw his fate bright and shiny. Heard his destiny loud and clear.

"Cut me loose, Benson," he said calmly into the phone. "It's the right thing to do for Darkwater. Besides, if I don't do this, I'm no good to Darkwater anyway. No good as a SEAL. No good as a man. So hang up and walk away, Benson. I'll see you and the boys in hell. Hooyah."

17

Benson hung up, but he didn't walk away.

Instead he swiveled his brown leather chair away from his desk and faced the large picture window overlooking the lush Virginia forest behind his two-story home. Morning was breaking somewhere beyond the thick dark trees.

He watched a yellow bird with red stripes settle on the tip of a leafy branch. It was singing at the top of its little lungs. The sound didn't come through the glass. It was bulletproof.

Maybe I'm being tested too here, he thought as he tapped his lip and considered his options. Maybe fate still has a few tricks I haven't seen yet. Maybe the universe is reminding me that quantum mechanics is about probabilities that change when choices are made. Like how the pattern in a kaleidoscope changes when you turn it.

"Cody's made his choice," he muttered as he stood and started to pace. The pinewood boards where he and Sally had made wild love in younger days creaked beneath his leather brogues. "Now it's your turn to choose, John. You've got to make some choices too, old man. Do you cut the SEAL loose? Do you send in the rest of

Team Darkwater with guns blazing and knives shining?"

Benson paced to the wood-paneled wall and leaned against it as he thought. Boro's compound was basically a military fortress. Yeah, four SEALs could inflict a lot of damage, but it was dicey. Benson couldn't send in Blackhawks with cannons and rockets to neutralize guard towers and Jeep patrols. Didn't have that kind of authority anymore—not for a mission like this.

So if he sent in backup, it would only be Team Darkwater. Four SEALs against an army. Casualties would be almost certain. Fatalities would be possible, maybe even likely.

Ax and Bruiser were family men now, Benson considered. Of course, Amy and Brenna were no ordinary wives. They were SEAL wives, military women now. But still Benson was uneasy about sending their husbands into a battle where they'd be greatly outnumbered. He felt more personally responsible for these proud, brave men and their families than he ever had working at the CIA with double-crossing snakes like himself and Kaiser.

No, Benson decided. Cody is a recon guy. Stealth and silence is his game. Kills like a shark in the night. He's got a better shot at Boro alone than with a team of cowboys, no matter how good the rest of the guys are.

He started to pace again, going over what he knew about Malone.

She was fifty-six years old. Hadn't started in government, instead working at Credit Suisse Bank in Boston. She'd been promoted to Vice President of Investment Banking in her first year.

Capturing Cate

She was just twenty one years old at the time. Performance reviews called her a superstar who could work around the clock. Maggie doesn't need to sleep, her boss had commented.

Malone got another promotion and was sent to the bank's headquarters in Zurich. Within three years she was managing the bank's operations for most of Europe: Switzerland, Germany, France, Austria, and Italy.

"Italy," Benson said aloud, frowning as he thought about it. "Where in Italy, I wonder."

He strode back to his desk. Pulled open his unmarked black laptop. Logged into the master databases that Kaiser had authorized off the record.

The Patriot Act had opened the door to a mindboggling array of information on U.S. citizens all over the world, and Benson took some time tracking Margaret J. Malone's European travels from when she was an investment banker, before she'd joined the Drug Enforcement Agency.

Benson ran the searches and sat back as the results popped up.

Rome. Milan. Naples. All short stays at luxury business hotels near Credit Suisse offices or other local bank affiliates.

Then something struck Benson as odd.

A ten-day stay in a small Italian township about forty miles inland from the coast. Town called Santo Silenzio.

Not a tourist spot, but that didn't mean anything. Malone could have picked the place for a vacation to unwind. Maybe she was burned out and needed to recharge.

Benson made a note to look into the town a bit more later. Then he moved on.

Switched databases. Scanned through client lists for major European banks. Wasn't surprised to see that Romero Bonasera had credit lines at most major European banks. Deutsche Bank. Barclays. Banque Paribas. And Credit Suisse.

"Huh," said Benson, a tight smile coming to his face. It wasn't hard to put the pieces together. Wasn't a stretch to think that after she joined the DEA, Malone used her old banking connections to get an audience with Romero Bonasera. Maybe she was able to use it to broker a different kind of deal.

A different kind of merger.

A marriage bargain.

It didn't surprise Benson. Nothing really surprised him. It was smart, in fact. It would be easier to get Boro to agree to a deal that pulled him out of the American market if Malone could offer him a direct path to the European market as a compromise.

Malone was good. Slick. Benson admired that maneuver. It was something he would have done. Hell, it was something he *had* done once during his wheeling and dealing with the Sheikhs of the Middle East.

So no surprise at all.

Not there at least.

But there was still one unknown.

One potential surprise.

Why had Maggie Malone joined the DEA?

He checked her bank accounts and investments.

Capturing Cate

Malone had left Investment Banking when she was just twenty six.

She'd saved a very nice nest egg. She was worth eight million dollars. There was no sign of anything sketchy in her finances. She wasn't on the take. Wasn't being investigated by Treasury or FBI. She was clean that way.

Benson stretched in his chair. He turned to look at that bird. It was gone. The sun was coming up through the trees.

Benson stretched again, turned back to his laptop. He felt the connections start to form in his head. Felt that tingling in his spine. It was that sixth sense that made him love the game so damn much.

Now the black push-button phone on his desk rang. Benson almost jumped out of his chair.

He grabbed the phone, excitement brewing in his chest. This was exactly how fate worked its games. These tiny coincidences that nobody noticed unless they were tuned to the right frequency.

"What you got for me, Patty?" Benson said.

It was Patty Duprey from the American Embassy in Costa Rica. She'd helped Bruiser and Brenna when Benson asked for a favor during that wild ride in search of Damyan Nagarev. Now Benson was asking Patty to do something for him again. She owed him more than she'd ever be able to repay.

Though of course Patty would do it anyway. She loved sneaking around. She was damn good at it too.

He listened. Nodded. Made a note.

"Get me full details of the report. I want names, descriptions, everything. The whole damn thing. I'll decide what's relevant." He paused to listen. "Yes, I know the Puerto Vallarta PD still keeps paper files. You'll have to get the file and take photos and send them to my phone." He listened to Patty complain some more. "Yes, I know you'll have to bang the nice-looking police officer in the filing room," he said with a sigh. "Don't pretend like you haven't already. Thanks. Give my regards to Henry when you get back to the Embassy. Does he still hire those twenty-five year old gay pornstars as cabana-boys? Good. Taxpayer money at work."

Then Benson was on his feet, head buzzing louder than the beehive in the trees outside his bulletproof glass. Cody was sharp to pick up on the Puerto Vallarta reference. There was something to it. Especially since there were no travel records in the database.

And that meant a lot.

It meant Margaret J. Malone didn't want anyone to know she'd visited Puerto Vallarta all those years ago.

Benson already suspected the reason, but he wouldn't know for sure until Patty did her thing in the filing room. He looked at his watch, sat back down, let his mind drift back to the question he'd been pondering.

Why had Maggie Malone joined the DEA?

Why does a smart, driven, superstar banker join the Drug Enforcement Agency?

Benson closed his eyes and went over what he'd learned about people in forty years of manipulating them.

There were two types of people drawn to the Drug Enforcement Agency.

One type joined because of the enforcement part.

The other joined because of the drug part.

Now Benson thought back to Maggie's performance evaluation.

Maggie doesn't need to sleep.

He chuckled. Shook his head. Wall Street bankers loved cocaine. It kept them up. Kept them focused. Kept them confident. And best of all, it was out of your system in twenty-four hours, so you could always beat the random drug tests.

Again Benson wasn't surprised. Recreational drugs weren't his thing, but he never judged anybody for it so long as they did their jobs well.

Besides, it wasn't like the DEA was full of cokeheads. The folks drawn to drugs weren't usually addicts. They were driven, ambitious people but with an edge. They'd experimented in their youth but gave it up when they learned it could destroy you.

Still, the dopamine surge you get from cocaine stays strong in your memory, which was why some former users were drawn to the Agency. Didn't hurt to know what you were fighting against.

Benson didn't judge Malone harshly for it. Maybe Maggie used when she was working crazy hours as a banker. Maybe she'd turned against the whole thing and joined the DEA to fight it.

And maybe the buried arrest report from thirty years ago in Puerto Vallarta was just a simple cover-up. Nothing more than a young Margaret Malone hiding a mistake she made on vacation with some friends.

Except that didn't explain why Malone had covered up more trips to Puerto Vallarta where she *hadn't* been arrested. Once a year. Every year from ages nineteen through twenty-five.

Benson glanced at the dates for Malone's last trip to the Mexican vacation spot.

Then he went back to his notes.

Looked at the dates when Malone had taken that ten-day break to the small Italian township of Santo Silenzio.

And something struck him.

Feverishly he typed in the name of the town and searched the Internet. Furiously he read through the major attractions. There weren't any attractions of note.

Nothing remarkable except a large hospital that served the region.

A hospital with a maternity ward.

A maternity ward supported by a church.

A church which was remarkable in one strange way.

It had run one of the last old-world orphanages in Italy.

Now Benson leapt from his chair. His eyes were wide and his fingers were curling into fists and opening up again as he realized he was missing something.

He'd underestimated the twists that fate can throw at you. He'd forgotten that destiny weaves a web that involves many people's fates, all intertwined like how the underground roots of ancient trees fuse and merge until you don't know where one starts and the other ends.

"I need to talk to Cate Bonasera," he muttered, grabbing the phone and dialing the Beechwood Motel. The front desk guy put the call through to Room 69.

Nobody answered.

Benson slammed the phone down and grabbed his jacket off the wooden chair in the corner. His patted his trouser pockets to check for his phone. Pulled open the top desk drawer and snatched up his Smith and Wesson 9mm handgun in its brown button-down holster.

Then he was tearing down the stairs, running out the door, heading to his gray Crown Victoria.

As he raced down the driveway and screeched onto the turnpike heading for Dulles Airport's private terminal, he went through a map of the United States in his head.

Colombia was at the Northwestern tip of South America.

Cody was heading to Colombia.

But how?

Cody no longer had access to a private jet.

He wouldn't risk flying commercial with Malone possibly monitoring the passenger lists.

He wouldn't drive all the way through multiple border crossings.

So not by air.

Not by land.

And oh yeah, Cody was a SEAL.

He'd head straight for his beloved water.

Straight for the Texas coast.

Cody was a Texas man.

He would know that Colombia was a straight shot across from Corpus Christi.

"Corpus Christi," he said into the phone. "Thanks, Nancy. You looking forward to being a grandma? Good. No, don't mention it to Brenna. Keeping this on the downlow for now. If she tells Bruiser, those SEALs might not be able to hold themselves back from going full cowboy in support of their brother. Thanks again."

Satisfied with his decision, Benson ended the call with Nancy Sullivan, who was now Team Darkwater's Head of Finances and Operations. She was also Brenna's mother, and a former Treasury Agent. She'd have a plane ready with a flight plan for Corpus Christi.

Now all Benson had to do was see about the rest of the plan.

The rest of fate's plan.

The rest of destiny's decree.

To see if even after forty years of playing the game, Benson could still be stunned by how it played out.

How the universe did its dance of chance and circumstance, of choice and possibilities.

How when two lovers make the choice to be together even if it means destroying the world and themselves with it . . .

The universe rewards their choice by giving the lovers a way out.

A way home.

A way to their ending without destroying the world and themselves with it.

Of course, right now it was just a hunch.

Just intuition.

He didn't know enough to put all the pieces together.

And he wouldn't know enough until he spoke to Cate Bonasera.

And ask her if she knew anything about an Italian orphan who would be around thirty years old now.

18

"Her name is Marya," said Cate with a smile. "She's around my age, maybe a year older. Maybe younger. The nuns did not disclose her exact birthdate when my parents adopted her to be my playmate."

"Around your age . . . " Cody said as he pulled the blue minivan back onto the highway after filling up the tank for the second time that day. "So like twelve?"

Cate frowned down at her boobs and shrugged. "I would be the most popular twelve-year old in the history of the universe."

Cody grinned. He reached over and ran the back of his hand over her breasts. She gasped as her nubs perked up at his touch. His fingers caught in the neckline of the black V-neck tee shirt that was part of her new wardrobe.

"Stop or it will tear," she said, using both her hands to pull Cody's arm away. "You cannot keep tearing my clothes. I do not even have a bra."

Cody sighed, slammed both hands onto the steering wheel, pretended to sulk. She straightened her neckline, patted down the wrinkles in the fresh cotton. It was a Hanes Beefy undershirt. A nice deep black.

Capturing Cate 239

Cody bought a 3-pack of them at the Walgreen's in Beechwood. It was the only place open when they left the motel before sunrise. The cotton was thick enough that the outline of her large nipples didn't show.

Thankfully Cate had managed to salvage her black jeans. They were badly stretched out at the waistband, almost torn apart at the seams from when Cody had pulled them off her and spanked her bare bottom for stabbing him in the chest. But the Hanes tee was long enough to cover the worst of it.

Cate didn't know where her panties were right now. They'd left the motel room in a hurry.

She glanced out the window. Read the big green highway signboard with white lettering. It said HOUSTON 86.

"Texas is so big," she said. "We have been driving in Texas all day, and we are still in Texas."

Their stolen blue minivan slowly crept past a lazily gliding green Cadillac. There were no child-seats or toys or cartoon DVDs in their minivan. It was OK to steal, they'd decided. The police would find it eventually when they ditched it before getting to Houston. No harm, no foul, Cody had declared as he brushed two wires together like he had done it before.

Cody's tanned face cracked a smile. He glanced out his window, gazed into the distance, then looked back at Cate before focusing on the open road again.

"Hundred or so miles thataway," he said. "It's where I grew up."

Cate leaned forward and looked past Cody. It was

miles of patchy grassland. Flat and endless. She blinked, nodded, looked down at her hands folded in her lap. She saw the tan line on her left ring finger. She rubbed it. It did not go away.

"Tell me about it," she said quickly, not wanting to let her mind wander too far ahead.

The closer they got to the Texas coast, the larger Boro's gold front teeth appeared in her mind.

Of course, she'd seen Cody's strength. She trusted his skills. She understood why he wanted Boro dead. She wanted Boro dead too. He would never stop looking for her.

But surely Cody could not defeat an army of men. This was not a cowboy movie. One man does not kill a hundred and then walk away with the girl in the end.

"Not much to tell," said Cody after a long pause. "Small town. Oil workers in the early days until the wells in the area ran dry. Cattle ranching kept the town alive, but it wasn't prime grassland, so nobody was getting rich." He shrugged. "We did all right, though." He rubbed the back of his neck, shifted in his seat.

Cate thought of what Malone had said about the girl. She looked at Cody, studied the proud jawline, the hints of sun-lines around his deadly eyes.

She wanted to know, but only because she wanted to understand Cody. It would not change her admiration for this man. Her belief that although he was a rough man who could turn a switch and go cold like a killing machine, he was warm and good in his heart.

But he was a silent man, she thought as they drove past

a sign that said FRESH EGGS AND BISON. They'd talked about many things over the eighteen hours of driving, but there had been long stretches of silence.

The quiet was peaceful, though. Cate knew they were communicating even through those periods where neither of them spoke a word. She was aware of every movement in Cody's big hard body. She thought she could even read his mind.

Now she looked at him and smiled. He had talked about his hometown. She hadn't asked him.

It meant he wanted to go there in his mind, wanted to take her there, wanted to let her in. He was inviting her into some part of him that had been private for a long time. He was opening the door just a crack. Seeing if she would walk in.

Perhaps afraid that she would turn around and walk out again.

"It does not matter what you did or did not do," she said softly. "It is impossible for me to pass judgment on anyone else. I benefited from violence and crime and injustice. It took me so many years to break free. All those years I was safe in my castles and mansions. A captive partly by birth and marriage, but sadly also by choice. It took an act of circumstance to force me to run. If not, perhaps I would have sat there like a coward for the rest of my life, eating fine food and wearing nice clothes, all my needs provided for." She looked at him, blinked and looked down.

Perhaps not all my needs, she thought.

Perhaps none at all.

My body was nourished but my soul was starved. Now it does not matter if I never eat a good meal again or feel fine silk against my skin. Not when my life feels this good, this fine, this perfect.

Cody shifted again in his seat. He glanced at her and nodded. She smiled as a warm ripple of emotion went through her body.

He can read me too, she thought. We do not need to say everything directly. He understands that I understand. That I want to understand more. That understanding transcends judgment, just like duty transcends right and wrong.

"Just carelessness," he said softly. "That's all it was. Carelessness that killed a kid who didn't deserve to die."

Cate swallowed hard. She nodded. Stayed quiet.

Cody shrugged like he wanted to shake it off. "We were drag racing down near the old oil wells outside town," he said. "Used to do it every Saturday night. Mostly old Camaros, Vipers, Mustangs. Souped up best we could afford." He shrugged again. "It was the beginning of summer. First weekend after school ended. I was seventeen, end of my junior year. Most of the kids had come out to watch. There was some drinking going on. Cheap beer. Some whiskey." He took a breath, blew it out hard. He shot a quick glance at her. "Not me. Not a damn drop." He overtook a black Ford pickup truck with a lot of shiny chrome. "My old man died drunk behind the wheel," he said, that coldness flashing in his eyes. "Put my mom in a wheelchair while doing it." There was no emotion in Cody's voice. Just a soldier repeating facts. "Anyway, kids were getting lit up. Cheering. Hollering. We were revving our engines. My buddy Steve against me. He'd won the last weekend, and I was gonna take this one."

"In front of the whole school, yes?" Cate said, smiling when she saw a hint of competitive fire behind those green eyes.

She could easily see him as a seventeen-year old hotshot cowboy behind the wheel of a rumbling muscle-car. He wasn't that much different now, she thought with a little smile.

Cody chuckled darkly. "I was so pumped up on myself back then. Reputation mattered. Your position in the hierarchy of men was important. Winning was everything." He paused a breath. "And doing it with a crowd of cheering girls was even better."

Cate blinked. She felt some heat in her cheeks. She imagined a line of pretty Texas sixteen-year old cowgirls taking their tops off for the hotshot boys in their muscle-cars.

She blinked again. Forced a sweet smile. This was about understanding him, she told herself. Certainly you are not the only girl Cody has touched.

But I damn well better be the last girl he touches, she thought as that annoying heat made her cheeks burn.

"We were revving the engines," Cody continued. "Getting ready to burn rubber. Steve's girl had her dad's gun for a starter pistol. She had it cocked and pointed at the stars, finger on the trigger." He paused and swallowed. "Then suddenly this random girl pulls open the door and jumps into the passenger seat next to me." He took a breath, shook his head. His jaw was tight like a wire. She wasn't sure if Cody was angry at himself or her or the whole damn world. "And the starter gun goes bang just then. So I shoot off without thinking. I'm all wound up, you know? Eyes on the finish line."

Cate touched his thigh. He was tense. She'd already guessed the ending to this story. But she also knew Cody needed to tell it more than she needed to hear it. She nodded and listened.

Cody's voice sped up. "Steve got the jump on me. I pulled in behind him to catch the slipstream and slingshot myself around him." His grip on the wheel tightened. "Then Steve's car blew a tire. He'd pumped it too full before the race." Cody shook his head. Shrugged. "Steve spun out. I was too close to stop. Smashed into the side of his back wheel." He swallowed. "The girl flew straight through the windshield. No seatbelt." Now Cody's chest filled out, and he exhaled violently. "One word from me would have prevented that death. All I fucking had to say was *Seatbelt* and it would have been fine. Steve and I walked away from that crash. That kid didn't. She was like fifteen or something. Whole life ahead of her." He bit his lip, almost crushed the steering wheel to powder with his grip. "You know, I've slit men's throats while they slept and never even thought about it again. I've planted explosives that I know killed more than just the target. I've done recon missions to scope out territory that later got firebombed to hell. And none of that ever got to me like this one thing." He shook his head vigorously. "These tiny, insignificant decisions that change lives, you know? All those small events happened together. If the gun had gone off a few seconds later, I would've had the time to either kick her out of the car or tell her to strap in. If Steve hadn't gotten ahead of me, I wouldn't have been right behind him. If he hadn't overfilled his tire, it might not have blown."

Cate nodded, blinking away some wetness from her eyes. "That is how Marya says fate works," she said. She looked at him. "Small coincidences that seem meaningless at first but send you down a path that is very meaningful in the end." She thought a moment. "You feel responsible for her, Cody?"

Cody nodded immediately. No hesitation at all. "I was driving. It was my responsibility to keep everyone in the car safe. Pretty simple in my eyes."

"Was there trouble for you with the law?"

Cody shook his head. "Wish there had been. Would've made me feel better."

"How do you feel about it now?" she asked.

Cody smiled. "You my psychiatrist?"

"I had been trained by years of Spanish soap opera melodrama," she replied very seriously.

Cody laughed. Then he went quiet. Thought a moment.

"I don't feel as bad as I want to feel," he said finally. His tone was soft, unsteady, almost like he was ashamed to admit it. "Maybe I never really did. Maybe that's why it still gets to me. Makes me wonder if I'm incapable of remorse. Just a stone killer who really can walk away from the people he kills. Just turn away and never think about the bodies I leave in the dust."

"But you still think about the girl." Cate pointed out. "So maybe you are not that bad."

Cody shrugged, kept driving. She looked at his eyes. There was a lightness in them now.

She smiled and looked down. Her heart fluttered a little. She understood that Cody was feeling guilty about *not* feeling too guilty. He was admitting that there was a coldness in him, a switch that could turn him into a machine, shut out the world, walk away from violence without letting it get to him.

"You are a good soldier," she said softly. "You use that part of you to serve your country. A soldier must have that cold, machine-like part in his heart or else he will kill a little bit of himself each time he kills another."

Cody raised his left eyebrow at her. "You get all that from the Spanish soaps?"

She laughed. "My whole life has been a soap opera, Cody."

He reached out and took her hand, squeezed it hard. "Well, now it's a cowboy movie."

Cate smiled, but the anxiety came back anyway. She stared at the road. It was very clean and very black.

"We cannot go to Colombia, Cody," she said softly. "You will be killed. Then I will be killed. It is not a good cowboy movie ending."

Cody's expression barely changed. "It's not going to end that way."

"How can it end any other way, Cody? It is impossible. There can be no plan that allows us to escape from that compound after killing Boro."

Cody kept staring at the road. His eyes were like arrows. Focused and sharp.

Then he turned that gaze towards her. A cool smile eased its way onto his lips.

"Who says the plan is to escape?" he whispered. He turned back to the road, that confident smile still hanging lazily on his lips. "We aren't going to be leaving that compound, Cate. We're going to be staying. Staying forever."

19

"Once Boro is dead, Malone's deal is dead too," Cody explained as they passed an abandoned Exxon station that was now a nest of rattlesnakes. "She'll have to cut a new deal."

"With whom?" Cate asked.

"With the person who takes over Boro's operations." He looked at her. "Which will be you, Cate Bonasera."

She laughed shrilly, clapped her hands twice like it was a grand joke.

Then she saw his dead serious expression and her eyes widened.

"You cannot be serious."

Cody shrugged. "You're still technically married to him. His estate passes to his wife."

"You are crazy," she said firmly. "Nico will take over. Nico is the first in command. He knows the troops and the operations."

"Nico is the guy who wears diamonds?"

Cate gulped. "Si."

"The guy who's expecting to wear your diamond on his pinky finger?"

Cate blinked. "Thumb."

"What?"

"All his fingers are used. Only two thumbs are available."

Cody's blood heated up. "Remind me to cut off his thumbs and stuff them up his ass before I break his neck."

Cate nodded absentmindedly. She stayed silent.

"What?" Cody said. "You don't like the plan?"

"It is not a plan," she declared. "It is madness. You are an American soldier. You cannot operate a cocaine smuggling operation."

Cody rubbed his stubble. "Benson would be totally into it. That crafty old bastard would think I'm the greatest strategic mind since Machiavelli."

"Then this man Benson is equally insane."

Cody grunted. He agreed, but didn't admit it out loud. He waited and listened to Cate.

Cate went on. "Anyway, even if by some miracle we kill Boro and Nico without being shot or blown up, what makes you think the rest of his men will just drop their weapons and surrender to us?"

Cody scratched his neck. "You think they'd shoot you even if Boro and Nico are dead?"

"They are thugs and mercenaries," Cate said. "They would shoot their own mothers. Some of them have done precisely that."

"Mercenaries won't shoot their mothers unless someone pays them to do it," Cody pointed out. "Worst case Boro's men loot the place and hit the road."

"There might be some men of ambition in Boro's

army," Cate said. "They may decide to seize control if Boro and Nico are both dead. I do not interact with Boro's men much. They have no respect for my authority outside of Boro's presence. I barely leave the mansion, Cody. Do you believe I am some queen and commander of a drug empire? That Boro's army of thugs will just bend the knee at my throne once their king is dead?"

She laughed, the tone shrill with nervousness. Cody immediately knew she was telling the truth. She was more prisoner than princess in Boro's world. She was there as collateral. Nothing more than a transaction. A hostage bound in silk. A hummingbird in a golden cage.

Cody relaxed. He took a breath. A sly smile escaped his lips.

He kept his eyes on the road, hoped Cate didn't see the smile.

Cate didn't miss it.

"You bastard," she whispered, her eyes going wide, her mouth hanging open. "You were testing me! You wanted to see if I went for the idea! If I truly was a part of Boro's operations. If I would be happy to continue destroying lives with that white poison powder. You *bastard*! How could you doubt me?"

Cody grinned. "And how could you think I would consider taking over a drug empire? I'm a SEAL, Cate. Not a damn druglord."

Cate crossed her arms tight over her breasts instead of under them like she'd done before. Cody was banned from pinching those poison-deadly nipples. She pouted in silence.

Cody grinned at the road. He wasn't sure if he'd been testing or teasing, playing or probing.

Maybe a little of both.

The game was still on.

Hell, the game would never end with her. Not with this woman.

And that was just the way he wanted it.

"Stop sulking," he said. "Here's the real plan. Listen up."

She huffed noisily. Looked over at him. Still pouty. Still pretty.

Still his.

"The first part of what I said still holds," Cody said, his voice slipping into the steady monotone that he used on missions, after the battlefield humor was done and the seriousness set in. "Once Boro and Nico are both dead, Malone's deal is dead too." He glanced at her. She was listening. "If one of Boro's men steps up, then she can cut a new deal with him. If the men just loot and plunder and the coca fields go unharvested, then maybe the other cartels take over the territory. Maybe the DEA places a stooge in charge. Either way, Malone will be forced to deal with it. Sort out her own mess. She can try to do damage control and blame Benson or Kaiser or some SEAL gone bad, but that'll be her last resort because she'll be burning her own career in the process. So I think she'll work out a new deal. Try to play Boro's death in her favor."

"But without me the Italian seaports will be closed to Boro's product," Cate said. "Malone might still need me to pressure my father into allowing Boro's successor to keep shipping to Europe."

Cody frowned. He didn't know enough about Malone's history with the Bonasera Family. He didn't even know if there was any. Not for sure, at least.

He wished he could call Benson, but he'd already committed to going solo, to cutting ties with Darkwater to protect the team in case Malone tried to bring everyone down with her in the end.

"You said you've never seen Malone before, right?" Cody asked. "You don't know if she was involved with the arrangement between your family and Boro."

Cate shook her head. "She never came to the house in Italy that I saw. Perhaps she was involved, but I cannot be certain."

"Tell me about the arrangement."

Cate shrugged. "My father was wiped out. Deep in debt to every bank in Europe. The Bonaseras were looked down upon by the top Italian Families. We were Sicilian scum. They would not cut us into any new operations. We were trading on old reputation. My father used his last remaining influence at the small Italian seaports to make the deal with Boro." She glanced away from Cody, out at the endless expanse of Texas. "Boro paid my father's debts and then some. In return my father gave him free passage to the seaports where he still had influence." She didn't look at him. "And I was the collateral. The guarantee that my father would continue to honor the deal even once his debts were paid and he was financially secure again."

Cody took a breath, glanced at her, then looked back

at the road. "The mafia in America work the same way. Kings and queens in the old world did that too—sent sons to enemy courts as wards, daughters as brides. Treaties secured by blood."

Cate nodded. She looked at him. Her expression was cold. If she hated her father, she didn't let it show. There was some stone-cold killer-queen in her blood. Hopefully their kids wouldn't be complete psychopaths.

"You and Boro never had kids," Cody said, his voice hardening a little.

She glanced at him. Looked away. Shook her head. Said nothing.

"From the first night I knew I would run," she said finally after a long period of silence.

Cody listened as she explained about the plant contraceptive, about Marya's warning, about the discovery that forced her to run.

"So you see, I knew if I had children, I would not be able to run." She swallowed hard, then looked at him, that hardness in her eyes again. "But it was not just that. I was . . . I was also scared that I might not be able to love a child that carried Boro's blood. I feared that I might . . ."

She trailed off. Cody didn't push her. He'd already seen the darkness in her. Already accepted it.

Already loved it.

Cody reached for her hand. They drove in silence, holding hands, their connection growing, their bond strengthening. There was so much to this woman, so much more to discover.

But they had the rest of their lives for that, Cody

thought as the landscape started getting more urban. They were getting to the Houston suburbs. Not much longer. Cody needed to set the plan up right.

And make sure Cate followed it.

"I'll be leaving you in Houston," he said, keeping his tone casual in the hope that it might lull her into a non-violent reaction.

He tightened his grip on her hand as she dug her nails deep into his flesh and tried to wrench away from him. Not too violent, he thought. At least he wasn't being stabbed in the face.

"I have to leave you there, Cate. No argument."

"Well, that didn't last long," she said with a loud sigh. "I saw this in the third season of *La Familia Degenerate* on Univision. The man seduces the woman. Takes her innocence. Then he says he has to go somewhere but no problemo, he will be right back, honey baby plumcake." She sighed with melodramatic sarcasm. "Then he goes back to his wife and family and plays with his children and pets his dog. He never comes back to the innocent lovely girl. Does not answer her desperate calls. Ignores her pleading messages. I believe it is called ghosting a woman." Cate rumbled air out through her lips like a child. She shrugged innocently. "So of course the betrayed woman kills the evil man and his bitch wife and his ugly children and then tragically takes her own beautiful innocent lovely life. The end."

Cody laughed until it was hard to see straight. "At least the dog got away."

Cate giggled. "Yes. The dog was fine in the end." She looked at him, the smile changing form. "I understand you want to keep me safe, Cody," she said. "But we are bound together now. You cannot keep me from the action. I will be there with you. Besides, without me, why would Boro let you into his compound?"

"He'll have seen the video of us on the freeway," Cody said. "He'll figure that either I'm a freelance ex-military guy looking for the bounty, or I'm a Black Ops guy looking for a deal in exchange for bringing his lovely innocent wife back home." He shrugged. "I'll show him a photograph of you and me and today's *Houston Chronicle* headlines. Tell him that I want half the bounty transferred over before I give you up. The wire transfer will take at least a day. He'll have to keep me alive."

"He will keep you in a cage," Cate said.

"There's no cage that can keep me," Cody said softly. "I'll get out in the dead of night. Find my way to Boro and Nico in the dark. Slit their throats and watch them drown on their own blood."

"That is very romantic, honey," said Cate. "But then what? How will you escape?"

Cody frowned to make sure she knew he was insulted. "I'm a SEAL recon specialist, Cate. Getting behind enemy lines is the easy part. Any SEAL can do that without being detected. Getting back out without being caught is where a recon specialist makes his money. That's why I'm the best of the best. Maybe the best that's ever been."

Cate attempted an eye-roll but she couldn't pull it off. She tried to blink away her admiration, but Cody saw it come through in her dark shining eyes. He chuckled inwardly. Clearly there was still a part of him that liked getting the glory.

And getting the girl.

Now the towers of downtown Houston popped up on

the horizon. Cody knew the city well. He headed for a residential neighborhood on the west side of town. They could leave the minivan in a legal parking spot and it wouldn't get called in for days.

Didn't matter, though.

Because Benson would find Cate within hours.

Because Cody was going to leave a breadcrumb for Benson.

Just in case this stuff about fate and destiny was bullshit after all.

Just in case Cate was stuck waiting forever for Cody to return.

Just in case these two days were all they would ever have.

20
TWO HOURS LATER
CORPUS CHRISTI
TEXAS COAST

"That two-timing piece of shit," grumbled Benson as Nancy Sullivan's sharp, professional voice read out the address she'd just picked up.

The address was two hundred miles from where Benson stood. It was the Grand Hyatt in Downtown Houston.

A guest named Tex Johnson had just checked in to the honeymoon suite. It had triggered a flag in Team Darkwater's system that was now under Nancy Sullivan's expert control.

"Technically Cody isn't two-timing anyone," Nancy said somewhat coyly. "He's leaving you a breadcrumb. It's one of Cody's Darkwater identities. He's in Houston, John. Or at least that's what he wants you to think. Maybe it's a triple-cross and he's actually in Christi after all. You'll have to call it."

Benson adjusted his sunglasses and rubbed the back of his neck. He was already feeling the sunburn. Or perhaps it was the burn of embarrassment. That SEAL had gotten Benson at his own damn game.

"No. He must have figured I'd try to head him off at the docks in Corpus Christi," Benson muttered. "So he went to Houston instead. He's flying to Colombia after all."

"Think you're right," said Nancy. Benson heard her fingers clatter on the keyboard. "I see a transaction on his crypto account. He may have paid someone under the table for a plane." She paused as she checked something. "He's trained and certified to fly small aircraft. Probably halfway to Colombia by now."

"Shit. Shit. Shit," Benson muttered. He glared at the line of boats bobbing in the blue water off the pier. He'd figured to head Cody off when he tried to get a boat.

Except Cody led him out to sea. Misdirection at its finest. Cody was a wily sonofabitch. No way was Benson cutting him loose. He was too damn good.

Benson thought a moment. Hotel room at the Grand Hyatt. The Hyatt would have good security. Nobody goes in without being stopped by the front desk. A good place to keep something important. Something you want protected.

"Guess I'm going to Houston," Benson said as he strode back to his Ford Taurus rental. He got in and slammed the door. "Works, since I need to talk to Cate anyway."

He hung up, then saw the photographs come through

Capturing Cate

from Patty Duprey in Puerto Vallarta. He scanned the files as he drove.

Then he dropped the phone and stepped on the gas.

Two hours and thirty eight minutes later he was impatiently tapping the brass knocker on the honeymoon suite at the Houston Grand Hyatt.

He heard footsteps on the carpet inside. Saw the peephole go dark. He grinned like a coyote. Knocked again.

Finally she opened the door. Benson strode past her, running his hand through his gray hair. He was already pacing the thick carpet before he got a good look at Cate Bonasera.

And what he saw made him relax.

Because one look at the sparkling energy in those dark eyes and Benson knew.

One glance at the poise in her step and Benson knew.

He knew that Cody had made the right choice.

He knew they were for real.

That fate was still real.

Destiny was still real.

And the game was still the same.

The only game in town.

The game of love.

21

I never told her that I love her, Cody thought as he angled the four-seater Cessna that had cost him a good chunk of cryptocurrency—mostly because he couldn't guarantee that it wouldn't be either destroyed or implicated in all sorts of illegal activities.

He gazed out the small double-paned window. The landing strip was long and wide. A Boeing 747 could land there if the pilot was skilled enough and could get his wheels down just past the treeline.

Impressive, Cody thought somewhat grudgingly. For all his shortcomings, Boro certainly thought big. Yeah, if he built an airstrip that big on his compound, he was definitely ambitious.

Not to mention arrogant. After all, no way even the top cartels could cut a deal that lets a cargo jet of uncut cocaine fly into American airspace. You'd need to cut everyone in on the deal, from the White House down through the Joint Chiefs to the entire Air Force High Command.

"No harm in thinking big, Boro," Cody muttered as he lined up for landing and gently pushed down on the controls. "But c'mon, man. Get a grip on reality."

But reality seemed very far away from Cody as he got closer to the ground. He'd decided to fly directly into Boro's lair. It was the most dangerous option but also the safest.

He'd been more worried about Malone's guys staking out the Bogota and Medellin airports and cutting him off. Not worried about getting past them—more like getting past them without leaving them all dead. Too messy to leave bodies at international airports. Not to mention driving all the way to Boro's compound. This was easier.

So long as he didn't get gunned down in the sky.

Cody hadn't bothered to contact anyone at Boro's compound on the radio. His Spanish was bare-bones and anyway, he didn't see any major ground-to-air weaponry.

He did see a line of men forming up along the edge of the runway, though. They looked like stick figures dressed in green-and-brown camo, with bare arms that were deeply tanned.

They carried rifles, and as Cody came in low to land, he saw that the weapons were German-made H&K fully automatic machine guns. They could unleash a hailstorm of a thousand bullets every thirty seconds. This was not a gunfight Cody could win.

Of course, he didn't expect this to be a gunfight.

He didn't bring any guns.

Cody had left his Sig Sauer with Cate at the Hyatt. He wondered if she'd shoot Benson in the face.

That's Benson's problem, he decided. I got my own fish to fry. My own sheep to skin.

The Cessna landed hard, bounced twice, then screamed

down the runway as Cody opened the flaps and eased in the brakes. The plane slowed well before the end of the runway, and Cody circled round and slowly made for the line of machine gunners.

"Hola," he said, popping out the door and sticking both hands out immediately so they knew he wasn't coming out shooting.

He waited for the men to take positions around the plane. Cody watched as a short man with a black mustache and three grenades on his flak-vest made his way over.

"Take me to your leader," Cody said with the friendliest grin he could muster. He wasn't nervous or tense in the least. He just wasn't good at friendly grins.

"Are you loco, gringo?" asked Mustache in broken English.

Then he blinked and cracked a huge grin. Glanced over his shoulder, rattled off something in Spanish.

A murmur rose up from the other men. The guns stayed aimed at Cody's center mass, but there was recognition on the men's faces.

"Ah, you saw my YouTube video," Cody said. "I'm an internet celebrity now."

"Si," said Mustache. He approached somewhat cautiously, his eyes darting towards the other windows.

"Solo flight. Cate is safe in America" said Cody. He tapped his head. "Because she is *not* loco."

He slowly stepped out of the plane. Stood straight with his arms out to the side.

Then he carefully lifted his black tee-shirt up past his

abdomen. Took a lazy circle to show he had no weapons. With two fingers he gently reached into his jeans and pulled out the burner phone he'd picked up in Houston.

He tapped to the photographs of Cate and himself with the *Houston Chronicle* showing the date. He'd made sure she didn't look too happy.

Made sure she didn't look like a woman in love.

"Show this to Boro," Cody said, gazing dead on at Mustache.

It wasn't a threatening look. It wasn't a challenge. It was simply eye contact that made it clear that if not for fifteen machine guns pointed at his chest, Cody would be king of the jungle right now. Hooyah, babycakes.

Mustache glanced at the photograph. Then he blinked, rubbed his throat, and stepped off to the side.

Cody saw him talk low into a black phone. He watched as Mustache took a photo of Cody's photo and then tapped it off, presumably sending it to Boro or Nico or whoever was next in this cute little phone-a-friend system.

Cody waited. He leaned against his plane. Grinned and nodded at the men.

They shifted on their feet. Grenades clinked against metal buckles and loops on their flak vests. It was late afternoon and the sun was moving down but was still very hot. Not long before it went below the treeline, Cody thought.

He scanned the surroundings. The airfield was in a large clearing. There were wide dirt roads that could handle two-way traffic. There was dense jungle about a quarter mile off on three sides. The fourth side had some low buildings.

Two barracks-style buildings, long and low. Three hangars that presumably housed Boro's air fleet. And a series of windowless barn-like structures that Cody figured for warehouses.

Cody couldn't see the border walls. He'd scoped out the compound from the air before landing. Saw the white walls from above, but they were too far away to see from the ground.

Cate was right. The compound was gigantic. Miles from the walls to the well-fortified main mansion. No sniper could make that shot. Hell, there was no rifle on earth that could generate enough velocity and spin to get a bullet that far without it being as harmless as a pebble tossed at a giant.

Boro isn't a giant, though, Cody thought as he saw a black armor-plated Humvee drive up in a furious cloud of red dust. Cody had pulled up some file photos of Boro and Nico before leaving the hotel. Didn't go too far into their files. Just enough to gauge their physical attributes. What he was up against.

He was more concerned about the layout of the private mansion. That wasn't part of any files. Cate had drawn him maps. He'd explored them.

Then he'd explored Cate again.

Carefully.

Deeply.

Lovingly.

And possessively.

Cody straightened up as the black Humvee stopped and all four doors opened at once.

Four men got out.

Boro was one of the men.

Cody knew from his outline. He was short and very thick. His shoulders were heavy. Powerful arms with forearms thicker than Cody's head.

He slammed his door shut and grinned at Cody. Boro had been driving himself, Cody noted. Setting an example. Just like Cate said he liked to do.

Gold flashed in the sun. Boro's teeth.

Cody grinned back. It occurred to Cody that he was here to kill the husband of the woman he'd just taken as his own.

It felt strangely righteous in a sick, twisted way. Like perhaps that was how it played out in some old world system where there was no government to settle your disputes. There was no divorce court and marriage counseling. No law other than natural law.

The oldest law in the book.

You saw the woman you wanted.

You took her.

You made sure nobody could take her back.

Cody grinned as he thought of Cate. She would say that this was Cody's own version of a cowboy movie. A standoff in the red dust to seal the deal in blood.

Then Cody lost the grin. Boro wasn't coming within twenty feet of Cody. There was going to be no duel for the right to claim Cate Bonasera. No six-guns at dawn. This wasn't gonna be a cowboy movie after all.

Boro snapped his stubby fingers and barked out orders in crisp Spanish that was beyond Cody's comprehension. Didn't take long to figure it out, though.

Within seconds Cody was face-down in the dirt, being patted down hard by rough hands. They searched his pockets and ran dirty fingers through his hair. Took off his shirt and made him remove his boots. He wondered if there would be an anal probe. This was going downhill fast.

He took long breaths. Slow exhales that would calm down his system. No point burning all the adrenaline right now. He would need it later.

Cody was ordered to stand up. He took his time. A show of power, even though he was surrounded by thirty men and about a million bullets. He saw machetes stuck in some men's belts. He hoped they were for the jungle, not his balls.

Cody blinked away sweat that was running down from his forehead. He glanced up at the sky. Blue as death. Not a single cloud. Sure as hell no Blackhawk squadron of Flyboys to save his damn ass. No SEALs parachuting down from a C-17. He was on his own.

This was the plan, he reminded himself as Boro finally walked towards him.

The short, thick man came close enough to smell. It was still about ten feet away from Cody.

Boro's scent was as thick as his neck and twice as leathery. Cigars, gunpowder, and sweat. Cody had smelled worse. Bruiser and Dogg didn't smell like roses after a three-day mission in the Gobi Desert.

"Houston Chronicle," said Boro, holding up Cody's phone and grinning. "So I presume she is not actually in Houston. Certainly you would not give up her location."

"I'm not that smart," Cody replied.

"Or perhaps you are too smart," Boro said, losing the grin with deadly quickness.

His weathered face settled into a scowl that had worn tracks on his jowls over the years. He kept a goatee that was well-manicured. It was thick and dark. So was his short hair. Eyebrows too.

Cate was right. Boro was a thick man. He was mid fifties, Cody figured. Cate had said Boro didn't know his exact age. Apparently he hadn't cared to ask Sister Francesca before he and Nico skewered her alive.

"Never been accused of being too smart," said Cody. He stayed expressionless, kept his voice in a steady monotone.

Boro rubbed his goatee, then flicked some sweat off his fingers before wiping his hand on his crisp green-brown khakis.

He wore a white linen shirt, short sleeved and open down past his hairy chest. The pants weren't cargo-style, but he wore a belt-harness for an evil looking H&K machine pistol.

The belt and harness were fine leather, probably Argentinean. Cody wasn't a fashion guy, but he knew good leather.

He also knew good guns. The H&K was a masterpiece of German engineering. The machine pistol was almost as powerful as the full-strength models slung across

Boro's soldiers. It wouldn't matter how bad a shot Boro was. He wasn't missing with something that sprayed hollow-point 9mm bullets like a shotgun sprays buckshot.

Boro's dark, sharp eyes studied Cody's face.

"You are Special Forces," he said definitively.

"Former," said Cody.

No point bullshitting. Boro had studied the video. It was hard to disguise those kind of hand-to-hand skills. You don't get that kind of training as a street thug. Or the kind of experience that turns training into instinct.

"Army Ranger?" Boro asked.

Cody bristled. "Navy SEAL."

Boro blinked twice quickly. "What do you want?"

Your wife, Cody thought. "What do you think?" he said.

Boro took a step closer and stopped. Not close enough for Cody to leap at him without getting shredded by six thousand bullets.

Boro sighed. "Bounty is paid upon delivery."

"Half up front."

"Then what?" snapped Boro. His face darkened. "My whore wife drops down from the clouds?"

Cody kept his gaze cool and steady. "I call my associates. They bring her to you. Air mail, just like I got here. Three hour turnaround after I see five million in my account."

Boro moved his lower jaw side to side. Then he reached for his machine pistol. Pointed it at Cody's chest.

"You told the truth about being a SEAL," he said. "But the rest is a lie."

Cody stayed calm on the outside. Inside him the adrenaline was trickling into his bloodstream.

But he'd anticipated that it might not be straightforward. Sure, he'd hoped Boro would agree, then toss Cody in a cage until the five million went through and Cate arrived as promised. But that was best case.

Clearly it was not going to be a best case scenario.

No problem.

Just so long as it wasn't the worst.

Cody shrugged. "If you think I'm lying, just shoot me."

Boro grinned. Then he sighed. Lowered the machine pistol casually.

And pulled the trigger.

Cody felt two 9mm bullets slam into his left thigh. He stifled a shout, dropped to one knee, felt the pain roar through his torn muscle.

He blinked rapidly, tightened his jaw to control the pain. He wasn't going to cry out, no matter what.

Three quick in-out breaths and then he managed to hold in some air and exhale slowly to steady his racing heart. He stared at the red dirt as he forced himself to evaluate the situation.

Boro had fired a three-round burst. Two bullets had struck his thigh. One bullet had gone clean though. The other was still in there.

It was not a hollow point bullet, he realized with relief. Which meant it hadn't ricocheted off bone and torn its way through so much tissue that he would bleed to death in minutes. He also knew that Boro had missed his femoral artery. Boro knew the human body, and he knew how to shoot.

Cody relaxed.

The wound would not be fatal.

Boro put the gun back in the belt-harness. He said something in Spanish.

One of his guards pulled out a black walkie and relayed something in faster Spanish.

Cody picked up a familiar word.

Medico.

From his position on one knee Cody saw a white Humvee speeding over along the dirt road. It pulled up in seconds.

The back opened up. Four men dressed in white cargo pants and white tee shirts jumped out. They pulled out a stretcher.

Cody was impressed. Boro was running a full-scale professional operation here.

"Thanks, but I can walk," Cody said. He pushed himself to his feet.

The blood roared in his ears, throbbed in his thigh. He swallowed his pain, blinked his eyes back into focus.

He'd been shot before. This was nothing. The embarrassment hurt more than the damn bullet. He'd messed up. Played it a little too cool. Maybe even underestimated Boro a bit.

Not good. Perhaps Cody's judgment had been clouded by his possessiveness over Cate. Those ancient instincts of claiming your mate from the other cavemen was overriding his training. Bruiser and the guys would laugh their asses off. He'd better not tell them that he'd gone full caveman over this woman.

Boro nodded, raised a hand to stop the stretcher-bearers.

A murmur rose from the troops as Cody walked to the ambulance. He did it slow and casual, using his strength of will to keep his expression calm.

He climbed into the back of the white Humvee. Sat down on the cushioned bench. Stretched out his wounded leg.

He stuck his fingers into the torn cloth of his jeans. Ripped the jeans clean down the leg to grant access to the wound. He'd rather not lose his pants. A hospital gown open at the back was not a good look. Too easy for that anal probe, he thought with a grin.

That grin turned grim when Boro walked over and pulled out his phone. He took a picture of Cody with his open wound. Tapped his phone screen. Shot Cody a disconcertingly triumphant look before putting the phone away and grinning.

"You were right. Nobody should accuse you of being too smart," Boro said causally. "Brave, yes. Tough, certainly. But smart . . ." He shook his head, strode away on his short, thick legs towards his black Humvee.

Before getting in he turned his head sideways. He eyes were like black marbles. "I know you do not want the bounty, Cody Cartright," he said with some degree of satisfaction. "Even if I had not been warned I would have known. Nobody is so stupid as to disrespect me by asking for payment before delivery. That would mean the man doubts my word. Doubts that I will make good on my bounty offer. A man's reputation is his most valuable asset. Even more so in the underworld, Cody Cartright."

Cody winced. It was not from the bulletwound.

Boro knew his name.

Knew he didn't want the bounty.

Knew he wanted Cate.

"Malone," Cody muttered, more to himself than anyone.

He issued the termination order in his mind. He'd given Maggie Malone a pass for her misdeeds so far. She was just doing her job, he'd told himself. Malone was no worse than the other wheeler-dealers in America's clandestine three-letter agencies.

But he'd been wrong.

She was worse.

She'd given him up.

"Do not judge Ms. Malone too harshly," Boro called out as he leaned on the Humvee's open door. "She made me promise to kill you with a bullet instead of a machete."

He smiled thinly, then parted his tobacco stained lips to show his gold headlamps. "Malone believes you have no intention of giving up my wife. She says you would like to keep her for yourself." He sighed, shook his head, cracked his thick neck by moving it side to side. "And when I see that you arrive here alone like a madman in love, I suspect it is true. Which puts us in an interesting situation. This is a fascinating turn of events. We shall discuss it at dinner."

Cody glanced at him. Said nothing.

Boro didn't say anything more. He just tapped the side of his head and clambered into his black Humvee.

Cody watched as Boro's chariot roared off in a cloud of red dust. He leaned his head against the metal wall of his ambulance and thought silently.

But he wasn't thinking about Malone anymore.

He was thinking about that photograph Boro had just taken.

22

Benson glanced at the photograph. It had just come through on one of the three phones he always carried. It was his official CIA number that Kaiser had let him port with him when he quit the Agency to start Darkwater. It was a number that anyone in the U.S. Government could access without much trouble.

Instantly Benson made the connection. It didn't surprise him that Malone would have passed his number on to Boro. Benson knew it the moment he read the Puerto Vallarta police reports that Patty Duprey had sent him.

Benson took another look at the photograph. Cody looked somewhat annoyed at being hobbled with what looked like two nasty bulletwounds. There was a message from Boro below the image. Benson read it quickly and then put away the phone.

"What is it?" Cate asked. "Your face went white. Now it is red again."

Benson smiled. He walked to the room-service tray near the hotel room window. Poured himself another cup of black coffee from the porcelain carafe. Sipped it slowly as he stared out over downtown Houston. Glass and metal towers. Cold and dark, but brutally beautiful.

He'd been with Cate Bonasera for less than an hour, but he'd known within the first three minutes that even though she'd tried to kill Cody twice, she was ready to die for him.

Except Boro's offer was worse than death.

Benson couldn't bring himself to tell her about it.

Mostly because she might accept.

And that might end in disaster.

"What is happening, Mister Benson," came her voice from behind him. It was strong, but with an undercurrent of anxiety. "What is our plan?"

Benson glanced at his watch. The same old black metal Fossil from his Navy days. The time didn't matter. He was just stalling. Thinking. Deciding.

He turned and looked at Cate. She was in black jeans and a black V-neck tee shirt that was thankfully thick enough that Benson didn't turn red again. She looked bright and clean and very alert. She did not look like a woman who'd just been through two days of hell.

She looked like a woman in love.

Benson sipped his coffee and turned to the window again. He went over what they'd talked about over the past hour. As was his way, Benson had revealed almost nothing about what he knew or didn't know.

Nothing about Puerto Vallarta police reports that showed a young, skinny wide-eyed Margaret Malone in a Mexican mugshot next to an equally young but very thick Boro.

Nothing about Margaret Malone's annual visits to the Mexican vacation spot.

Visits that stopped after four years.

Six months before that ten-day trip to Santo Silenzio.

That small Italian town with a hospital.

And a maternity ward.

And an orphanage.

No, Benson kept all of that to himself for now.

He'd gotten what he needed from Cate.

He'd asked Cate questions to get answers to the questions he didn't want to ask yet.

Because it was all still speculation.

But speculation backed by intuition.

Intuition that Benson couldn't ignore.

Benson knew the signs of serendipity. He knew how space and time bent back over itself from the power of human choice.

Especially when that choice was powered by love.

Love that asked you to fight for it.

Risk everything for it.

He'd seen it because Benson knew what to look for. He knew that if fate and destiny were doing their ancient dance of mystery and mayhem, if the universe had indeed brought Cate and Cody together in its favorite game of man and woman, then that same trickster universe would provide them a way out, a way through, a way home.

Home to their forever.

And so he finished his cup of black coffee, dabbed his mouth with a clean white serviette, then turned back to Cate Bonasera.

He'd made his choice.

Cody had made his choice.

Capturing Cate

Now it was Cate's turn to choose.

He handed her his phone.

It was unlocked. Boro's message was on the screen.

She blinked three times when she saw the photograph. Swallowed hard and then read the message.

Then she handed the phone back to Benson.

"Let's go," she said calmly.

She turned and walked to the door. Pulled it open. Strode down the hall and hit the elevator call button three times before glancing back at Benson. "You coming?"

Benson felt that familiar excitement race up his spine and grab him in a chokehold. He felt his face turn red again. The game was ancient, but it never got old. It was new every damn time.

He grinned and grabbed his jacket. Hurried to the elevator and slipped in with Cate just as the steel doors glided closed.

He pulled out his phone and called Nancy Sullivan, told her they didn't need a flight plan because they were flying to a private airstrip eighty miles out of Medellin.

Then he hung up and looked at Boro's message again.

Read through it as Cate stood straight as an arrow next to him, her eyes focused like arrowheads, the energy in her heart burning like a furnace hot enough to melt steel.

Dearest Catherine:

I am deeply moved that you have found true love. Our marriage was a business arrangement, and I am not a fool to think there was any love between us. I am also a believer that we all have our fate, and if this is yours, who am I to stand in the way?

It so happens I have decided to abandon my European operations and turn my attention back to my beloved United States. So I have no use for our arrangement or your family anymore.

Indeed, I have no use for you anymore.

Alas, I have already promised Nico that he can decorate his thumb with what he takes from your broken fingers. You know how I always keep my commitments.

Unlike you.

Still, out of my curiosity to understand the wonder of true love, I will make you an offer, sweet Catherine:

Present your cheating, whoring, treacherous self to the court of Boro.

Accept your punishment from Nico in front of the troops.

Then, if you can still walk straight, still see straight, still fuck straight, you and your cowboy may ride off into the sunset.

Happily ever after.

It sounds harsh, but of course, there is another option, Dear Catherine.

You may simply walk away.

Go make a new life in America.

I will retract the bounty.

Set you free.

All you have to do is pay the price.

Turn around and walk away.

Just walk away.

23

"Of course she'll walk away," said Margaret Malone with a snort. "I said *he* was infatuated, Boro. Not her. Cate doesn't give a damn about him. She manipulated his protective instincts to get out of a jam. And now you're giving her a free pass."

Boro puffed on his cigar until the cherry burned red like a sunset. He blew the smoke across the open verandah, watched it swirl around Margaret's perfectly coiffed hair, smiled as she made a face and waved it away.

She has aged well, Boro thought as he glanced down at her long, slender frame that was perhaps a bit frail these days. He wondered if her body would hold up to the powerful, violent thrusts with which he used to take her back in that seaside hotel in Puerto Vallarta thirty years ago.

Of course, Boro had seen her again a decade earlier, but that was not a time to revisit the distant past. Margaret was climbing the ladder at the DEA, and she was negotiating a complex deal that involved all the Colombian Cartels plus the Mexican and Venezuelan kingpins.

Back then Boro was not powerful enough to get his

way. Though in truth, none of the cartels were powerful enough to go against the DEA when the American War on Drugs was at its height. The DEA had the military support and federal funding to burn every coca field in South America. They had the clout to wipe out every drug lord and his entire bloodline.

Though of course that was not the endgame. People wanted cocaine, just like they wanted alcohol and cigarettes, sugar and salt, sex and violence. These things triggered powerful pathways in human bodies and brains, and the DEA knew that as surely as the pusher on the corner does.

They could not stop the human demand for drugs. The DEA knew that unstoppable demand means there will always be a supplier. Destroy the Cartels and you spawn thousands of smaller dealers that crop up like ants, strike like mosquitoes, are harder to kill than cockroaches.

Better to manage the big cartels, the DEA had decided. Move things around now and then to make it look like the war was being won. Sleight of hand. Smoke and mirrors. Snakes and ladders.

Some go up. Others go down.

Then the pattern reverses.

Now it was time for Boro to climb the ladder once more.

And Cate's betrayal might have put him on the first rung.

Started a chain of events that forced Boro's hand. Forced him to pull the plug on the Bonasera arrangement. Roll the dice with America again. Go for gold. Reach for the stars.

"Perhaps there is something to this whole fate and destiny thing, yes, Margaret?" he said softly as he ran his gaze along her long neck and up past her hard cheekbones into her water blue eyes. "After all, this mess with Cate has brought you back to me."

"I am not *back*, Boro," she snapped.

Boro shrugged those heavy shoulders. "You left. Now you are back. It is our fate to be together, Margaret."

He grinned, licked the back of his teeth, let his gaze wander down her body. She had arrived in a gray pantsuit. Her jacket was inside on the couch. She was in a black sleeveless blouse. Her arms were thin but tight and wiry, with veins running down her slender forearms. Her skin was white and the veins looked grayish green.

"We were never together," said Margaret. Her voice was not as hard now. She had seen his eyes.

He stood from his armchair, strolled across the open terrace, stood before her.

She looked up at him. Her eyes were paler blue than he remembered. He reached down and ran the back of his hand over her cheek.

"Boro, don't," she said, turning her head to the side.

Boro turned his palm around and grabbed her by the throat, forcing her to look up at him. He stared into her eyes silently, letting her know that this was his domain and she was in the lion's den. She had much to lose with this whole situation. He knew she had ambition. She wanted to be DEA Director. Maybe even a Senator later in life. He could do anything and she would be forced to submit.

Boro waited until those sharp blue eyes blinked and looked down. He grunted and let go of her neck.

She blinked and swallowed, then rubbed her thin arms and stared darkly out towards the reddening sky beyond the distant jungle.

Boro forced himself to calm down. He reminded himself that he had much to gain from his connection with Margaret. Already he had gained much, he thought.

After all, it was Margaret who negotiated the European deal with the Bonasera Family. Without that Boro would have been the odd man out amongst the big Colombian Cartels. The DEA might have chosen to wipe out Boro and his operation as a show of force, to show that the War on Drugs was proceeding with satisfactory violence and ruthlessness.

Still, it could go either way if Margaret was up for DEA Director soon. Perhaps she would decide it was better to erase all connections with Boro.

In fact Boro was mildly surprised she had not simply sent in a wet team, a hit squad, perhaps even one of those drones that could fly in through his bedroom window and put a miniature missile right between his eyes.

"Why have you come here?" he asked coldly.

He heard Margaret sit back against the cushion of her wood-framed armchair. "I need you to continue your European operations for a couple more years," she said. "Just until I get through the vetting process for Director. Then we can talk about reshuffling the deals with the Cartels. Get you back into the U.S. market."

Boro strolled to the parapet and looked out over his estate. His verandah faced north towards the United States. "My arrangement with the Bonasera Family is dead. Cate betrayed me. She has to die. My reputation is at stake."

Margaret laughed. A short, scoffing laugh. "Betrayed you? With that plant-remedy contraceptive that the village whores use?" She laughed again. "Boro, you never wanted kids. You hate the very idea of bloodlines and inheritance. You were probably thrilled Cate never got pregnant."

Boro turned, a golden grin breaking on his face. "Ah, you know me so well, Margaret. See, we should be together. It is fate, just like I said. Come. Take off your blouse. I would like to see your nipples again. Are they still small and tight like buttons?"

Now Boro saw color rush to her bone-white face. Her eyes flashed and her neck moved as she swallowed.

She looked away, touched her styled hair, then looked back at him. She was all-business again. But Boro knew he had struck a blow. There was still something there. He smiled in the growing darkness.

"You are correct," he said finally. "I do not give a shit about a child. Do not care a damn about a legacy or a bloodline. I came from nothing. No bloodline. I fought my way to the top. Nobody will be *given* my empire. They will have to fight for it. Let chaos reign once I am gone." He chuckled, his black eyes shining. "That is what has kept me alive this long, has it not, Margaret?"

Finally those thin lips spread into a smile. "Yes," she said, letting a glint of admiration show in her blue eyes.

"It wasn't clear what would happen to your operation if you got assassinated. The other cartels might go to war for the right to claim your fields and facilities. Much easier for the DEA to keep you alive." She lost the smile. "Alive, and away from the American market. Two more years, Boro. Three tops."

Boro shook his head. "Cate's betrayal cannot go unpunished. I punish traitors amongst my men, and it is important they see that my rules are absolute. Perception and reputation is what gives me power. I must protect it. Grow it." He shrugged, puffed his cigar, blew thick smoke rings into the twilight sky. "Besides, it is too late," Boro said. "Nico is already on his way. We have passed the point of no return."

Margaret sat forward. "On his way where?"

Boro held up his left thumb. "Italy."

Margaret stood up. "Why?" she whispered, her eyes revealing that she'd guessed the answer.

Boro answered anyway. "Romero said not while Cate's mother still lives." His grin widened.

She closed her eyes and rubbed them. "You maniac," she groaned. "Oh. God, Boro. I wish you hadn't done that."

Boro grinned. "And I wish you had never left."

She glared at him. "Fuck," she said. She started to pace. "I came here to convince you to hold off on doing anything drastic about the Cate situation. Either let her run or if she comes back then let her live. But now it doesn't matter. Fuck."

She took quick, snorting breaths as she paced. Boro thought of those days when Margaret would snort white lines of powder as he took her from behind like the young bull he was back then. He would always pull out just in time, finish on her tight narrow ass.

Well, almost always pull out it time. Thank God she hadn't gotten pregnant.

The thought sparked a strange melancholy in Boro. For a moment he wondered if their lives would have been different if Margaret had gotten pregnant by some accident of fate.

He dismissed the whimsical thoughts of possible pasts. Focused back on the here and now.

"Shit," she muttered under her breath as she passed him. She paced up and down twice, then stopped abruptly and looked at him. "We'll have to kill them all," she said, her eyes widening slightly like she was surprised. She shrugged, her eyes still wide. "Cody. Cate. Benson. Romero Bonasera too, I guess." She tapped her lip, blinked three times, then nodded firmly. "Tell Nico to do Cate's father since he's in Italy anyway," she said.

Boro raised his chin. Stroked his goatee. He did not like people giving him orders, but he stayed silent and thought it through.

Perhaps Margaret had just included Boro in her mental list of people she wanted erased. Common sense told Boro to break her neck and bury her in the jungle. She was here off the record. No DEA search would include the jungle within Boro's compound. They might connect the dots and eventually guess the truth. But they would never know for sure, and they would perhaps leave the bodies buried, let the skeletons turn to dust.

But of course, eventually the score would be settled.

The DEA would not let one of their own go unavenged.

No, he should not break her lovely neck yet. Better to wait and see. Perhaps fate was still in play here. After all, Margaret was here again.

"Would you like to sample my new strain of fine powder?" he whispered as he watched her eyes dart left and right.

She blinked and shook her head violently. "Of course not. That's why I ended it between us, Boro. Now are you going to call Nico or not?"

Boro frowned deep, his thick brows overlapping above his squat nose. He scratched his goatee, then finally nodded.

He strolled back into the living room, snatched up his phone, made the call. Then he walked back out to Margaret.

She was on the phone.

"Told my guys to drive up to the compound," she said after hanging up. "Will have to clean that up too. Easier to do it here."

Boro grunted. "Where are they?"

"Posted them at Bogota and Medellin airports to watch for Cody," she said. "Not that I expected Cody to actually show up here. Didn't figure he was *that* far gone."

Boro nodded. "It is curious, I will admit." He looked up. "Why do you think he came?"

Margaret shrugged. She was quiet for a while. "I think he came to kill you," she said finally.

Boro rubbed his chin. Nodded slowly. "I think so too," he said quietly. "I saw it in his eyes. He came to claim Cate from me. He is not a man who steals like a coward and runs away with his prize. He came because it is the right thing to do. If you want to take a man's woman, you face the man and you say so."

"Well, he *didn't* say so, did he?" Margaret said with an eye-roll. "He made up some story and showed you a staged photo."

Boro swiped at the air. "That means nothing. The real communication comes from the eyes, not the tongue. He said so with his eyes. His heart." He took a breath, cast a lingering glance at her. "He loves her, Margaret."

Margaret laughed. "Sucks for him, then. Because he's never going to see her again."

"You do not think she will come?"

"To get torn apart by Nico in front of Cody and a hundred cheering men? Cate isn't stupid, Boro."

"What if she loves him?" Boro asked, frowning as he watched Margaret sit back down on her armchair, cross one long leg over the other knee. "Loves him enough to suffer through that to save his life. To save their chance at being together."

Margaret shook her head flippantly. "No woman can love a man enough to put herself through that. Not in the real world, at least. Maybe in some ridiculous romance novel. Or a Spanish soap opera."

Boro shrugged. "Cate and that maid of hers . . . Marya. They watched Spanish soap operas day and night. Perhaps Cate has picked up some romantic ideals from there."

"Well, it'll certainly tie up the loose ends for me if Cate brings her bouncy butt back here to save her man," said

Margaret. She snorted. "Not that coming here would save either of them."

Boro shrugged. "It might."

Margaret raised a thin, well-plucked eyebrow. "You can't be serious about honoring that ridiculous deal you offered."

"My word is law. It is the cornerstone of my reputation." Boro shrugged. "And I am curious about this matter of love now. Curious how it makes people do irrational things. It made the soldier fly into the lion's den without even a toothpick to arm himself." He took a slow breath, picked up the half-smoked cigar from the heavy glass ashtray, puffed on it until the cherry burst back to life. "And if Cate shows up to accept what I admit is a gruesome punishment, then perhaps she deserves a chance at true love, at her soap-opera ending."

"Doesn't everyone die at the end of a Spanish soap opera?" Margaret said with a twisted smile that made Boro's cock move.

"Everyone except the dogs," he said with a grin. "Come. We can discuss more over dinner with the loverboy SEAL. The nurses will have patched him up by now."

24

"You don't look like a nurse," said Cody.

The pleasant looking woman dressed in clean blue cotton trousers and a white linen tunic smiled at him. She had thick black hair done in plaits and watery blue eyes that stood out against her olive brown skin.

She placed another piece of clean white tape over the gauze covering his wound. Then she glanced around the infirmary before leaning closer to Cody.

"I am Marya," she whispered. "I am Cate's—"

"Oh, shit, Cate is so damn worried about you," said Cody, immediately recognizing this pleasant young woman even though he'd never seen her before. Cate's description was enough. Marya radiated sweetness like the sun radiates warmth. "She'll be thrilled to know you're all right." He paused, took a breath, considered whether to say what he wanted to say, decided to say it. "If it works out, I can try to take you with me," he said stiffly, not wanting to promise something he might not be able to deliver.

Cate hadn't asked him to do it, but from the way she'd talked about Marya, about how they were like sisters and best friends more than mistress and maid, Cody had decided to keep an eye out for her, see if it was workable.

"If what works out?" she asked, looking down and cutting off another long strip of tape so she could stay close to him. "Why did you come here? Boro will never let you leave. He will kill you. Probably in some horrible way to set an example to the troops. He is a monster. A filthy, ugly monster. I curse him every day and pray for Satan to take him back to hell where the demons can torture him with their fiery pitchforks." She placed the tape carefully over his dressing, patted it down gently, then smiled sweetly at him. "How do you feel?"

Cody grinned and shook his head. "You're just like Cate, aren't you? Sweetness and darkness rolled into one."

Marya shrugged like she understood. "I am so happy Cate is free. So happy she ran. So proud of her courage." She smiled, then frowned. "But why have you come. I do not understand. Is it for the money?"

Cody shook his head. "I have plenty of money."

"Then why?"

Cody swallowed. He looked at her sweet round face. He would have trusted her even without Cate's gushing reference.

"I have to kill him," he said softly. "Or else Cate will never be free."

Marya looked up at him. She blinked several times. Looked down and then up again.

"You love her?" she whispered.

"Yes."

The word came so fast and naturally that Cody felt

his heart fill with a sudden exhilaration, like admitting it out loud had infused him with a superpower.

Marya grinned like a giddy schoolgirl. "Then you will win," she said matter-of-factly.

Cody almost laughed out loud at her innocence and optimism. He glanced around the infirmary. It was a large open room with gurneys and drip-stands and stainless steel medical carts. There were offices along one wall. A large door leading to the waiting room.

He could see four armed guards in the next room. There were no windows anywhere. Running was not an option anyway. His thigh was numb from a local anesthetic. He'd fall on his face.

"Where is Nico?" he asked.

"The men who work at the airfield say he has gone to Italy."

"Why?"

She shrugged. Shook her head.

"You don't know?" Cody asked. "Or don't want to say."

"Madam Renata," Marya said. "She does not answer her phone today. She always answers my calls. Then I called Master Romero. His phone is off."

Cody frowned. Nico goes to Italy. Cate's parents don't answer their phones when their daughter is missing.

Not a good sequence of events.

Boro was cutting ties to the Bonasera Family in his own vicious way.

He was committing himself.

Going past the point of no return.

"When will Nico be back?"

Marya shrugged. "I can find out."

Cody nodded. He glanced towards the door. There was some activity outside. The head guard was on the walkie. He said something into the walkie, then looked at Cody.

Cody grinned and held up his middle finger. What were they gonna do, shoot him?

The head guard's face darkened. He barked out something in Spanish.

Three guards marched into the room. The doctor who'd stitched Cody up stepped out of his office, pointed to a wheelchair. The guards waved him away. No wheelchair. They surrounded the gurney where he was sitting.

Marya said something to them in Spanish. They all laughed. She went back and forth with them, laughing and talking. They knew Marya. They liked Marya. Cody made a mental note.

"They are taking you to dinner," she explained.

"Is that before or after the anal probe?" Cody deadpanned.

"Sorry?" Marya said. "My English is not so good."

"Probably for the best," Cody said with a wink.

Marya smiled and did a little half-bow and ran off like a kid playing hide-and-seek. She seemed to know her way around the compound. She'd probably be just fine if the shit hit he fan.

When the shit hit the fan.

Cody nodded at the guards.

Show time.

Ready to rock.

Fate was on his side.
Destiny was in his corner.
Cody slid himself off the gurney.
And fell flat on his face.

25

Cate kept the flat smile on her face. It was the only way to hold herself together, to not lose her mind in front of this man John Benson.

She stared out the small window of the Cessna plane. They'd been flying for an hour. They were over the gray sea, just past the southern coast of the United States. It was getting dark outside and Cate could see her reflection in the double-paned window.

She did not look into her own eyes.

She already knew what she would see in them.

"You see what I mean?" came John Benson's voice through the roar of the twin jet engines. He was in the front seat with the pilot, his head turned towards her, smile on his well-lined face, a sparkle in his sharp gray eyes.

"I think so," she said. "You are saying that it will work out even though we cannot know for sure exactly *how* it will work out."

"Something like that," said Benson. His eyes crinkled at the corner from his smile. She wondered how old he was. His hair had streaks of gray and silver, his forehead had signs of many moments of great strain. But those eyes were bright with a strange mix of a young man's innocence and a sage's wisdom. "Trust me, kid. It's pure science."

She frowned. "How so?"

Benson laughed like a wolf. "Hard to explain. But I think you already understand." He looked at her with something that was either envy or admiration. "That's why you're here, Cate. That's why you didn't even think for one damn moment before walking out the door and hitting that elevator button."

She smiled. Looked down. Blinked and looked back up. "Perhaps I knew that if I thought about it, I would realize it was madness. Nico will not leave me alive." She swallowed. "And Cody will not be able to watch it. He will either kill them all or die trying." She laughed once. "Or perhaps Cody will kill me first for being stupid enough to show up."

"Nah, I'd be number one on his kill list for letting you come," said Benson. "For bringing you with me."

She was quiet. "You are risking your own life," she said after a breath. "I am doing this because there is no choice for me. If I walk away, then my life is meaningless. But you do not need to do this, John Benson."

"Call me John or call me Benson. Not both," he said with a wink. "And yeah, I do need to do this. I brought Cody and the rest of the SEALs into my world, forced them to play the game by my rules. It's a tricky game, though. It's about probabilities and choices. Leaps of faith. Finding that balance between the heart and the mind." He shrugged. "The real twist is that fate isn't a sure thing. Destiny isn't a guarantee. That's why just believing in fate isn't enough. You can't just sit there and wait for your destiny like it's a guarantee from above. You have to act. You have to choose. You have to roll the dice, risk it all, throw yourself off the damn cliff with the faith that you'll find your wings before you get smashed against the rocks." He took a breath, let it out slow. "That's what Cody did when he went to face Boro against all reason, all odds, all common sense. And now you're doing the same thing, Cate. You can't fake those kind of choices, and destiny sees it. The universe sees that you aren't going to sit and wait for your happy ending. You're going to fight for it. And when you do that, the universe turns in your direction, Cate. You'll see. That's why I'm still playing this game." He grinned. "The game where you bet it all on the feeling in your heart and roll the dice. It's the only game in town, kid."

Cate stayed quiet. Her heart thrummed like a song without words. She thought John Benson might be insane, but then maybe she was insane too.

Because that feeling in her heart was real.

It was powerful.

It was freedom.

26

"Instead of freedom you chose to come here," Boro said from the head of the long wooden table. He sliced off a chunk of rare Argentine ribeye, then pointed the bloody serrated knife in Cody's direction. "Why? It makes no logical sense. I would like to call you stupid, but SEALs are not stupid. Their minds do not break under pressure."

Cody felt the pressure of the stitches on his wound as he flexed his quadriceps. The numbness from the local anesthetic had worn off. His muscles were operational again. That's why the SEALs never used local anesthetics in the field. The pain won't kill you. Losing control of your muscles for even a few minutes might.

Cody didn't answer. Instead he held up the white plastic knife that was the third one of the evening. The first two had snapped as he tried to cut his steak.

Boro shrugged as he chewed. He glanced at Maggie Malone, who was sitting to his left.

Cody was at the far end of the long table. His ankles were shackled to iron rings drilled into the studs beneath the floorboards. His wrists were loosely bound to the arms of the chair. He could eat, but he couldn't extend his elbow enough to throw anything at Boro.

"Death by humiliation," Cody said. "Maggie, will you cut my steak for me?"

Malone didn't look at him. She had barely touched her steak. She took a sip of sparkling water from a crystal glass.

Cody glared at the paper cup of plain water before him. Even his plate was just flimsy disposable wood fiber.

Cody finally pushed the plate away and leaned back in the wooden chair. He was used to going days without food. He fought better on an empty stomach anyway. Like those wild dogs that Cate had told him about. Hungry and angry.

"I am not angry that my wife is with you," Boro said, sawing off another piece of steak. "I am simply curious as to why you are here." He grinned, leaned back, dabbed his goatee with a red serviette. "I am even more curious to see if Cate will show up."

Cody's breath caught. He said nothing. He'd already figured that Boro had sent the photo to Benson. A message along with it. Some kind of trade. Cate for Cody or something like that.

"She isn't an idiot," Malone said. "She isn't coming."

"But if she is in love," said Boro. "Then perhaps she will come."

Malone laughed. Her helmet of hair moved. "If she convinced this SEAL that she loves him, then she's even smarter than I thought."

Cody didn't take the bait. None of this interested him.

Things were still roughly on plan. He was in the mansion. He was alive.

He watched Malone and Boro mock him and Cate. The words had no impact. He was taking in the details behind the words. Their hand movements. Facial expressions. Body language. Eye contact.

They know each other, Cody thought. More than just from some DEA negotiation from ten years ago.

Puerto Vallarta, he decided. He wondered if Benson had looked it up. Found anything interesting.

Malone pushed her chair back and stood up. She took one last sip of water and looked at her watch. It was a digital watch with a silver metal band.

"I have a couple of calls to make," she said, walking past Cody towards the ornate black-iron spiral staircase that led to a stone courtyard within the mansion walls.

As Malone walked past she looked at Cody. He raised his paper cup and grinned. She didn't say anything.

Cody drained the water from the cup as something about Malone struck him.

Her eyes.

Watery blue eyes.

He'd noticed them on the freeway in LA, of course.

But they meant more this time.

Because he'd seen those eyes before.

About an hour ago.

Watery blue eyes set in a sweet round face, framed by thick dark eyebrows and deep black hair.

Cody felt a thrill go through him as he watched Boro's eyes follow Malone to the stairs.

That thrill escalated as he watched Boro move his thick dark eyebrows, stroke his deep black goatee.

Cody saw it.

He saw it and he stored it away.

He wasn't sure how to use it yet.

But he was damn sure it meant something.

It meant that Benson was right.

Fate had a trick up her sleeve.

Destiny had a plan in motion.

Cody just needed to stand his ground.

Hold his line.

Wait for his shot.

"You will not get a shot at me," said Boro, forking the last triangle of bloody steak into his mouth. He chased it down with the dark wine he'd been drinking all night. Then he leaned back and stuck a half-smoked cigar between his teeth. "You came here for nothing, SEAL. Curiosity aside, we both know Margaret is right. Cate will not come here. You will be executed in front of the troops tomorrow. I will keep my word and remove the bounty on Cate. But I cannot stop Nico from going after Cate. She is Nico's now, you know." He struck a long match on the wooden tabletop and puffed his cigar to life. "He will wear Cate's ring on his thumb." He held up a stubbly thumb, then slowly turned it downwards and shook his head.

Cody gazed into Boro's eyes. He pushed away the possessive anger rising up his neck and making his temples thunder.

He'd already tested the strength of the iron rings and

the chains tethering him to the floor. Cody could deadlift a horse, but he knew it would be impossible to rip the bolts out of the studs in the support beams of the building.

Besides, that H&K machine pistol was still in Boro's belt. There were two guards behind Cody, three more outside the door, two on either side of the dining room flanking Boro. The man wasn't taking any chances. Cody would get his shot, but this wasn't it.

Might as well talk, Cody decided.

"You sent Nico to kill Cate's parents," he said in his military monotone. "Every son-in-law's fantasy."

Boro frowned briefly, then flashed a grin. "That nosy maid . . . Marya . . . she told you," he said.

Cody didn't answer. He studied Boro's face.

There was no reaction.

He didn't know about Marya.

He barely knew her name.

Cody tucked away the information. Added it to the knowledge that Boro had made an offer to Cate, and was at least waiting until the next day before executing Cody. That meant he was honoring some kind of timeline. Giving Cate a chance to accept his offer even though she'd be crazy to do it.

"What exactly was the offer?" Cody said at last.

He knew it wasn't wise to show interest. It was admitting that he gave a damn. That he was vulnerable. Still, Cody needed to know. It would help him plan for tomorrow.

"It will be a surprise," said Boro. He grinned, then

swiped at the air. "Ah, no matter. She will not come. You will get a bullet in the head. It will be quick for you."

Cody shrugged. "Then why wait?"

Boro puffed his cigar. Blew out the smoke. Watched it swirl in a gray-black haze. Didn't answer.

"You think she might come, don't you?" Cody said.

Boro shrugged. "There is always the tiny chance that she believes she loves you." He took a breath, looked at the burning tip of the cigar thoughtfully. "Or that she *actually* loves you."

Cody blinked. He glanced at Malone's chair still pushed back from the table. Her lipstick-smudged napkin was folded on the seat.

"Malone doesn't believe that kind of love exists," Cody said.

Boro snorted. "Margaret is cold like a snake inside." His eyes softened for a moment. "That is why we were so good together."

Cody smiled. "And that's why you're curious to see if Cate shows up. It would mean there is such a thing as love that's completely irrational, feeling so deep that it transcends the flesh." He lost the smile as he looked into Boro's eyes. For one strange moment he felt a connection to the man he know would soon die by his hand. "You want to believe that fate draws people together. That destiny decides who gets their happy ending. Me and Cate. You and Malone."

Boro roared and thumped his palm on the table. Cody's uneaten steak shook like jelly.

"Enough," he gasped through laughs and coughs.

"The guards will overhear and tell everyone that Boro and the SEAL are like two girls talking about Spanish soap operas. I will have to be extra brutal at the festivities tomorrow to salvage my reputation."

Cody grinned, shrugged his shoulders. "I heard everyone dies at the end of a Spanish soap anyway."

Boro nodded very seriously. "I have heard that too. Everyone dies except the dog."

Cody laughed, and was about to thump the table himself when the sound of dogs barking came through from the open balcony at the far end of the dining area.

Boro stood from the table, said something to the guard, then walked briskly towards the balcony. He stood at the parapet and leaned out into the night. He turned his head and frowned.

Then Cody heard the sound. Twin engines of a plane. He prayed it was Nico returning from Italy with Renata's ring on his thumb and Romero's head in a bag.

But when he heard the sounds of men shouting in the distance and the mansion guards' walkies crackling to life, Cody felt the sickness of dread rise up in him like a snake.

He cursed Benson under his breath. Blew out strong exhales of air to calm himself. Gulped fresh oxygen to slow the pounding of his heart.

But when Boro turned from the balcony and cocked his head at Cody with a strange look in his eyes, that dread was chased away by an irrational exhilaration.

Boro said nothing, but there was something in his dark eyes that said everything.

The game was on.

Someone was gonna get their happy ending in this violent soap opera.

And hopefully it wouldn't be just the dogs this time.

27

The dogs howled all through the night.

At first Cate thought she was dead and already in hell, but then she saw Marya and knew it couldn't be hell.

"My sweet Marya," Cate whispered in Italian. "Thank God you are alive. I would never forgive myself if you paid the price for my sins."

Marya didn't reply. She was speaking in hushed, urgent tones to the guards.

Cate laughed to herself. Sweet Marya was trying to use her influence to see if the guards would let Cate take a walk in the prison courtyard. Cate knew how Marya's childlike friendliness had won over everyone including the angry wild dogs. But of course no guard would go against Boro's orders.

Finally Marya sighed, thanked the guards, and stepped into Cate's prison. It was an empty cell with red walls and two long barred windows that overlooked a concrete courtyard. The building was unpainted concrete, and it had two floors of cells. It was mostly unused. Boro did not care much for imprisonment. Why waste food and water on someone who deserves to die, he'd reasoned.

The metal door closed with a thunk. Marya rushed to Cate and they hugged like lost children reunited. Cate tried not to cry. She thought of what Benson had said. She wondered where he was.

"The silver-haired man is at the other end of the hall," said Marya in Italian. "Who is he? Why did he come?" She frowned, her sweet face still pleasant, her blue eyes still bright. "Why did *you* come, Cate?"

Cate blinked. She hadn't really thought about it. There'd been no thinking at all, really. It had seemed obvious that she would come. There was no walking away from Cody. No running away from this feeling.

"Because . . ." she started to say. Then she stopped.

"Because you love him," Marya said, closing her eyes and biting her lower lip. She nodded and opened her eyes. "He said the same thing."

Cate blinked as heat rushed to her cheeks and her head buzzed like a bee. "Cody said he loves me?"

Marya cocked her head, closed one eye, raised the other eyebrow. "He did not say it to you?"

Cate shook her head. It sounded crazy. They'd known each other two days. Lived a lifetime together already. Were about to die together perhaps. No soap opera would dare get away with such melodrama, she thought.

"He said it to me," Marya said proudly. Then her eyes went wide. "About you, of course. He said it about you. To me. But about you."

Cate laughed and hugged Marya again. She smelled like a flower. Cate kissed her cheek and pulled back again.

"What is it?" Cate whispered when she saw Marya's eyes.

Marya parted her lips to answer but the sound of the door clanging open made them both jump back against the wall. They turned and looked.

It was Nico.

He stood in the open doorway. Cate could smell him from across the cell. If Marya smelled like a flower, Nico was the dung fertilizer. Except nothing good would grow in his filth. She almost spat onto the concrete floor to rid herself of his stench that was so thick she could taste it.

"I am looking forward to your taste in my mouth, Senora Bonasera," he whispered to her.

He stepped towards the two women. Reached out his left hand. Cate saw the diamonds shine in the white fluorescent light. She gasped when she saw the new ring on his thumb.

She recognized the diamond.

It was her mother's.

"You *dog*!" Cate screamed, launching herself at Nico as images of her mother being ravaged by Nico invaded her mind.

Her eyes focused on Nico's throat, but her hands never got there.

Nico caught her by the hair and hurled her against the wall. Marya screamed and leaped forward. She hung onto Cate's arm and managed to slow her down so Cate wouldn't crack her skull open. The two women grabbed each other and turned to face Nico, their backs against the concrete wall.

"Save it for tomorrow, eh?" said Nico with a grunt. He grinned and cracked his knuckles, then raised his other thumb and wiggled it. Suddenly his grin vanished when he glanced at Cate's left hand and saw no ring. "You cunt," he growled. "That will make it ten times worse for you. Your mother's end was a peaceful stroll in the garden compared to how you will be sent to hell."

Cate stared up at him as hatred like she'd never felt burned in her heart. There had been dark moments when she'd cursed her father and mother for selling her like a slave to Boro. Perhaps there were times she wished them dead. But they were family and Nico was filth. Her mother did not deserve it.

"You, I will kill myself," she whispered in Italian. "My man will kill Boro, but you will die at my feet. By my hand. I am Sicilian, and I declare a vendetta on you."

Nico did not speak Italian, but Cate saw his expression change. He touched his rat-like ponytail. The stench of death flooded the room as he exposed his armpit.

He shrugged, grunted, then turned to the guards at the door.

"Keep the Italian maid in here tonight as well," he ordered. "She will be the opening act at the show tomorrow."

28

Cody wasn't going to show his cards yet. He'd prepared himself mentally all night. He knew he had to stay cool and unaffected, flip the inner switch he knew so well. He needed to become that machine, cold and hard inside, silent like death, calm like the sea before a storm.

But when the time came to become that machine, he was all man.

Just a man.

Possessive as hell.

Pissed off as fuck.

"You're going to die screaming," he snarled in Boro's direction when the guards brought out his woman like she was an animal about to be slaughtered.

She looked at him with those dark eyes that he'd kill for and die for. Her hair was wild like a nest of snakes. Her bare feet were cut and bruised along the sides.

She wore that same Hanes Beefy tee shirt. Her wrists were bound in black silk that made Cody see red. He looked at his chains but held himself back from wrenching at them. It would only made the scene more darkly surreal.

The sun was rising over the distant jungle treetops. They were on a circular section of raised concrete set in the red dirt of a wide clearing. There were heavy iron rings set into the concrete at various intervals.

There was a ten-foot by twenty-foot concrete wall standing at one edge of the circle. It was riddled with bullet holes. Streaks and spatters of black dried blood made it look like a work of modern art—the kind Cody understood.

Towards the center was a concrete stump like a chopping block. It was streaked dark red and black along the top and sides. Cody remembered Cate explaining how Boro liked to take people's fingers, toes, limbs, and sometimes heads.

Cody had been brought out here at night, shortly after the dinner party. Perhaps Boro sensed it would be unwise to keep him anywhere near the mansion. Cody's ankle-chains had been looped through a set of rings near the shooting wall. The center of the grisly theater-in-the-round was forty feet away.

Cody's wrists were cuffed. He'd glanced at the drowsy guards saddled with watching him all night out in the open. Sank down against the concrete wall slow and careful. He was stiff in more than one place.

The night sky had been clear at first. A big moon and lots of stars. Too bright to work, so Cody dozed off just long enough to recharge.

When he woke, the clouds had returned. The moon was gone. The stars hidden.

Show time.

The guards were lounging about, smoking hand-rolled cigarettes, talking sleepily in Spanish. They looked over at him every so often to make sure he hadn't disappeared or perhaps banged his head on the wall to kill himself. Cody knew of captives who'd done that rather than face the torture of the day.

Not Cody's style. He was looking forward to the day. This was for all the marbles. It was what he was born to do, what he was trained to do, what he damn well loved to do.

Win.

For almost an hour after waking Cody stayed completely still, motionless like the concrete wall. He studied the guards' patterns. Timed how long it took for them to finish a cigarette, roll a new one, smoke it down to the butt. He got into the rhythm of how often they glanced in his direction.

Without moving his head he'd examined the cuffs. They were standard police restraints. SEALs were trained to pop these suckers open with anything from a toothpick to a blade of grass.

No grass in sight, though.

No toothpicks handy.

Didn't bother Cody.

Next he studied the nifty ankle cuffs. Simple padlocking system around the side of each cuff. A large bolt holding the half-moons of the cuff together on each ankle. Almost too easy. There were about six different ways to get out of those cuffs.

Satisfied, Cody waited for the next round of cigarettes

to be rolled. The guards sat around the cutting block where they'd laid out the tobacco. They sipped from stainless steel mugs. Someone made a joke and they all chuckled. The joke was not on Cody.

Not that joke, at least.

But there was another joke unfolding on the scene.

A private joke.

A joke that would stay private forever.

Though technically the private joke wasn't exactly *on* Cody.

It was *in* him.

Cody grimaced as he shifted his muscular butt on the rough concrete floor. Gingerly leaned over to one side. Raised one buttcheek off the concrete.

Grimaced again, then smiled when he thought of what Bruiser and Dogg would say about this.

No way he was telling them.

No way he was telling anyone.

There were many classified secrets that Cody would take to the grave with him, but nothing as dark as this.

Nothing as deep as this.

"Good thing they skipped the anal probe," he muttered as he flexed and released his sphincter in quick bursts until he felt the cool metal of the thankfully still-retracted switchblade slide out of his virgin SEAL butthole. He wriggled it down his trouser leg onto the concrete floor.

It landed with a muted clink, and Cody quickly straightened up as the guards lit up their smokes. He took several deep breaths, feeling his cheeks burn as he imagined the one-liners Bruiser and the guys would come up with.

Then he shook his head firmly, reminded himself that he'd been trained to do whatever it took to win the day, accomplish the mission, get the girl. Besides, if nobody ever found out, it was like it never happened, right?

"What goes in must come out," he imagined Bruiser saying like he was spewing Confucian wisdom.

"Go deep or go home," Dogg would say with a head-nod and a fake-fierce game face.

"Can you keep this safe for me, buddy?" Ax would say innocently as he handed Cody a full-sized M-16 rifle butt first.

Somehow Cody managed to stay composed as he waited for the next round of cigarette rolling.

Then he got to work on the handcuffs and the anklets.

It took him four minutes to pick the locks.

Another three minutes to put them back together to make it look like they were still secure.

When it was done he slipped the knife into the front pocket of his jeans.

Then he sat tight and waited for the sun to rise.

29

"Good morning, Sunshine," came Benson's sparkly voice as Boro's guards led him over to Cody's shooting-wall.

Benson glanced at Cody's ripped up jeans where he'd been shot. The wound had bled through over the night. Cody didn't give a damn. There would be lots of people bleeding before the curtain came down on this circus.

"I should kill you first," Cody said without moving his head or feet or even his lips. He was gazing at Cate. His Cate. "You're an asshole for bringing Cate here."

Benson leaned against the wall. He smiled at the guards as they locked his ankle-chains to the rings set in the floor.

Cody's breath caught as he glanced at his own chains. He exhaled when the guards finished up with Benson and then strode away.

Finally Cody looked at Benson, who was a bit disheveled but seemed all right. Though Cody wouldn't have minded if they'd roughed him up a bit.

"Speaking of assholes," Benson whispered as he looked straight ahead with a disconcerting smugness. "What else you got up yours?"

Cody's stone-cold focus broke for a second. He shot a look at Benson. Swallowed hard. Said nothing as his cheeks burned under his tan and stubble.

Benson grinned. His gray eyes flicked down towards Cody's ankles and wrists before finally settling on the slim outline of the switchblade in Cody's jeans pocket.

Cody stretched his neck and considered whipping out that switchblade and cutting off Benson's tongue so the old fox couldn't tell any tales. He settled down soon enough, though. Exhaled and cracked a tight smile.

The old man didn't miss much, Cody thought with grudging respect. Still, some secrets needed to stay hidden.

Benson lost the smile quick, though. Battlefield humor was only good for a quick strike. You ease the tension, then ratchet it up again. Tight like a wire. Coiled like a snake.

Both men surveyed the battlefield with silent focus.

Boro was in a freshly pressed pair of brown linen trousers and his trademark white linen shortsleeves. The black hair on his arms was thick and curly. His goatee looked combed. Thick neck freshly shaved.

The H&K machine pistol swung loose in the leather belt harness. He was standing in the center of the round, one foot up on the chopping block, arms crossed over his thickset frame. He was watching his troops gather. Waiting for the audience to arrive.

Boro glanced over at Cody and grinned. His gold teeth flashed like he'd polished them for the show. He winked at Cody, glanced at Benson without much of a reaction, then turned away and said something to Nico.

Nico was taller than Boro by at least a foot. He was broad but lean and weathered, probably a few years older than Boro. He was balding on top but kept a gray-streaked ponytail that he stroked like it was a pet python.

His flak-vest held a short, curved blade that Cody knew would be good for cutting fingers off at the joint. The stench from his underarms pervaded the air. It must take effort to smell that bad, Cody thought.

It also took effort for Cody to stand still and wait for his shot. Right now Boro was still setting the stage like a director before the final act. The troops were gathering in the red dirt, smoking cigarettes and milling about. Clearly a public execution was not new to them, but Cody sensed some tense excitement amongst the men as they looked at Cate and then glanced at Nico before muttering to each other.

Although the troops were gathered informally, they were all armed with H&K machine guns. There was almost zero chance that Cody could kill Boro without being perforated like a cardboard target of Osama Bin Laden at a U.S. military shooting range.

Maybe Cate would make it out alive, but probably not. Not with the current stage positions.

Cody knew he had to wait for something to change.

Something to happen.

Something to give them a chance.

But what?

"What are you doing?" came Cate's voice suddenly from where she was standing to Boro's left. She lunged at him, raising her silk-bound arms and trying to break through the line of guards. Two guards grabbed her by the shoulders, easily restraining her as she screamed at Boro in Spanish and Italian and then English. "She has no part in this, you sick bastard!"

Boro ignored her. He gestured towards the gathering crowd of troops. Said something in Spanish.

Two guards dragged Marya onto the platform.

She didn't struggle, but she was trembling. It was a subtle tremble, involuntary and heartwrenching.

Cody clenched his fists and screwed his boots into the concrete.

Wait for the shot, he told himself.

Wait for your window.

Something's happening, but it hasn't happened yet.

Wait for it.

"Wait," said Boro to the guards. He turned to his right, waved someone up onto the stage.

Maggie Malone stepped up reluctantly. She stood like a statue at attention. Those watery blue eyes gazing over the heads of the troops.

Boro grinned, grabbed Maggie's slender arm, pulled her a bit closer like he wanted the men to see her. She shifted on her feet. She looked uncomfortable. Impatient, maybe.

She shot a quick glance at Benson and Cody, then looked at her watch before glancing towards the distant gates of the compound. Her eyes were cold blue in the sun.

She glanced at Marya, sighed, tapped her foot on

the concrete, looked away like she was saying just get on with it.

"Santo Silenzio," said Benson just then. Cody frowned, looked over at him. Benson was calling out to Malone. "Santo Silenzio."

Malone turned her head, then her body.

Those blue eyes paled, narrowed, then widened.

She cocked her head like a bell that had just been struck.

"What?" she said.

"You heard me," Benson said. "I know. It's all there, Maggie. The breadcrumbs are all there. From Puerto Vallarta to Santo Silenzio to right here, right now, right in front of your damn eyes. Those watery blue eyes. Don't you see it, Maggie? Don't you see her?"

Malone's long slender body twitched. She stared at Benson.

Then slowly she turned to Marya. She cocked her head like she didn't understand, then looked at Boro in puzzlement.

It struck Cody that neither of them seemed to know, but right now wasn't the damn time to sort out their family drama. Cody knew the window of opportunity was close.

So damn close.

Cody let his mind go still. Benson could handle the talking. Right now Cody needed to let those battle-instincts blaze through him.

He'd been taking in every detail, knew every player's position on the stage.

With practiced control he quietly kicked off the unscrewed ankle cuffs.

He snapped off the handcuffs.

Slipped out the switchblade.

Clicked it open.

Locked the blade in place.

Made sure to keep it covered so it wouldn't reflect any light.

Benson kept going, manipulating everyone's attention like a maestro conducting a deadly orchestra.

"Look at her, Boro," Benson hissed. "Look at her damn eyes, Boro. Don't you see? Don't you see her? She's yours, Boro. Both of yours."

Boro was staring like he was in a trance.

His eyes flicked from Malone to Marya and back to Malone.

Malone was breathing in spurts now, like there was something in her chest that was crawling up her throat.

It took Boro another long moment, but then it clicked.

"You . . . you never told me?" he whispered to Malone. His eyes widened, then narrowed with rage. "You never *told* me?!" he roared, taking a step towards Malone, his thickness amplified by his anger, the dark hair on his arms and face and head and chest all bristling and alert like a mad dog about to pounce. "About my *daughter*, Margaret? You never told me about my *daughter*?! *Our* daughter?"

Malone just stood there as the shock worked its way through her body.

Then her shoulders slumped.

She shrugged.

Touched her coiffed hair.

Whooshed out a breath.

Her eyes moved side to side like she was doing math in her head, calculating some complex equation, working through a problem of logic.

Then those blue eyes went still.

She had decided.

"There's nothing we can do about it now," she said briskly, like it was an agenda-item at a status meeting. "Just get on with it. Finish it."

Boro looked at Marya, then turned to Malone.

The silence was so thick and heavy that Cody could have swum through the air like he was underwater.

Then things started to slow down in that brutally beautiful way it happened in battle.

Cody saw Boro's lips move in slow motion.

The words were lost because space and time had splintered apart for Cody.

There was nothing in his sphere of attention except the cold steel of the knife in his hand and the warm blood throbbing through Boro's veins.

Cody watched as if in that battle dream where all warriors past and future fight for eternity.

He saw droplets of angry saliva hurtle through the air from Boro's lips.

He saw Boro's thick hairy arm move towards his belt.

He saw Boro raise that machine pistol and point it at Malone.

He saw the three-round burst slam into Malone's chest.

Capturing Cate

Then Boro roared and turned his body to look for Cate.

Boro saw her and raised the gun.

Boro's thick neck turned as he aimed.

Turned just enough to expose that special part of the brain stem.

The part that controls motor movements.

Such as a trigger finger spasming in the throes of death.

Now suddenly everything sped up with breathtaking precision.

Cody stepped forward onto his injured leg.

Hurled the knife with everything he had.

Put his body and soul and heart into the shining tip of the blade.

Then watched as it struck home.

True as an arrow.

Focused like it was fate guiding the throw.

Like it was destiny delivering the blow.

30

Cate blew past the stunned guards and dropped to her knees. She wasn't thinking, but it felt like she knew exactly what to do, that something was guiding her.

Instinct or intuition.

Fate or destiny.

Panic or providence.

Didn't matter. It was happening like in a dream. A part in a grand play. A role written just for her.

Boro lay twitching on his side, his eyes bugged out, his tongue pinkish-black. The knife was lodged above the base of his neck, right in the stem of his brain.

As he died, Cate placed her silk-handcuffs on the small portion of blade still exposed.

The blade sliced through the silk with the smoothness of butter.

Cate grabbed the knife and pulled it out. Blood spurted from the death-wound. Brain fluid followed.

Cate could hear pandemonium in the crowd. Guards shouting in confusion. The words sound garbled, like it was playing in slow motion, an old tape recorder that was dragging.

She understood that time had slowed down for her, that sound wasn't keeping up with the fury of the fight.

The smell of dung and death came through with the same slowness.

The stench of Nico.

Cate saw her mother's ring on his ugly thumb.

Still on her knees she held the knife with both hands.

When Nico came she lunged forward, putting her entire body weight behind the thrust.

She felt it sink into his abdomen.

She felt herself push up with her powerful thighs.

She felt the knife tear through skin and tissue.

She felt the warmth of Nico's filthy blood rush down over her hands.

She heard herself scream in Italian as Nico's guts slithered out through the cut.

Then, as Nico's body slammed down to the concrete floor, Cate took that curved short knife from the loop on his vest.

She put her knee on his arm.

Cut his thumb off at the joint.

Took her mother's ring off and tossed the thumb.

"Get down!" Cody shouted as sound sped up to normal speed.

She saw Cody flying through the air, his arms spread wide.

She realized a hundred of Boro's guards were raising their weapons as they recovered from the shock of the past three seconds.

She screamed and went down, felt Cody smother her with his body.

Cate closed her eyes and took a deep breath. Cody's smell filled her lungs.

She smiled like it was the sweetest dream in the world. The happiest ending she could imagine.

To die in the protective arms of your man was melodrama that she and Marya would laugh like girls about when they met again in the afterlife. Heaven or hell, it did not matter. After all, this life had a bit of both, did it not?

She felt that old sadness threaten to break through again as she waited for the thunder of gunshots, steadied herself for the bullets to tear them apart as they held each other.

But the sadness did not break through all the way.

And no bullets came.

She felt Cody stir and sit up.

She felt the sunlight on her skin.

But it was splintered sunlight.

Splintered by a shadow that fell upon the two of them.

A figure with arms spread out wide like an angel

It was Marya.

Her sweet Marya.

She stood in front of them as a shield.

A hundred rifles pointed at her chest.

Not one man able to shoot.

"Remind them who you are," came Benson's urgent call from where he was chained by the wall, a shadowy stage-director in the wings.

The guards were shifting on their feet, looking at each other, at their unit commanders, perhaps the more ambitious of Boro's men.

Things were starting to unravel.

Cate could feel it.

Benson's voice came through again. "They heard Boro call you his daughter, Marya. You have legitimacy here. You need to claim your birthright. Claim it as yours, before everything falls apart, descends into chaos. Do it, Marya. This is who you are. This is your fate too, Marya. It's your destiny too. But you have to claim it before all of this slips away. Destiny will knock on the door, but you have to answer. You have to make the choice. Nobody can make it for you, Marya."

Marya turned her head and looked at Benson.

Those blue eyes were wide and wild.

Scared.

Uncertain.

She looked at Cate, her lips trembling.

Cate nodded.

Cate smiled.

Then Cate stepped back and let Marya have the floor.

31

"Floor it," said Benson to the pilot as the twin-engine Cessna barreled down the runway. The front wheel lifted off the tarmac. The plane made it into the air. Nobody was shooting at them.

Cody looked at Cate. Her face was pressed to the window. She was craning her neck to see if Marya was still all right, if she was still in control. She'd refused to leave with them. She was staying.

"They'll listen to her," Cody said. "I saw the effect she had on every damn guard we came across. I saw how they couldn't bring themselves to shoot her. Hell, I bet even those starved, beaten dogs wag their tails when Marya comes by."

Cate finally leaned back in the seat and let Cody put his arm around her shoulders. "She sneaks food to the dogs that are starved the worst. She pets the dogs that are beaten the most." Cate sighed. "She is an angel. How can she have Boro's blood in her veins? And how could Malone give up a sweet child like that?"

"Not once but twice," said Cody grimly as he thought

about Malone's final decision to just shrug and say it was too late so they might as well get on with it. "Still, Malone could have ended the pregnancy thirty years ago. Something in her couldn't do it."

He looked over at Benson, who was strapped in beside the pilot.

Benson must have felt the eyes on him. He turned his head sideways and looked at them. His gray eyes were shining with a mist that made Cody hold off on threatening to break his neck for bringing Cate down there in the first place.

"None of them knew," Benson said gently. "Boro. Malone. Marya. None of them knew. This wasn't some twisted plan by Malone to secretly send their daughter to Boro's compound. Malone didn't place Marya with the Bonaseras. It all just played out this way. Coincidence that makes it so clear that there's no such thing as coincidence. This was about people being drawn together by those forces that demand resolution. Forces that bend the knee to the greatest force in the world. The only damn force in the world. Hell, every time I think this shit won't get to me, it hits me harder than ever."

Benson turned away. Cody was grateful. He didn't want anyone to see the look in his own damn eyes.

He kissed Cate's hair that was thick with red dirt. She looked up at him and he kissed her lips that were sweet and dark, just like she was.

Cody smiled but stayed quiet. Couldn't stay quiet for long, though.

"I told Marya I loved you," he said softly.

She glanced up at him, raised an eyebrow, then giggled and nodded. "I told her that too."

He kissed her nose as the plane circled to head back north. The sky was very blue. The clouds were startlingly white. The sun was bright and exactly above them.

Cody sighed. "So this isn't a cowboy movie ending," he said. "No sunset to ride off into."

Cate nodded with dramatic seriousness. "But it is not exactly a Spanish Soap Opera ending either, because everyone is not dead."

They grinned and pulled each other close and kissed. The plane was vibrating their seats like the magic-fingers of a motel-room bed. The roar of the engines was comforting in its all-encompassing loudness.

Then Cody's sharp ears picked up a strange sound.

"Circle round again and take it down low," Cody said to the pilot.

The pilot did it. Cody and Cate leaned close to the window. The sounds came through clear now.

It was dogs barking.

Cody gazed down at the pack of Boro's beaten, starved dogs running like a dust cloud on the hunt. He saw three men in the distance, also running. One man was limping. His knee wasn't working right.

"It's Malone's thugs," Cody said with a half-grin that almost made him feel guilty. "She must have called them in. Probably so she could tie up all the loose ends."

"Well, it appears the loose ends are about to be tied,"

Capturing Cate

Cate observed as the fastest—and perhaps hungriest—of the dogs caught up with the slowest of the loose ends.

The plane did one more circle as the dogs descended on the last two thugs. Howls that signaled dinner time rose up from the swirling red dirt. The dogs were getting theirs.

Cate sighed and rested her head against Cody's shoulder. She looked up into his eyes with all the sweetness and darkness in her soul.

Cody grinned, shrugged, leaned down to kiss her once more.

The plane rose up again at a sharp angle.

For a moment it pointed directly at the sun.

If someone were looking from below, it would appear that they were riding off into the sunset.

And if someone were listening from beyond, it would appear that fate let out a sigh.

Destiny let loose a giggle.

And the universe kept playing its game.

The only game it ever played.

The game of man and woman.

The game of always and forever.

The game of love.

∞

EPILOGUE
THREE MONTHS LATER
TEXAS COAST

"I love the cake," said Amy. "Black velvet. Red borders. Darkness and sweetness."

"Yes, it's perfect for you guys," said Brenna, pulling away her infant daughter's hand from her breast.

She rolled her eyes, then glanced at Cate's belly and smiled.

Cate was starting to show.

Cody hadn't said anything, but Cate knew he was hoping for twins. Ax and Amy had twin boys. Bruiser and Brenna had twin girls. The competition never let up with those Darkwater SEALs.

Cate exhaled, relieved that the other Darkwater wives seemed OK with her choice of a black wedding cake. She lifted the bottom of her shining red wedding gown that Marya had gotten hand-made down in Sicily. Then she smiled when she saw Cody in a double-breasted black tux that made him look like a cross between Sheriff and Outlaw in this Texas wedding.

Cody was out on the sprawling front porch of the

beachview house they'd bought shortly after getting back to the United States. They'd waited two months before settling on the place. Cody had wanted to lie low, move around between rentals until things calmed down. Until he was sure Cate was safe.

"Nah, we sorted things out with the Caliente Crew," Cody was explaining as the four SEALs strolled back into the main room. The wedding had taken place on the beach, and there were long tables with black tablecloths and legs bowed under the weight of food fit for druglords, mafia princesses, and elite warriors the size of giants. "Benson dropped a backdoor message that it wasn't a good idea to put a hit on a woman supported by a team of former SEALs."

"Speaking of backdoors," came Benson's perky voice from the bar inside the main room.

He was holding a champagne flute and grinning like a Cheshire cat. Cate glanced at Cody, saw him turn a fiery red under his manicured beard.

She tried not to laugh. He'd told her about the switchblade. He'd also warned her that he'd use it on her tongue if she ever told the guys.

"Benson . . ." Cody growled, his neck thickening, his fist almost shattering the glass he was holding. "You piece of—"

Benson flashed a look of pure innocence. He gestured towards the back door at the end of the open kitchen. "It's a blast-proof firedoor. You two expecting trouble in paradise? Told you I fixed that Caliente thing for you guys. You're welcome, by the way."

"Nobody thanked you, Benson," said Cody. "You owe

me for letting you off the hook. You risked Cate's neck by letting her fly out there."

"What about *my* neck?" Benson demanded with an indignant grin. "I'm a senior citizen, you know."

Ax, Bruiser, and Dogg all laughed together. Cody finally broke a smile, raised his glass to salute Benson.

Benson nodded and saluted back, his gray eyes shining with affection.

Cate was about to say something when she saw Marya come back into the house through the beachside French doors.

"The caterers are all set up for the reception," Marya announced excitedly. She'd insisted on helping Cate with the wedding, even though she was running a military-sized drug operation in Colombia. "Oh, and I put out some product samples from Colombia on a side table out there. That's all right, isn't it?"

Ax, Bruiser, and Dogg all stared at Marya. Benson took a hurried sip of his champagne and rubbed his chin. Marya shrugged under her blue tunic made of watered silk.

"What?" she asked, her face darkening as she saw their confused faces. "Didn't Cate or Cody tell you guys what I do for a living?"

"Yeah," said Bruiser uncomfortably. "We know about how it went down in Colombia. But we didn't know you . . . kept it going."

Marya shrugged again. "There are hundreds of men who depend on me. They have families who live on the compound. We have farmers who grow and harvest the crop. Packers and processors. Pilots. Drivers. Guards. Dogs. Doctors. Nurses. Janitors. Cooks. Oh, and laboratories with researchers and scientists."

She smiled, her blue eyes brighter than Cate remembered. Her hair was thicker and darker than before. She had both Boro and Malone in her. But she was her own person.

Marya glanced at Cate, then slumped her shoulders and scolded her in Italian.

"Don't yell at me," Cate protested. "Cody had me locked up tighter than when I was his captive. I didn't even meet the rest of the Darkwater folks until this morning before the wedding!"

Every head turned towards Cody. He cleared his throat, shifted in his shining new cowboy boots. "Cate and I have been laying low since we got back. Wanted to make sure it was safe for her. Wanted the Caliente Crew hit to get called back. Wait for the news about Boro to spread through the underworld so nobody thought the bounty was still in play. Also had to clear up some delicate legal things with her family estate and inheritance back in Italy." He shrugged, rubbed the back of his head. "Kinda forgot to mention that Marya decided to keep the operation going."

"Shall we sample the buffet tables?" Benson said. He smiled at Nancy Sullivan, who'd just emerged from where she'd been talking to some guests.

Benson offered Nancy his arm. She took it and they led the group of four Darkwater SEALs and three Darkwater wives out through the French doors, down the wooden steps, onto the head of the beach where the sand had been packed down hard and tight.

Benson walked past canopy-covered tables filled with everything from caviar on ice to slow-cooked Texas brisket still simmering in its own juices. He stopped at a table set to the side.

On the black tablecloth sat a row of polished silver bowls. Each bowl was filled with little plastic baggies. Each baggie had three capsules inside. All the capsules were filled with fine powder of varying shades of white, green, and brown.

In front of each bowl was a tented placard. Marya picked one up and read from it.

"A Relaxing, Soothing Formulation of Herbs and Extracts from the Jungles of Colombia," she announced proudly. "It is for reducing stress. And this one helps with digestion. This one is for headaches. And these big pills are for . . ." She trailed off, blinked, and shrugged off a smile. "They are for . . . you know . . . if a man wants some extra energy in his nocturnal activities."

There was much hemming and hawing and beard-rubbing amongst the men. Some cracks about how a SEAL's nocturnal activities often involved slitting an enemy's throat while he snored.

Then Ax, former SEAL Team Thirteen Leader, nodded at Marya.

"You're making herbal supplements now," he said, chuckling and nodding again with admiration. "Using Boro's infrastructure to make a different class of powders."

Marya shrugged, her cheeks glowing with pride. "There are many powerful plants in the Colombian jungles. And we have smart researchers and genetic botanists at the compound." Now her blue eyes narrowed mischievously. "We also produce raw materials that I sell to American pharmaceutical companies. They use it for painkillers. Anti-psychotics. Anti-anxiety." She smiled. "Big money, and it helps people instead of destroying them."

Cate hugged Marya and planted a wet, sisterly kiss on her cheek. Then she laughed when she saw Bruiser and Dogg shoveling fistfuls of the "male enhancement" pills into Cody's pockets.

"Take two hundred of these before bed," Bruiser instructed with the seriousness of a doctor.

"Then report back in the morning," Dogg added.

"We expect full details of nocturnal activities," Ax threw in.

"What happens behind closed backdoors, stays behind closed backdoors," said Benson wickedly.

Ax, Bruiser, and Dogg shot perplexed glances at Benson. Cody almost just straight up shot Benson.

Cate looked down and snorted into her cleavage. Then she blinked and gasped when she remembered what was tucked in there. She wondered if Cody had seen the glint of polished steel between her boobs that were already getting heavy for what she hoped would be twins.

Soon the guests started filing in through various doors of the open ranch-style house on the Texas coast. Many were in military dress. Cate was introduced to Marines and Army Rangers and a group of men in mirrored Aviators that Cody called Cocky Flyboys.

The champagne glasses clinked and the black velvet wedding cake's red borders were breached. The sun moved lazily across the sky as the champagne flutes were replaced by wine glasses and whiskey high-balls.

Army and Navy competed for bragging rights as to who could make the biggest fools of themselves on the beach. Marines stepped in to show off what they could do after mixing bourbon and beer. Finally the Flyboys won the pennant by racing each other on the beach wearing nothing but their Aviator sunglasses.

Laughter and cheers chased the sun across the Texas sky. The reception slowly wound down.

The caterers brought in the leftovers and folded up the tables. The barmen counted the bottles and took out the empties. Finally even Marya took off for the airport because she had a morning meeting in New Jersey with some pharmaceutical executives. The sun was sinking over the horizon. It was just Team Darkwater left on the scene now.

Cate watched the group admire the sunset out on the front porch. She felt her heart filling up and then overflowing in a way that made her want to burst into tears. She wondered if it was that old sadness that had been in her heart for what seemed like forever.

But it wasn't that sadness.

It was something that didn't have a name because it was so overwhelming and all-encompassing.

So expansive and exhilarating.

So private and perfect.
That perfect mix of sweetness and darkness.
Of violence and passion.
Captivity and freedom.
Always and forever.

∞

FROM THE AUTHOR

Hope you liked that one!
And I hope you read the next one!

Cody and Cate have ridden off into the sunset,
but Dogg and Diana's wild tale is about to begin.

Get DELIVERING DIANA now!

And do consider joining my private list at
ANNABELLEWINTERS.COM/JOIN
to get five never-been-published forbidden epilogues
from my SHEIKHS series.

Love,
Anna.
mail@annabellewinters.com

∞

Printed in Great Britain
by Amazon